For Mum, Dad and Michael, with love

£1-50

24/07

SUSAN FLETCHER was born in the West Midlands in 1979. *Eve Green* is her first novel and won both the 2004 Whitbread First Novel Award and the 2005 Authors' Club Best First Novel.

For automatic updates on Susan Fletcher visit harperperennial.co.uk and register for AuthorTracker.

'Few coming-of-age novels have the beguiling power of this one . . . its lyrical intensity reminiscent of Laurie Lee. This is a precisely observed, immensely compelling and ultimately redemptive first novel'   *Sunday Times*

'Evokes with a beguiling lyrical muscularity the peaks and troughs in the life of seven-year-old Evie'   *Guardian*

'Susan Fletcher is a gifted storyteller'   *Independent*

'Around this clear-eyed portrait of childhood, Fletcher spins an unsettling mystery'   HEPHZIBAH ANDERSON

'An exceptional debut of grace and subtlety'
                                        ROBERT McCRUM, *Observer*

'Beautifully rendered, the story moves easily from past to present, sensuously descriptive yet hauntingly sinister. *Eve Green* is an enthralling first novel from a major new talent'   *Waterstone's Books Quarterly*

SUSAN FLETCHER

Eve Green

HARPER PERENNIAL
London, New York, Toronto and Sydney

Harper Perennial
An imprint of HarperCollins*Publishers*
77–85 Fulham Palace Road
Hammersmith
London W6 8JB

www.harperperennial.co.uk

This edition published by Harper Perennial 2005
16

First published in Great Britain by Fourth Estate 2004

Copyright © Susan Fletcher 2004

PS section © Eithne Farry 2005

PS™ is a trademark of HarperCollins*Publishers* Ltd

A catalogue record for this book
is available from the British Library

ISBN 0 00 719040 9

Set in Sabon by
Palimpsest Book Production Ltd, Polmont, Stirlingshire

Printed and bound in Great Britain by Clays Ltd, St Ives plc

White Paper

On white paper my mother has written,

Last night I walked where he had. My legs took me there. Through the bracken, and I sat on the gate again. What makes freckles? I shall ask him. The bats were out, and I watched them for nearly two hours.

I don't know his surname, I don't even know his age. But this is the start of something. I stand on the edge. I write it and know it.

She was right, of course.

BOOK ONE

Departure

Three things happened when I was seven years old.

In the spring I learnt how to spell my full name. It took weeks, but when I'd finally grasped all fifteen letters I wrote them wherever I could – in books, on furniture, on my plate in ketchup, on my arms in biro, in spit on windowpanes. Once I etched my name above the skirting board in the downstairs loo. My mother never found it, but I knew it was there. I'd sit, swing my legs, and eye my handiwork under the sink. It shone out in blue wax crayon.

Then in the summer I burned. I'd spent the day in the garden, digging for worms. The paving slabs were too hot to walk on and the shed roof softened. By evening I was scarlet. She lowered me into a cool bath and dabbed on calamine lotion, but still I wailed. For three days I couldn't sleep. I was feverish, grizzly, and the bed sheets stuck to my blisters. Two weeks later more freckles appeared.

And ten days before Christmas I lost her.

What do I remember? Every little thing. From my frayed pyjama bottoms to the eerie blue light that city rain brought with it. You don't forget. For twenty-one years I've picked away at my memory of it, lifting up moments, testing myself. Believing I might have finally healed to a neat, white scar.

I know it was a Friday. That I woke to a quiet house. That when I crept downstairs the mail was still on the doormat and the milk in the fridge was yellow. The kitchen curtains hadn't been opened yet.

My mother was curled up on the sofa under the patch-work rug. I shifted from foot to foot, saw the tissue in her hand, the full ashtray. She smelt of jasmine. She always did. In my mind it was her scent, as if somehow she made it.

And I thought it strange that the dustmen hadn't been yet. They always came on Fridays. I liked the rattle and roar they brought with them, how they slung our rubbish with one hand, how their dustcart munched up bin bags and burped out a vegetable stench. I'd wanted to be a dustman. I'd wanted to wear a green jacket and matching cap, to hang off the side of the van as it shuddered through the streets. They would whistle and wave when they saw me. Dustmen made things better. That morning I'd wanted them there.

Perhaps I felt it. Perhaps some secret part of me knew what was to come. Can this happen? Can death be sensed, like a shift in the weather? I've wondered. In my quieter moments, when half drunk or ill or tired, I've succumbed to the notion that I could have somehow stopped the deaths – both of them. For my mother's was only the first. Another death was yet to come – a swift, snatched death. It made ditches seem darker and sleep harder to find. It meant that if the wind picked up quickly enough, and without enough warning, I'd run.

I've been looking back too much of late. New frown lines and bitten nails prove it. I've been distracted, lost, having strange dreams; I find myself gazing out of windows, listening to silence. But I have reason to now.

I have to remember everything that my mother's death led me to, as I felt it, as it took place. I have to write down every glance, each whisper in my ear. How hot that summer was. How moths bumped against the window-panes at night. How easy it was to hide in bracken. The purplish bloom of damaged skin. Nettle-rash. How a man's hand felt on me. The lies I told. The fire.

There's no doubt that there was a strange hush to the day she died; that our cold terraced house seemed to hold its breath. Later, as a teenager, I would imagine loss to act like a stone flung in a pond, sending dark waves into every distant corner. Maybe some reached me as I rested my chin on my knees in the window.

Maybe not.

At any rate, the dustmen never came.

My mother stirred at lunch time. She raked her fingers through her hair, and when I heard the front door close I scrambled up onto the windowsill so that I could see all the way to the shop. This was forbidden – I'd been told I could fall through the glass that way. But I knew she wouldn't look back to see it. She gazed up past the telegraph wires. The wind was picking up. The sky over the city was steely and low.

When she came home she carried a plastic bag, and for a while our house felt lived in again. There were noises in the kitchen. I heard the loo flush and the scuff of her slippers in the hall. In the fridge I found a bottle of milk that didn't smell sour or have lumps in, and it had a lovely bluish tinge when she slopped it into a glass for me. I held it with both hands. She seemed well again, happier. So I went back up to my room and began digging my name into the paintwork with a penny. I felt better. The trains trundled past the end of the garden in the rain.

Four o' clock came. The clock in the hall whispered it. As I lay on the floor, fitting whole biscuits into my mouth and flicking through my comic books, the banister creaked. She trudged past my room. Twisting a strand of hair between her fingers she said, 'Are you all right in there?'

Then she ran a bath.

I loved the sound. It made me sleepy, and when I closed my eyes I'd think of magic waterfalls and little dipping boats. She always took long baths. She loved thick body creams and scented talc. She loved washing the city out of her hair and combing it as she drifted through the house, switching on lights, and she loved fluffy white towels, candles on the windowsill, water so hot there'd be a red line round her waist afterwards, and that afternoon I smelt her jasmine scent and cigarettes, heard her clothes drop to the floor, and my mother shut the bathroom door at four sixteen, as the Snow Hill to Marylebone train rolled past the house, sounding its horn into the damp air.

I know I was humming, reading my comics with my chin cupped in my hands, when she died.

Mrs Willis next door made the phone call. I stood on the back step in my dressing gown and slippers watching the frost, not wanting to go back inside. She wore a dark-red knitted cardigan with buttons that looked like boiled sweets, and she smelt of washing machines. She came out to me with the patchwork rug, knelt down and arranged

8

it over my shoulders. It felt heavy. She rubbed warmth into my hands, tried to smooth my hair back. She covered my ears as the sirens came, pressed me into her chest, but I still heard them.

When she went to let them in, I pattered down to the shed, tugged at the lock and crept in. My bicycle was kept in there. There were old pot plants, bricks, and a watering can. The place smelt of petrol, soil, damp wood, and I wedged myself between the wall and an old deckchair, nestled into the rug, stared at the darkness and crouched there until they'd gone.

I stayed with Mr and Mrs Willis for the next two nights – who else would have had me? I slept in their spare bedroom at the front of the house which had a fringed pink lampshade and cracks across the ceiling. At night headlights scooted over the walls, and I'd listen to the click-click of high heels on the pavement. These things were new to me, because I'd only known the back of the house before. But I could still hear tomcats yowling on fence tops. Freight trains still rumbled like thunder through the dark.

Mrs Willis didn't stray far. She turned up radiators, told me Bible stories, brought me boiled egg and soldiers, sat on the end of my bed and patted my feet, and one night, when she thought I was sleeping, she whispered about me on the telephone. I hugged my shins at the top of the stairs and picked at the leafy wallpaper. I was being taken away. I didn't know where to, or how long for, but I knew I'd never sit at the top of Mrs Willis's stairs again. 'It's a four-hour journey!' she hissed into the phone. 'Can't I drive her there? The child's seven years old, for pity's sake!'

Next morning it was explained. Mrs Willis said she was too old to keep me, and Mr Willis was older still.

He was poorly, she told me, and needed rest. I knew this anyway, because he never seemed to leave the faded armchair that faced the back garden, and he watched the bird table with watery eyes, coughing into a wad of cotton wool. I only ever used to see him when I went round to get my ball back – a waxy, thin man with striped pyjamas, half-moon glasses and big jowls that trembled when he spoke. But for those two nights, I got to know what he smelt like, how his fingernails had a strange rind underneath them that he peeled out with toothpicks. At night, as the headlights wheeled over my head, I'd hear his breath rattle through the bedroom wall, and wonder if he'd die soon too, and who would find him.

So one slippery white-sky morning in December I was put into a car. Mrs Willis helped me. I felt like a parcel in my duffle coat and scarf, clutching Dog by the ears. My eczema itched beneath my red woollen tights. It was quiet in our street. Before shutting the car door Mrs Willis gave me a satsuma and a slice of soggy fruitcake for the journey.

'God be with you,' – she smiled – 'and try to be good.'

As the car pulled away, Mrs Willis tried to keep up. She began blowing kisses, mouthing something at me I couldn't make out. I thought maybe she'd changed her mind, that she was trying to catch me, to pop me back into the front bedroom with the frilly lampshade. I put my hand up against the glass. I willed her to run faster but she grew smaller and smaller. Through the rear window I saw her standing by the letterbox at the bottom of our street, her left arm raised with a balled-up hanky in her hand. That was the last I ever saw of her. As the car turned the corner, her white apron shone out through the gloom.

*   *   *

10

Strictly, I'm a Midlands girl. I've never been back there, and no longer see it as home, but I've not lost the accent completely. I can still describe the smell of canals in August. I like to think I still have atoms of coal dust in me, that M6 traffic fumes still inch through my veins. That if I ever walked down New Street again I'd feel like I'd never been away.

Until she died, I knew nowhere else. I'd been brought to Birmingham before I was born, before my mother knew if I was going to be a boy or a girl. She said she'd sit in the bath and watch my elbows poke up under her belly like chicken wings. We didn't live near the chocolate factory, but sometimes I was sure I could smell the cocoa beans and cream. I'd lean out of my bedroom window, close my eyes and breathe.

My weekends, when I was old enough, had been spent crawling under market stalls in the Bull Ring, chasing grimy pigeons, being pushed on the rickety swings in the park. I picked up the accent at school. I learnt football chants from the playground and bellowed them out in the bath. When I was six I sat myself down at the edge of Gas Street Basin and dipped my feet in the water, and my mother tugged me out because of the greenish scum and the floating things. She scrubbed my feet till they tingled. I wasn't allowed there again.

And the Indian takeaway from three streets away made our house smell spicy when the wind was right. And we could hear the noise from St Andrew's when there was a home game. Mr Hardy from the corner shop always gave me a free penny chew. In queues and over washing lines people still talked about the Irish bombs, and I'd listen, even though I was only four when it happened, and couldn't really remember the bangs. There were toads in the wet leaves on the embankment. If I stood on my tiptoes, I could see the Rotunda from our bathroom window.

11

They took me away from there. As we turned out of our road I saw our postman on his bicycle. Outside the chemist I saw old Mr Soames with his missing thumb and bloated dog. Then my redbrick school flashed by. The mosque with the turquoise roof sped past, and the bingo hall, and the indoor market that smelt stuffy, and I squashed my face against the glass when I saw the signs for Moor Street station, because she'd taken me on the train once, just so that we could see what our house looked like from the tracks. I'd left Dog in my window, and glimpsed him as we rolled past. When my mother wasn't looking, I'd stuck two fingers up at the track workers for no reason, and they'd straightened their backs and wiped their brows. That was two summers before, when she was having a good spell. The pink plant on the shed roof had been in flower.

I didn't want to go. I grappled with my seat belt, tugged at the door handle, banged my fists against the glass so that people on the pavement looked up and stared. I wanted Mrs Willis. I wanted my beanbag and a glass of milk and the warm smell of my mother's hair. I wanted the silver bell on a chain that swung round her neck, but when I called out the woman next to me took hold of my wrists. She fought me. She used a voice with warning in it, and I wrenched away from her and buried my face in Dog. He smelt of home – jasmine, laundry, cigarette smells. I quietened. I stroked his nose with the pad of my thumb.

The rain came with the motorway. Birmingham thinned out to a few grey factories, car parks and graffiti. Then to nothing at all.

As children can at the strangest of times, I slept.

The car was hot; the rain drummed on the roof.

I woke with a sore head. Things looked different. The light in the car was stranger, sharper. I twisted in my seat. The woman beside me was reading. I looked from her to the driver to Dog, and waited. Something had changed. The wheels crunched on gravel.

I knew I'd seen the countryside before. There had been a school trip to the Lickey Hills once, and I'd eaten my packed lunch under an oak tree, amongst its dropped little acorns that looked like busy eggcups. My birthday present when I was six had been a blue and yellow kite, and we'd flown it on Cannock Chase amongst the badger sets. Mrs Willis used to promise to take me to Stratford. She said we would go boating and have cream teas. She never took me there, but I could picture it. I knew there'd be willow trees and ducks to feed, and in my head it never rained in Stratford. My River Avon was always sparkly blue.

But Wales was nothing like that.

It was empty and wet. It had stiff grey grasses and a big dark sky. Rain was like flung grit. The car lurched up the hillside, throwing me from side to side. I banged my head. I dropped Dog by my feet and was too padded and strapped up to reach him.

Outside there were rocks and mud and trees with no leaves on. I saw no other houses. No homes, no lights in the distance, no hidden gateways or drives. There were no other cars, no passers-by. The car plunged into a pothole.

'That's home for you now,' the woman said.

I couldn't see anything but stones at the top of the lane with a feeble light and a chimneypot. When I turned back to her, I saw the crumbs of Mrs Willis's fruitcake scattered in her lap.

Wales. Five letters, four hours and a whole world away. Nothing like Birmingham. Nothing at all like any city life.

To a seven-year-old with no mother any more, the differences would seem huge at first, and fearful. But, given time, some would prove so subtle they could be missed altogether – tap water tastes cleaner in Wales; wet earth has a real, incredible smell to it; clouds are bigger; birds come closer. Flowers seem much brighter out here. I don't know why, but they do.

And it would take months for me to get used to Welsh nights.

In the summer months, Birmingham nights were pinkish. Streetlights fuzzed on one by one. The birds never seemed to rest, and I'd lie awake with one leg dangling, listening to them through my open window. Stars were hard to see there. My mother said that stars were the souls of babies that hadn't been made yet. They were up there, hovering quietly, waiting to be picked out by mothers, brought down and turned into children. I didn't really believe her, but I wanted to. When I asked about my father, she always went back to her theory on stars. I'd sit by the window with Dog, gaze up at the few lights bright enough to be seen, and wonder whose babies they'd be, what sort of life they'd have down on the ground with the rest of us.

Welsh evening wasn't like that. It rolled down the valley like a fog. It was a proper darkness – as black as car oil or the inside of a letterbox. I looked for stars but there were none. As we pulled into the yard I saw someone standing there. I stared at my feet, at my holey red and grey trainers. I knocked my ankles together.

I knew my grandparents had come to visit me when I was born, that they bought me a cow mobile that hung in my bedroom for years and twirled when the radiator was on. They sent me pop-up birthday cards and pressed flowers, and my mother posted them photographs back. I knew she'd sent them my first school photograph – me, aged five, with unbrushable hair and no order to my freckles. I hadn't wanted to smile for the camera. The teachers had coaxed me, pulled faces, and at the last minute, when everyone had grown tired of my pouting, I'd flashed my very best smile. My mother liked the picture. It made her laugh, and she used to keep it on the mantelpiece, next to the crispy dried rosebud and the well-thumbed postcard of Limerick Bay.

My grandmother opened the car door. She looked down at me with dark, thick-lashed eyes, and she lifted her hand to her mouth. I knew then that I looked terrible – swollen, sweaty, wretched and struggling in my woolly tights and heavy coat. I could smell the farmyard – straw, dung, petrol, the stench of dead water, the tang of wood smoke. I whimpered. I held out my hands and flexed my fingers at her, and she knelt down to unfasten me then. She worked quickly, with rough pink hands. I could see the down on the lobes of her ears, and the little grey strands in her hair. I felt her hands on my waist, and she lifted me and Dog and my duffel coat up, out of the car and into her arms. The skin on her neck was soft and warm. 'Hello, Evangeline,' she said, kissing my hair. 'Hello.' She wore a cream flowery blouse underneath a pale-blue jumper, and I grasped the collar with my fist, would not let it go. I breathed in the smell of her, and she said, 'It's OK, my love, it's OK.'

She held me tightly, and I could feel her shaking.

Over her shoulder I saw the wind in the trees, heard the trees creaking, and my grandmother kept saying my name.

The Shoebox

Evangeline. Five consonants, five vowels. A hard name to be saddled with when learning to write joined-up. A hard name still, even at twenty-nine, since it takes me an age to spell it out over the phone, and I've been accused of making it up altogether before now. Men, in particular, pronounce it wrong. They rush into the word, tangle themselves up in it as if it were wire. Slowness, as with most things, is the key.

I used to hate it, of course. I wanted a name that didn't pinch eyebrows together or have to be repeated. I longed for a name that could fit down the side of my lunchbox. Still, my mother liked it.

'It's good news, Miss Jones,' they told her, as I was first handed over, gluey with cradle cap and pedalling the air. 'A healthy girl. All her fingers and toes.' The midwife smiled and whispered, 'I take it the father's a redhead?'

I was born in the Birmingham Maternity Hospital at three in the morning on New Year's Day. Not the first Birmingham baby of the year, because a boy had been squeezed out in the next ward not long after midnight. But I was the first girl. 'Special from the word go,' my mother would say, knowing it soothed me when my skin hurt. 'Number one, you were. And we sat together by the window watching the very first morning of the year.'

I felt she made the story prettier than it was, but that was fine by me. I liked picturing me, just a baby, all wrapped up and cosy, with my mother's blue-black hair dropping round me.

Twenty-nine feels an important age. It has a seriousness to it, as though certain things will be lost to me once I've swung my leg over the stile into thirty. But like what? The few nightclubs I've been to I hated; fashion has always meant nothing; my only piercing has long since healed over into a small skin ball. Still, I know I've been viewed as wayward. I can see how I must have appeared during that first summer – solemn eyes beneath a thatch of hair, stubborn, solitary, ever my father's daughter without even knowing it. Ever ready to break rules whilst flashing an innocent smile.

All the same, this age is a landmark. Last night, unable to sleep, I decided that if twenty-nine were a colour it would have to be red – the colour of the dragon, of Mr Phipps's broken veins, of sour hawthorn berries: something to skirt round and respect. And I do respect it. How could I not, when so much will happen this year?

I've taken to hauling the worn brown armchair out of the back bedroom, across the landing, and next to the window above the porch. This is one of the few comfortable places left for me – my feet up on the windowsill, cushions in the small of my back, a mug of black tea, a notepad, a pen. Sometimes the cat joins me. She kneads my thighs as I write this story down.

And there's plenty to see from here – our yard, our blue barn roof with the fields behind it, Tor-y-gwynt in the distance, our sheep, Welsh sky.

But this is not the best view. That comes from the old shepherd's hut on the ridge. My castle. My mossy, windy outpost. I'd charge up there on clear days hoping to spy a distant, hazy Cardigan Bay. I'd lie in wait behind the stones for hikers or bird-watchers or deer, or a glimpse of Billy Macklin before he became my friend. And I had breezy picnics in that tussock grass, secret teenage cigarettes, long daydreams, and I hid there in rainstorms or when I just didn't want to be found. The stars have always been amazing there. I've spent hours watching satellites glide. When Halley's Comet blazed her ghostly way over our fields, she made my grandmother cry.

My strange first kiss. That, too, took place against those stones – a quick, dry, tasteless thing, barely a kiss at all. I remember not expecting it, how his teeth clinked against mine. I remember feeling cheated, even angry. I had no idea that there were far better kisses, from far better people, yet to come.

And my shepherd's hut was one of the first places the policemen looked that summer, once they believed there was a body to be found.

That was a fierce July. It changed lives. It brought shadows into the village. Worry hung in lanes with the last of the foxgloves. The men grew dark half-moons under their arms, and we slept with our windows half open. But there was nothing to find on the ridge, of course – nothing except bog grass, snagged wool and my footprints. And that view. Even the police paused, shielded their eyes and gazed for a moment or two. From our wild rhubarb patch I saw them do it.

The hut is too much of a journey for me now. I walk like an old lady, and doze like one. Reverend Bickley found me napping two afternoons ago, and he looked anxious at having woken me. He knows all about back pain. Eighty-four and arthritic, almost doubled over, and yet he still preaches once a month at St Tysul's, still exorcises when he has to, and he still makes the trip up here to check on me, although he always pretends he was just passing. He brings groceries I never asked for – leeks, dried apricots for iron, speckled pears from his own sagging tree. Those pears, though, are as lovely as they've ever been – juicy and yellow, with the warmth of summer still in them. I've learnt how to poach them in brandy, how to caramelise them and add them to cream, how to slice them, sugar them, and bake them in a pie. Or we just eat those pears as they are, Daniel and I – scooping out their flesh with our teeth, letting the juice run over our hands. I know the Reverend's knock on the window – it's soft, apologetic. And I know he misses my grandmother. I think he comes here to check that what's left of her is still coping. Plus I suspect he gets lonely – no wife any more, no children, and a three-bedroomed house out on the road to Tregaron that was flooded not long ago when the Teifi and the Brych burst their banks and the rain just kept on coming.

I worry for him sometimes. When I can't sleep I worry about his tired heart, and our tired farm, about fox kills and flystrike, sheep keds, nightshade, whether I can manage, whether I even want to any more, if it might not make more sense for Daniel and me to sell this place to someone else and move on, if it might not be better to turn from Wales, to leave everything that's gone before – the ghosts, the mistakes, the trouble – to start a new life and a new millennium in a brand-new place, with a whole new, serious purpose.

Just six weeks. That's all I have left of me, as I am. Not long. I count the minutes. I think of my grandparents, of the moss creeping onto their graves. I think of my mother. Of Billy. And I think of one man's hands, his mouth on mine in a market in the rain, his smooth appendix scar.

Rosie. In Cae Tresaint her name still whispers under doors, waves through the bracken. How can she ever be laid to rest? Whenever I walk under our lime trees, for a moment I think I see her, with her gold hoops in her ears and her roller skates on. She'd be thirty-three now.

And as if that story is not enough, there's one more that troubles me. It came back to me three nights ago – of how my mother, aged four, went missing on a day trip to the coast. My grandmother turned from a shop window to find her gone, and she darted down the seafront, screaming out, grabbing people, searching frantically for a girl in a lemon-yellow sundress with a lace trim. She called the police, wept and got sunburnt. She fell on the promenade and sliced open her knee. In the end, my mother was found in the penny arcade with jammy fingers and a missing shoe.

There are worse stories. For years this one meant nothing. But now it seems to tread after me. It makes me climb out of bed and snap on the light. I hear my grandmother's warning in it – that there exists a violent, flame-hot, blade-sharp kind of fear. Nothing else can match it, she promised. It shakes you breathless. It turns you into a thing with teeth and claws. *Just you wait,* she said. *You'll see.*

We all wait.

Someone pinned up a bead curtain in the porch yesterday to keep out the flies, and the Land Rover is clean for once, fuelled and ready. I can see it from the brown armchair. Daniel has painted the front bedroom a soft, eggshell yellow, and only this morning I came upstairs to find him running his thumb down the side of the door-frame, checking for splinters.

21

That's something my mother would have done. Even on her quiet days, she watched out for the little dangers – the rose thorns, the drawing pins, the things that might hurt me silently, without my even knowing it.

Fear is the price we pay for love. That's the deal. Despite everything that's happened, only now, with six weeks to go, can I see that.

In some ways I was an unobservant child. I failed to hear doorbells, ran in front of cars, and I caught a bad cold once from playing outside in wet weather. When my mother towelled me down, flashing her black eyes and demanding explanations, my answer was simple: I just hadn't noticed the rain.

But there were times, too, when my mind was as hungry as blotting paper. Odd things left their mark. This troubled my mother. One afternoon, as she walked me back from school, I asked her where Mrs Everett got her rings from.

'Mrs Everett?'

'Uh-huh. The lady with the white dog. The one who used to push me in my pram when you had to go to work.' I hopscotched over cracks in the pavement. 'Where did she get her rings from?'

My mother slowed, curled a strand of hair behind her ear and stared at me. 'You remember her? How could you remember her?'

'All those glittery rings. Were they real, do you think?'

Only when we got home, when my mother had made a pot of tea and curled around me in front of the telly, did she say, 'Mrs Everett was married three times. All her husbands died, you know. Those were her engagement rings.'

'*All* of them died?'

'All of them.'

I felt sorry for Mrs Everett, and told my mother so.

She blew over the top of her tea. 'Perhaps she was lucky. Three men wanted to marry her. Some people don't even find one.'

These were the things I stored away like humbugs in a jar. Nothing obvious – not faces, not stories they told, but the little bits of people that made no sense and left me wondering after lights out. When I thought of Mrs Barrett, my old teacher, all that came to me was her hat like a pancake and how she swept the puddles at break time. That bothered me – where did the puddles go? Terry Mulligan was my best friend for a week because he was double-jointed. Mrs Sima Singh at the end of our road made no noise when she sneezed; she just put the back of her hand up to her nose and shuddered.

My first partner, too, is a good example of how my brain works. I was fifteen; he was blond. I can't remember his surname, but I know he had a broken rib – a legacy from years in a rugby scrum. Under his shirt I found it – a jagged bone that was cool to touch, and smooth. It gently bumped against me. It fitted the palm of my hand.

As for my mother, her name was Bronwen, and she died when her heart stopped for no reason – it can happen, I've since been told. Her birthday was in April, and she was always happiest when the blossom in the road was out for it – she'd fill old coffee jars with their blooms. She danced dreamily in the kitchen to radio songs; she sang with a Welsh accent. She used to ride horses, and missed doing so. She had a birthmark at the base of her spine that she hated. When she was upset, I sometimes saw her hit herself there, as if it was all the birthmark's fault. I didn't understand that. I'd trip after her, anxious, hoping she'd stop. The mark was the colour of toffee and the shape of a boat and I liked it. I looked for it whenever she bent down.

She wore mascara sometimes. I clapped when she peeled apples in one go, and I was always impressed that a grown-up could still do backbends, even though there were solemn cracking noises every time she tried. Her cigarettes left a carroty patch on her right middle finger. She wore a silver bell around her neck – the only charm left from a bracelet she lost whilst still in Wales, before she was my mother. That bell tinkled when she ran. I knew, too, that the bathroom was her favourite room for crying in, that she thought I couldn't hear her over the gurgling of the cistern filling back up. But I did. I'd dawdle on the landing, sticking limbs through the banisters, listening to the two different watery noises choking away in the room next door.

One lunch time, when I was five, as I steered my Fisher Price lorry over the carpet tiles I saw something under her bed. It was a brown shoebox wrapped in coloured elastic bands. She screamed when she saw me picking my way into it. 'Give that here! Give it to me, Evie! What were you thinking? *Never* touch this, do you hear? It's not yours!' She whipped the box up and clutched it as if it were a brand-new baby that I'd been prodding too hard. I blinked, then wailed. Under her bed became a dangerous place after that.

Nor was I allowed to peep into her handbag, but I did anyway. It was full of wonderful things – sticky lip salve in a pot, flowered hairgrips, the photo of a man with the sun in his hair, her white headache pills, her rubbery red dragon key ring.

Most people thought she was lovely. Our postman particularly did. He rocked on his heels when she laughed with him, and always asked her how the little one was. Mrs Willis told me she was an angel, although I quietly doubted this since angels were honey-haired in my picture books, not dark smoky women with shoeboxes under the bed and a job making fried eggs for people. Still, Mrs Willis believed it. When I ran over her daffodils without thinking, she tutted, picked up the broken ones and wrapped them in newspaper for me to take home to my mother. 'A bright little something,' she said, 'for that saint of a mother of yours.'

The man who drove the ice-cream van always looked at my mother for too long. If she ever bought a cone from him he'd shower it with extra sprinkles, wink, and then lean right out of his window to catch a last glimpse of her swinging black hair. I never liked that. I sensed a danger to it, and one Bank Holiday, out of the blue, I unscrewed the valves on his tyres and vowed never to buy his ice pops again. I saved all my fifty-pence pieces instead, dropping them into an old flowerpot, dreaming of space hoppers and fluorescent little moons and stars that I could stick on my ceiling above my bed. My own night sky, for when I couldn't sleep. Whether it was a lie or not, I liked to peep at the stars from under my blankets, to believe that I secretly came from there.

But Mrs Saunders didn't like my mother. Nor did the woman who shovelled the chips in the chip shop. Some of the women didn't, Mrs Willis told me, because human beings could be bitter things. 'Jealousy,' she assured me, 'pure and simple.'

I pondered this in my den by the train tracks, not quite sure what my mother had that made other women so snappy or thin-eyed. Maybe it was the birthmark, or the white scarf that felt rabbity, or the way she got extra toppings on her ice-creams. I couldn't work it out. I was too young to understand beauty, and what it could do. Not even when Mrs Saunders came round one night, hammering on the door and screaming at us, did it make any sense. She ranted and sobbed and threw a jar of tree blossom at the wall. The jar smashed. The house shook. 'Evie, to bed,' said my mother.

Afterwards, she came up and tucked me in. I smelt her warmth, her jasmine. 'Why was she angry?' I asked.

'Because she's unhappy, and she's scared. But' – she kissed my head – 'it's not our fault. It's got nothing to do with us. Have you got Dog?'

A week later, as Mrs Willis pegged out her washing and I sidled in and out of the fragrant bed sheets, she told me that Mr Saunders had left his wife for a woman half his age.

'Grief shows itself in all sorts of different ways, my love.'

How true. Her words would come back to me whenever I saw glazed eyes or heard doors shutting quietly. My grandmother crammed her hand against her mouth some-times, as if trying to keep a secret in. Daniel's sadness took him walking, to Tor-y-gwynt or the gold mines, and often I followed him, scrambling through brambles, always keeping his broad shoulders and thick brown hair in sight.

And grief can turn a person mad, or as good as. It destroyed Rosie's mother, Mrs Hughes. If asked, my first and strongest memory of her is how she collapsed outside the White Hart pub in late July – like a puppet with cut strings, or creeping ivy when the wall's pulled away. No backbone to her, just slack skin and a low, animal groan.

That was grief. It's stealthy and comes in disguises on the whole, but for her, and for those of us who were passing by the pub at the time, it was unmistakeable.

Pencarreg

That night a westerly wind blew straight in off the sea. It swept over piers and grey beaches, over the mines and quarries and mill towns of Ceredigion, past rugby fields and cricket pitches, through the Teifi valley, the hidden lanes, the crumbling battlements, lost abbeys, empty market squares, and then further inland, rising up towards the Cambrians, the pine plantations, Tor-y-gwynt, our sheep and our squat farmhouse with its blue slate roof, and bringing with it a fat, heavy rain that woke me. Or rather, the ivy that clung to my windowpane did. It rattled the glass as if seeking entry. I stayed beneath the blankets, wide-eyed.

After breakfast I was shown the farm. My grandfather smelt of herby soap and dog hair, and he led me through the rain in my new rubber boots. I was skirted around potholes, lifted into the hayloft, shown an old jackdaw's nest and the rainwater barrel. I was beckoned into barns and dripping outhouses. A caravan rusted behind a line of firs. Chickens curled their feet and ogled me. I poked my fingers through the wire cage at the side of the house, where the sheepdogs licked me with grainy tongues. I followed him through the cowshed and the handling race and the holding pens and the sheep dip, and to the huge sycamore at the end of the drive where he said he'd broken his arm as a boy, by falling from it. I stared into the boughs and imagined him spinning to earth as its seeds did – beautifully, without a sound.

'Look at these,' he said behind the barn. 'Badger tracks.'

I said nothing. I studied the back of his head, the smooth pale skin behind his ear.

As for the cattle, they steamed quietly in the field at the back of the house, their hot mouths working on hay. I was a surprise to them. They lifted their heads and flicked soapy tongues at me. Their breath was warm, sweet-smelling. I could see my reflection in their conker-shiny eyes.

Beneath a grey sky I thought, *my mother is dead now.*

'Do you like them, Evie?' my grandfather asked.

I felt hard, as if full of stones.

'Yes.' There was no other answer.

As I followed him into the field, I turned and saw my grandmother in the kitchen window, watching me. She waved brightly, with a red tea towel in her hand.

So. My first home had been a red-bricked terraced house in Birmingham, with a railway line at the end of the garden and pigeon droppings on the doorstep, and a view of the city from the bathroom window. I knew how many steps it took to get to the corner shop. Rats lived down on the embankment, and once or twice I heard them shoot under our garden shed like firecrackers.

This was my second. Pencarreg. A word full of shadows and clicks that I rolled around in my mouth like a pear drop; a mossy farm behind a row of lime trees at the top of a blustery lane, with no carpet in the hallway, a furry moth by the light switch in the downstairs loo, dusty light bulbs and stairs that complained when I trod on them. Even when I held on tight to the banister the floorboards grumbled. The place smelt fusty. No curtains met in the middle. Cupboards had a churchy smell, as if they needed sun. There were pictures on the walls that I peered into, one by one. Fresh white flowers caught the dust in glass vases. And on my second evening I found a letter carved deeply into my window frame – *K*. Why K? The letter was straight, elegant, and felt smooth under my fingertips. My nail could slot into its groove.

No trains. No traffic noise. At night, my mother's old bedroom was so dark I couldn't tell if I'd shut my eyes or not.

No one lived higher in the Brych valley. I suppose we were – and still are – the village attic: cluttered, cobwebby, damp for most of the year. And the wind rarely left us. My grandmother told me over the top of her reading glasses that when people in Cae Tresaint woke to a slight shaking of the weathervane or a banging door, we were losing roof tiles. In autumn gales anything not tied down could vanish out into Ceredigion. She'd lost underwear off the washing line that way. I could picture it – white knickers skittering over the heads of baffled sheep.

'We've had some deep snow in our time,' she said, 'but it's the wind that's really our trouble. Have you heard it at night?'

I nodded.

'It whips in off the sea and heads straight for us. And then there's the rain . . . Mind you' – she leant forwards, gave me a wink – 'if it does snow, the lane is perfect for tobogganing.'

I blinked at her. Tobogganing?

'Ask your grandfather. He used to hurtle down there on a tea tray when he was your age.'

I took this thought to bed with me, along with Dog

and two hot-water bottles. Layers, she informed me, were the key. I nodded, wore jumpers on top of jumpers and kept my slippers on.

My grandmother was Louisa, a breezy whisper of a name. Except everyone called her Lou. She made me think of the neat little women on washing powder adverts – there was the same bustle about her, the same strong arms and briskness. In those early days her efficiency unnerved me – was I in her way? Was I a nuisance? As I spied on her through the banisters, it never once occurred to me that she, too, might be adjusting. To me, she just washed and scrubbed and peeled.

And she seemed to sniff a lot. I noticed, too, that she hummed when I watched her ironing, yet stopped when I went back upstairs. When Reverend Bickley drove up on my third day with more white flowers and a soft voice, my grandmother whisked out a proper teapot and a biscuit tin and pretended to be cheery. I knew she wasn't, because cheery people didn't stand in the hallway and stare at the floor for no reason, but she pretended well. She planted strong kisses deep into my hair at bedtime. And there was a belly to her, a soft wodge that Dog and I only noticed when she reached up for one of the saucepans that were slung on rusty hooks above the kitchen table. Dried lavender hung there too, and ears of corn. I awaited the day a pan dropped on our heads at teatime.

Although her hair was peppered with grey, and it wasn't so thick that she could hold it in place with just a pencil, it looked familiar. It swung the same. When I studied her through the crack of her bedroom door last thing at night I saw how it fanned across her back. Hair looked so pretty that way. I vowed that if I'd been born with such hair, I'd have always worn it like that. But she usually pinned

30

it into a wispy ball on the top of her head. I wanted to plunge my face into her hair and smell it. I wanted to ask her if it was true that all Jones women could touch their ears with their big toes, as my mother had claimed.

The kitchen was the only room that didn't have dark corners. There were shadows elsewhere, but here the light ran under dressers and filled up nooks and crannies. Sometimes the radio burbled on the windowsill, half listened to.

My grandmother seemed to brighten when I sat myself down at her table.

'Evie!' She'd smile. 'What do you fancy for tea tonight? Stew? Sausages? Chops?'

We'd eat in silence mostly. I'd pick at my eczema, study these people I was now living with, and secretly offer food to the farm cat under the table. She was never really interested. Too full of mice, I thought.

Some of those early days are blurred. If I press my temples with my thumbs and try to think of certain times, nothing comes. I can't blame tiredness or my hormones for this – it's how it's always been. I have spaces I can't fill, as though I sealed my head up for a while, or boarded up my windows against the stormy weather. I know I fell downstairs at one point, but I told no one, and I can't remember what part of me hurt. Something was grazed, and ached under the blankets at night. But what, exactly? The image of a broken plate comes back to me, too, although who broke it, and how, I don't know.

One day was too wet to go anywhere, so my grandmother sat me down at the kitchen table with a pastry cutter and pie trimmings.

'What are we making?'

'Mince pies,' she announced. 'Do you like mince pies?'

I was a poor helper. There was too much to look at in the kitchen at Pencarreg – mince pies took third place behind the yellow mug tree and the huge glazed trout in a box. There was hand cream by the sink, a sieve as big as my head, a row of black-edged cards on the sideboard, and there was a white china chicken that sat prissily on top of real, sometimes still feathery, eggs. When my grandmother bent down, I heard her knees click. It sounded like a pill bottle being opened. She kept tissues up her sleeve, so that when she produced them to dab her nose or wipe my face they smelt of her hand cream – warm and lemony, like sponge cake.

'What does K stand for?' I asked her. But she didn't seem to hear.

As for my grandfather, he was harder to find in the day. He left the house whilst it was still dark outside, sometimes not returning until it was dark all over again. He droned up the hills in the gloom, sometimes with the dogs, sometimes with shadowy men I hadn't met yet. Pots of cream for chapped skin turned up on the windowsill. Salt blocks and molasses wheels were left in the fields. The pregnant ewes required watching, he said, because the weather was bad and there were foxes about. I'd hear them barking in the evenings. That was a sound I knew.

When I went to visit the cows with kitchen scraps I sometimes saw him up there in the half-light with the sheep, a skinny man with a brown cap and straight back. He gradually made me think of the wooden clothes pegs I used to steal from back gardens and bring to life with a felt-tip pen. He had the same slimness, the same round little head. But those clothes pegs splintered after a time, aged by the weather. I had strange dreams that made me tearful in which I found him bent over a gate or a bale, his felt-tipped face running in the rain.

* * *

Christmas Eve. These days it's usually a drizzly walk down to the church where the aged Cae Tresaint carol singers do their best under umbrellas, and everyone casts glances at me. Lanterns have become torches. The crowds aren't nearly so big. Mr Phipps has shut up shop now and disappeared, thank God, but before that he would begrudgingly provide the paper cups for the mulled wine. Definitely not a man known for his festive cheer. He always saw me as a shoplifter. It made no sense for a while – why me? He never followed anyone else down the aisles; he never backed away from others if they came too close. But it's clear enough now. My father's fault – as most things would turn out to be. Out of all the soured minds in the village, his was the worst, and the darkest. Mr Phipps seemed to think criminality was passed down through the generations like a stutter, or a squint, or in my case red hair.

I did shoplift, eventually. His suspicion felt like a challenge, and my hatred for him was as strong as ever, so at thirteen I tucked a bottle of Swn-Y-Mor whisky under my school blazer and dared to thank him as I sauntered out of his shop. Gerry, my school friend, was in awe of me. I was unashamedly proud. We got drunk under the beech tree in the churchyard, and then poured the rest of the evidence into the Brych for the minnows.

I suppose Mr Phipps never worked it out. I was certainly never accused. But my point had been made: if someone expects trouble, they usually get it, in the end.

That Christmas Eve did not involve carol singers, but rather low mists and thermal vests, loud river noises, and I spent the morning thinking of home. I squatted by the chicken coop, picking at my skin. I hid from my grandfather but he found me eventually.

'Fancy a trip up the hillside, *cariad?*' he said.

We went up to the ridge on his roaring four-wheeled motorbike, bumping through potholes and skirting bogs. He pointed out the heart-shaped rock and the wild rhubarb patch. 'See that?' he asked. 'And that?' I hunched into his back with my fingers wedged through his belt loops. Our sheep scattered. The sun was a tired candle through the trees.

That's when I first saw the view. That's when I learnt what it felt like to be so high up that birds flew in the spaces beneath me, my eyes watered and the air felt thin. I dared to lift my arms out, and the wind nearly took me like a plastic bag. Under a slate of sky I stared at it all – the fields, the pine forests, hedgerows, our thin little lane, its passing place, the huge oak, the church tower, buzzards, shadows of gorse, bracken, the woods that would bring bluebells in May, the distant hill road that curled its way to Lampeter, the Cambrians, the distant promise of sea. The farm looked tiny, with its toy tractor and postcard chimney smoke. Wind flurried the tussock grass. And Tor-y-gwynt reared up behind me.

Tor-y-gwynt. Place of wind.

'What do you think?' my grandfather called.

I missed her. I wanted her there. Did I cry? No. But a secret part of me unfurled up on the ridge that afternoon. My loss billowed out before me, snapping at itself and pulling me with it, streaming out over the sheep hills like a funeral flag caught in the strong Welsh wind.

'Evie, there are one or two things you should know.'

We sheltered in the crumbling shepherd's hut, my grandfather and I. In the musty half-light he produced mince pies and a flask of sweet tea, and we munched for a while, watching the grass race outside.

I glanced over. 'What things?'

Rule number one, he said, was not to go beyond the rhubarb patch on my own, and to stay off the hills altogether after dark. When I asked why, he shook his head. 'Anything might be lurking up here at night.' There were vicious bogs hidden in the hillside – hungry brown bogs that were strong enough to pull a grown man down. Adders weren't unheard of, and the weather, too, might kill me. People had died of exposure, he said. That was a new word, full of whispered secrets – *exposure*. I tried it out in my mouth for size, along with the mince pie.

'I'm serious,' he said. 'Even in summer, don't ever guess with the weather.'

Good advice – I listened to it. It didn't take long to learn that, in Wales, rain is sly. It creeps up behind you, taps you on the shoulder. 'Take an anorak!' my grandmother would bellow from the kitchen window. 'You never can tell round here!'

Rule number two involved machinery – 'no playing near any.' This applied to tractors, shears, all things metal. I was offered tales of missing fingers as deterrence, and worse. Rules surrounded tubes and pots and aerosols, too – all the chemicals that were kept on the wonky shelf in the old loosebox were absolutely out of bounds. So they would, given time, become an interest. The lock on the door would prove easy to pick. I'd dip my fingers in grease, and test antiseptic spray till my nose fizzed; I learnt that iodine dyed skin fox-orange. My lungs, these days, must be gnarled, rotten things. Gerry and I took to investigating sheep dye one half term, and so must have breathed in all sorts of cancerous fumes. When he coughs on the phone these days I believe I hear more than a smoker's rattle there. But I try not to think about that.

Furthermore, I wasn't to pester the farmhands – men I hadn't met yet, but would. And I should never eat any berries or mushrooms I didn't know; nightshade grew in the lane, he said, and mushrooms came with the first autumn mists.

'Mushrooms?' The red-and-white kind that fairies lived in, if you believed in such stories? No – more like the brown teated ones that Lampeter students would appear with plastic bags for, and boil up into tea. That has never been my scene. My brain has its dark rooms, and I'd rather let it be.

'So make sure you wash your hands when you come indoors. Always.' And I nodded with serious eyes.

Nor was I allowed to paddle in the Brych, at least not till May – rivers claimed lives, I was told. And the sheep-dogs were there to work, not for playing fetch with. I wasn't to sneak up to their cage and slide back the bolt. Not that I'd intended to – dogs were smelly, wet, slavering things that my mother had crossed streets to avoid. 'I won't do that,' I told him, and meant it.

'And don't be afraid of talking about her,' he said, 'if you want to.'

Not a rule as such, but he seemed to view it as one.

Evening came by three thirty. I felt tired. I closed my eyes on the way back down to the farm, pressed myself into his back. I longed for bed, and for soft things. As we came into the yard I saw my bedroom light was on. It glowed out into the half-dark. 'I've thought of one more,' he said.

The last rule involved horses. 'Never go round the back of them.'

I asked, 'Why not?'

'Because the back leg of a horse is a powerful thing. Believe me, Evie. You don't want to startle a horse, not from behind. A man from the village was hurt that way.'

'Hurt how?'

'He was kicked in the head. Many years ago.'

I rubbed my eyes. In the head? 'What happened? Did he die?'

My grandfather shook his head. I was glad of it. 'No, he did not. He was lucky there. But it smashed his skull. Cracked his left side. Had to have all sorts of surgery there. And he couldn't walk for months, you know.'

'Can he walk now?'

'He can, but he's not as he was, poor man.'

Did a smashed skull look like a dropped egg, and did spilt brains look like cold porridge? Was the dent of a horseshoe still in his head? I didn't ask. But needless to say, I imagined a foul, purplish face, and I dreamt of twisted faces that night. Children are savage little creatures – they seek out ugliness, develop a hunger for it and look for it everywhere. Why is that? Such an irony – when we spend our adult lives looking through the madness for something easy on the heart and eye.

'Billy Macklin,' was the reply when I asked for a name.

So from the start those two words meant danger and sadness to me.

Nine rules – it could have been worse. I'd had more before then. But it was an odd number. Ten would make more sense, of course, so I think I knew to expect one more. Like a sentence without a full stop, I awaited a fat, dark certainty.

I should have known it would involve another man. *Don't let him go, when you find him, my love,* my mother had said, not long before she died. She'd been sitting on the landing with the shoebox, smoking in the dark. I'd woken to the creak of the floorboards. The glow from the streetlight had made her look old. She wasn't old, of course. Just twenty-eight when her heart gave up in the bath. *Don't,* she whispered. *Promise me?*

I was too young to fully understand her, and too sleepy – let go of whom? But I nodded at her solemnly, took her hand, and promised anyway.

October

I saw him again today. From the shop window I saw him wander across the square – jeans, white shirt with short sleeves, hand-rolled cigarette. Mr P was sour about it. He muttered, told me redheads had tempers and weren't to be trusted. Think of Judas, he said. But I didn't listen. I paid and left. I've never seen hair like it.

I followed him – was that wrong? Not very far. Just to the churchyard. He sat on the end fence, his feet in the nettles, his back to me. Three magpies – doesn't that mean good luck? I watched him from the vestry door. He lifted his head as he blew out the smoke.

A man can be beautiful, I see that now. It's not just a woman's term, not a word reserved for romantic, virtuous, elegant things. I don't think beauty is neat any more. It's unordered. It's unbrushed hair and a torn back pocket. It's bright and strange and lovely, and if I were to paint him I'd use all the warm colours – ochre, gold, plum, terracotta, scarlet, burnt orange.

I want him to see me as I saw him then. I want him to find me alone at the end of the day with the sun in my hair. I want his heart to buckle, too. I want him to

stop someone out in the square and say, who's that? Do
you know her? Where is she from?

I take this to be the first of my mother's accounts. There
are many scraps of paper in the old shoebox – on some
there are essays, on others just single words. I've read
them all, placed all in order, and this seems the oldest to
me. The words of a twenty-year-old, although her writing
is still childish – loopy, with wild flourishes. I remember
it this way. This is how she signed birthday cards; this is
the writing she used to leave orders for the milkman.

It is written on a piece of thin, yellow paper, and is
folded in half.

I like this account. I like it because it's true, she's right:
we all want our lovers to see us that way – unaware,
natural, serene. We want to change their world with one
glance, to stop their breath at the sight of us. I'm guilty
of it. I've pinched my cheeks to make myself look sun-
flushed, and have loitered in the lane when I've expected
him there. We practise the spontaneous look; we perfect
the casual air. I like knowing that she did this too, that
she wanted to look beautiful, having no idea that she
already was. Plus I like the thought of my father in a
churchyard, resting in the evening sun. It's a better image
than the one so many people have offered, over the years.

On the back of the yellow paper, in the same pen, she
has written her name. *Bronwen.* Dark and pure. The *o* is
as flawless as a star, as open as a window. I look at it
and something in me becomes seven again – I want to
crawl into that letter, right into the warm, wanting heart
of my mother, before it stopped beating in a jasmine-
scented bath.

Tor-y-gwynt

Mrs Hughes. Two nights ago I dreamt of her.

It was a pale, fluid dream, in which she was whispering at me through cupped hands, but however hard I tried I couldn't hear her. I felt bad, as if I was letting her down all over again. So in the afternoon I decided to take the very last of our heavy-headed roses down to her grave. They grow by the drain of the sheep race, elegant sugar-pink roses that used to send my grandmother into rapture every July. They have frail yellow centres, curling velvet petals and a scent so violently sweet it's almost obscene. The smell is an ambush. It races up noses and makes eyes water. That was my grandmother's favourite part – so little, she said, smelt good on a farm.

I felt them suitable. Dog rose – *Rosa canina*, the largest of the wild roses. I never really knew Mrs Hughes to talk to. Adults fell into two groups when I was eight – those who winked and kept my secrets, and those who side-stepped me in the street. She sidestepped. She wore shoes with heels and she smelt expensive, and rumour had it she wore red underwear. This part I never believed – who could possibly have seen it? Gerry took to dropping pennies in an attempt to confirm this. He'd stoop, and peep up

41

her skirt. We never knew for certain, but Mrs Hughes had a prim, reserved look about her, and it was thrilling to imagine such things. She was always so composed. She had a tidy, practised smile.

But this was all before Rosie disappeared. She changed then. She lost weight overnight. No more make-up, hands that couldn't stay still, two pleading, panicking eyes. In the papers and on the television she looked like someone else, someone older. She took to sitting in her bay window by the phone, watching the street and gnawing the skin on her hands. I remember sidling past her house with an ice pop once and catching her eye. I slowed for a moment, sticky-fingered. With her eyes she gave a faint smile. I hope I smiled back. Either way, I saw her differently from that day onwards, and that lost, tired smile came back to me when Mrs Hughes was found nearly four years later, crammed full of aspirin and vodka and stone-cold in her bed. No note, they said, but no accident.

I took a jam jar with me, and a trowel. It was a good afternoon, the drowsy late-summer kind that brings out midges and wood-pigeon calls. Her grave had white, feathery lichen creeping over it, so I spent an hour kneeling on a bin liner under the oak tree, scraping it away. Lichen is proof of clean air. It grows everywhere here, along with ragwort and chickweed – hardly how you'd picture a place that has seen such trouble in its time, but then we should never assume. That's a lesson I learnt. Just because a man smiles doesn't mean he's friendly; a plucked flower and promises don't mean love.

There's no one to look after Mrs Hughes now. I take it upon myself to tidy her grave – I dig up the weeds, as if by doing so I can somehow apologise for my part in things, lessen her anguish. Not that she has any these days. But I do it all the same.

A young woman came into the graveyard as the shadows were starting to get long – blonde, slender, carrying freesias wrapped in paper towel. I didn't know her. She glanced at me, noted my bump and stroked her own stomach as if reassuring herself she had no bump of her own. I rested back on my heels. She might live here now, I thought, in Cae Tresaint. She might be looking at me, wondering who I am, if I am just a visitor. Or maybe she knows exactly who I am. Maybe she's heard the rumours, and knows the story of Billy Macklin and me. Her hair was perfectly straight, the hair I'd always hoped I might one day wake up having. I shifted my head in greeting. She responded, but kept one hand on her belly. Was that a sign of disapproval? If I were as superstitious as some people are, I wouldn't have chosen to kneel there – a woman with child tending the grave of a woman whose child was lost.

Things aren't easily forgotten here. There's some comfort in that, I suppose, an immortality. I feel I've made my mark, pressed my thumb into Cae Tresaint's clay the way my mother, my grandparents, the other Joneses have. But history has been a burden, too. It has been a vast, smothering burden that I longed, for years, to throw off. Nothing is new. Each gate squeaks to remind us of all the other hands that have pushed it. Each pair of eyes that encounter me for the first time have memories shifting behind them, like sand under tides. *So you're Eve Green,* they seem to say. *At last.*

No one here lets go.

Take what happened that summer, my first Welsh summer, when fingers were quick to be pointed at the wrong man. Two decades on, and everyone in the village could still tell you exactly what happened back then, or their version of it – where they last saw Rosie, how the

43

culprit was singled out, whether that fire was a blessing or not. The fire that made my left wrist bubble and run clear. I believe I can still feel it sometimes.

Or take my father – thirty years since he came here and his name is still carved into brains. Reverend Bickley has a brown envelope of newspaper clippings from that time. I still have the photograph – the only picture of my father, the one my mother kept safely in her purse along with her loose change, stamps and tablets. A handsome man. A man with a wide smile, in a white shirt, the sun igniting his hair so that it looks like a halo, of sorts.

The Irishman. This is how he's remembered, as if his name is cursed. As if no one will get to heaven if they say his name out loud.

I felt tired in the graveyard. I left Mrs Hughes and went to find my grandparents. Theirs is a shambling grave, half hidden by hydrangea bushes and hollyhocks and sun-crisped offerings, and they wouldn't have wanted it any other way. I added a couple of the roses and lay down beside them.

I miss them. My grandmother's been dead for ten years now, my grandfather for not quite two, yet the house still creaks as if they're walking in it. My mother's death made no sense. It stung, shot out its poison as and when it chose to. But their absence is another thing. It's tender. I have to sit down with it.

I think I slept for a while. I awoke to find it was evening, that the bats were out and the grass was cool. I wanted to get home, but when I pushed myself up onto my elbows, I paused. Something made me smile. My grandmother always told me that her favourite thing in the whole of Cae Tresaint was the solitary gargoyle above the vestry door. It's easy to miss. Most people never notice it. Generations have been and gone and not known of its impish existence. But as I sat in the grass I glimpsed its weathered face peeking through the creepers. My grand-mother has the perfect view of it – something, in all the time I've lived here, I'd never realised before. It's a good thing, when a place you've known for so long can still have its gentle surprises.

Our village has always been tiny – just a dot on a map if it's on a map at all, with only one sign for it, out on the Lampeter road, although that sign is pretty well hidden by nettles for most of the year. Twenty or so homes, a church and a pub lie in a corner of the valley undetected. Even the gales often fail to see them, and so Cae Tresaint itself is generally unbattered and fully tiled, its only real trouble ever coming from the river, the Brych, which can bulge and spill over after heavy winter rain or sudden thaws. The ground can get boggy, too. For as long as I've known it, the grass by the war memorial has squelched underfoot. Someone always slips on Poppy Day. Even during the drought that lasted the whole of one of my teenage summers, it was wet there. Sludge bubbled up under my shoe, and I remember watching parched toads flop over the road to reach it.

Nor has there been a time when the church gate actu-ally shut, or when the pub sign didn't need painting, and the ancient red phone box still sits at the top of the village as if on guard. There's no road but the one you come in by, and those hedgerows can run riot in June. I like this disorder – such flaws only add to character. But in twenty-one years things have changed, too. The village hall has been lost to a holiday home. Amongst the sheep more pylons hum. Fighter jets roar through the valley on their practice runs. The huge oak I could hang upside down in, bat-like, was discovered to be rotten, chopped up and hauled away. I remember sitting in it with Gerry and watching the fireworks above Lampeter on the night of the royal wedding. The man with the green eyes has moved elsewhere, Mr Phipps's shop is just a house now, and there is a bus service, a bus shelter which is scribbled on, and I don't know a lot of people down there any more. Most of the young people have gone; it goes without saying that most of the old are dead. Mrs Jessop died as curiously as she lived, by sitting down on the church bench one Sunday in her tweed jacket and never standing back up. All day, everyone just thought she was snoozing. She was buried not ten yards from where she died, and my grandmother wore a floppy black hat that smelt of attics for the funeral. Mrs Hughes, Mr Wilkinson, my lovely Mrs Maddox and my grandparents are all buried near her.

Our lane begins just before the White Hart pub, winding up past the pink cottage, the passing place, through the Brych where it fords the road, under a tunnel of oaks, past the gate that once led to the derelict barn, and up, up, up towards our lime trees and cattle grid, ending with a turning circle, a wall of sky and a mass of blackberry bushes. It can be a tough walk – I've had many long, miserable, contemplative climbs back up to Pencarreg, usually in the drizzle, always with my legs aching at the end of it. None of Mr Phipps's paperboys ever had the stamina to reach us. They'd get as far as the passing place and then give up. My grandmother would find soggy bundles in the fool's parsley and demand her money back.

There are a few more visitors these days, but it's not so much worry that brings them. It's curiosity. I remain, to this day, a scandal. My baby is newsworthy, and my choice of partner even more so. I've heard us called distasteful. I've heard the age gap whispered about –

Sixteen years! Sixteen, I tell you! How can that be normal?
– and at first I cared, but no longer. I pity them. Perhaps they don't know love, or if they do, they know the safe, orderly kind.

But not everyone disapproves. There are some people who are genuinely pleased for us, and are counting the days down, too. Daniel fields the phone calls – 'She's fine,' he tells them. 'We both are.' The farm is viewed like a whole other world. All it is, I tell them, is a little wind-battered and muddy, and at the top of a pretty steep lane.

Hikers, though, aren't deterred by its steepness; they find their way to the cattle grid. Billy Macklin managed it often, despite his stiffness and his shambling gait – 'All puffed out,' he'd say, blowing through wet lips. And Rosie coped with it. Fly-tippers sneak up in the evenings, which I loathe, and which once led to my grandmother rowing spectacularly with a culprit in the lane. She was amazing that evening – flinging out her arms, brewing with a fierce, magic anger.

There are bird-watchers, too, and the occasional lost, lonely drunk from the pub. And it has been known for furtive teenage couples to make the trip up here and vanish in the overgrown bridle path, hand in hand. This is how I first learnt about sex – about what fits where, and the appropriate noises. My grandparents never told me these things, so I had no choice but to spy. I'd crouch in the undergrowth and watch teenagers fumble. A dark, brutal way of learning – and so much came as a terrible shock to me. I'd never seen breasts that way before, or the pale, persistent thing men carried in their jeans. At first I felt frightened – it awoke dark memories in me. And although I knew animals did it this way, I'd somehow expected something cleaner, *better* for humans. I was appalled. I vowed never to do such a thing.

Two decades on and I'm converted. The proof is curled

up in my belly and nearly eight months old. Yet the teenagers don't come as often as they used to. I find myself bizarrely relieved when I spot them in the lane. Mrs Watts, the weasel-faced woman who runs the pub, can't understand it – she asks why I tolerate it, why I don't shout out to them. Shameful, she calls it; she shakes her head and puckers her mouth. But how could I mind it? I would be a hypocrite if I did, since in my teens I came to know the path by the gold mines better than most. I know what it's like to open my eyes and see two skies above me – one made of air, one of flesh, and smiling. It's lovely. Whenever I glimpse a nervous couple edging into the bracken I almost feel happy, a surge of pride. I approve. There's a real, primitive beauty in loving intimacy outdoors. Of all the places to be close to someone special, and for the first time, I can't think of anywhere better.

Horse riders, too, come to Pencarreg. They clatter past in their anoraks and acknowledge anyone who happens to be in the yard. *The pony club,* Daniel calls them, with a wink. After rain the hooves echo through the valley, and it's a sound that always makes me think of the day I was left there, at the stable yard, with nothing but a packed lunch and a sense of being lied to. It was a run-down place then, full of dour faces. But now it's owned by a lady with more freckles than me, who's turned Bryn Mawr into a busy, whitewashed hotel. It has its own website, its own glossy leaflets, and whenever I go there, it feels like a completely different place.

It was after Christmas but not yet New Year. I was sitting at the kitchen table, dunking my soldiers into a boiled egg, when my grandmother peeled off her rubber gloves, blotted her forehead with the back of her hand and sat down. I sensed something. She picked up the newspaper, hid behind it and said, 'How would you like to go and see some horses tomorrow?'

I already knew about their existence. The home-made sign in our lane – *CEFFYLAU!* – warned of them. Old dung rotted in gateways and passing places.

'Why?'

My grandmother bunched her lips in a smile. 'We just felt it might be a nice change for you,' she said, 'a bit of fun.'

I retrieved a slice of eggy toast. 'Are you coming too?'

She turned the pages of the newspaper over without having read them.

'Your grandfather and I will have things to do that day.'

'Why?'

'We just do.'

'What?'

'Things.'

'What sort of things?'

'Just things, Evie!'

'Can't I go with you?'

'No, love, you can't.' She settled back in her chair, adding, 'You'll have all sorts of fun at the stables.'

Outside there was rain, and I thought of the cows under the trees, chewing, watching the weather. I kicked the table.

'Don't do that, love. It's old.'

I kicked it again. 'How old?'

'Very. Now,' she said briskly, folding up the newspaper, 'shall I tell Mr Wilkinson you're going? You'll like it. Maybe you could actually have a ride on one.'

I shrugged.

'Good,' she said.

'I don't want to.'

She looked at me. 'Evangeline, we all have to do things we don't want to do. I'm sorry. But it's only for one day.'

'Just one day?'

'Just one day. I promise. We'll pick you up as soon as we can. And we'll have something nice for pudding. OK?'

I squirmed in my chair, gave a nod.

'Good girl.'

She stood, moved back to the sink and busied herself with rinsing her mug. I sulked. What if I was kicked in the head, like Mad Billy Macklin? Hadn't she thought of that? Or was that, in fact, what she wanted?

'You never know,' she said, 'you might like it there.'

However long our lane might seem, we still aren't quite at the top of it.

High above the valley, beyond our gravelled turning circle and brambles and sheep, there are a group of rocks. They're jagged, strange to look at. I can see them from my bedroom window, how they change colour when clouds draw across them. My grandparents couldn't tell me much about how they happened to be there. I asked, but got silly replies – they were made, they said, by magic elves or feuding mountains. I'm eight, I'd mutter, not a baby.

Tor-y-gwynt is surrounded by peat bogs and grass so sharp that it can nick skin. Red kites are spotted there. Sheep and rabbit dung peppers its lower stones, and I've found many animal bones in the peat over the years – sheep, deer, others. And the wind is strong at the Tor. Hair flutters like a snared bird, and I used to like standing on the highest boulder, trying to keep my balance in the wind.

But it is a hard place in the winter months. Rain can tear up the peat like gunfire. Old sheep drop against boulders and die. There is a good tale about a farmhand who'd sought shelter there years ago, and three days later he'd wandered into the Royal Oak at Caio talking nonsense.

They said he went insane and died young. I wholly believed this. I thought about the hills at night, and wondered what might prowl there – wolves, ghosts, people who just couldn't sleep.

I know better these days. But between November and March people still stay away from the Tor. They slip legends and hearsay into their pockets and take them wherever they choose. They remember the bad things, always. They say that Tor-y-gwynt is haunted, and a dangerous place to go.

This is where my mother wanted to end up. She, too, must have liked the view. It puzzled me for a while – the grounds of St Tysul's, where my ancestors are buried, seemed a safer, quieter place. But she chose the grass and sheep bones. She chose Tor-y-gwynt, and my grandparents chose not to tell me. They believed that the thought of cremation was too much for me at that age. I still don't know if they were right.

So at the end of the year I was taken to Bryn Mawr – a rambling stable yard run by Mr Wilkinson, a glum man with broken teeth and an armpit smell. I was handed a packed lunch, my colouring things, and left by the mounting block. I loitered, not sure what to do with myself. A woman with a saddle lumbered by and ordered me to stay out of the way. I felt miserable. I traipsed to the nearest stable, reached up for the bolt and slipped inside.

The day was spent talking to their carthorse, drawing him with my new wax crayons. He was a solid, sweaty, friendly thing. He blew through fleshy nostrils and munched hay. I had no idea that as I sat cross-legged in the straw, under a tin roof, my grandparents and Daniel were letting her ashes go. They would have stood downwind of the bogs. Their coats would have billowed.

The carthorse shifted on feet as big as dinner plates. I stayed away from his back legs.

When I offered him hay, he lipped it up gently without even touching my hand.

It was getting dark by the time they collected me. I was sorry to leave the horse behind, so my grandfather came with me to say goodbye. He lifted me up to the stable door. The horse's bristly mouth quivered when I touched him.

'Can I find him some nice grass? Might they have a carrot for him? Do you think? Will you ask?'

'It's getting late,' he said. 'I'm sure you can come and see the horse another time. Let's get going now.'

'I want to feed him!'

'Evangeline, get in the car.'

I did as I was told.

My grandmother was as good as her word that evening. We had sugary doughnuts with bright red jam, and I forgot to be sullen.

And as my grandfather went to switch off the porch light, he found a tangle of mistletoe sitting on the doorstep. He picked it up, turned it over as if it might be a trick.

'Who is it for?' I asked. 'Who is it from?'

'No label,' he replied. 'I don't know.'

At any rate those branches were pinned to the ceiling in the sitting room. My grandmother reached up and ran her palm over them whenever she went past.

I see it as a ghostly, tragic gesture now – leaving anonymous presents like that. It's something only a lonely person would do. But stranger things would happen. And all I knew that night was that I'd been kept in the dark about something. I went to bed scratching, feeling the lie. So I didn't think too long or hard about the secret mistletoe, the shining *Viscum album*, who it might be for, or why.

My mother knew her flowers. I remember that. I remember her picking a solitary straggly wild pansy from the far end of Cannon Hill Park and popping it behind my ear. *Viola tricolor,* she told me – one of the easier names to learn. She had an eye for flowers. She'd find them in cracks in houses, on waste ground, amongst rubble. Some she'd leave, but most she took home – they would otherwise grow unnoticed and die unmourned. At least this way, on our kitchen windowsill or the television set, they were admired. They made her happier.

Plus they were a flash of Wales in her city home, I understand that now. Wild pansies used to grow by the ruined barn in Cae Tresaint, before it was set alight. They bustled for sun by the south-facing wall, next to the strawberry plant. I'd trample on them blindly when exploring there, ducking under eaves and emptying the place of sparrows and jays. She did that, too, I know it. She went there, lingered in the half-light. Mrs Maddox claimed to have seen her there, biting her nails, waiting for someone. *Waiting for him,* she'd assure me.

My mother's old shoebox confirms this. As I sit here now, on a warm September afternoon with the kettle singing downstairs and a baby in my belly, I have it next to my feet. My mother's treasure trove – and mine, too, in a way. A small grey room full of wine corks and beer mats and dried daisy chains.

On a scrap of brown paper, perhaps the back of an envelope, she has written in her looping childish hand – *met at the barn, 5pm, didn't hear him coming. All too hot now – need rain. He smelt of earth. When do I tell him? When shall I tell him the news?*

An erratic note, jumbled and hasty. But can't love make us do that? Love is blind, they say – but isn't it more that loves makes us see too much? Isn't it more that love floods our brain with sights and sounds, so that everything looks bigger, brighter, more lovely than ever before?

Viola tricolor. Too spindly to be my favourite flower – something robust is better, something brave. The daffodil would be an easy, fitting choice – *Narcissus*. Cow parsley, too, is good: some of the stalks would grow so thick and so tall it took much of my weight to pick them. But their smell makes me uneasy. It takes me back. Policemen battered the hedgerows back when Rosie disappeared, in the hope they might find a clue hidden there. Pollen was flung up into the lanes; Gerry's nose began streaming.

But I race ahead. That was the summer when I was eight, and I've not quite finished being seven.

Blue Eyes

I introduced myself! Although technically he spoke first. I felt him looking, then he crossed the yard and asked if he'd seen me somewhere before. Big blue eyes – the kind people could get lost in. I think he probably knows this, but that's OK with me. We shook hands. I liked that. His name sounds just as it should, and his accent is wonderful.

This is neat writing. She's used a proper fountain pen. I can feel the concentration, the focus on each letter to make it tidy, appealing. But by the last sentence the loops have returned, and the words start to slant as if a secret wind is blowing them. That's how I write – Daniel has said so. He's said my letters are clumsy, falling over, that they need propping up. As runner beans need staking? I'd asked indignantly.

His eyes are grey, not blue – although they can darken at times, and surprise me. I think of mists and feathers. The family eyes, he tells me. Like many things of his, I hope they'll be passed on.

Heritage

I don't cry, not as such. These days I am a little softer, but just as a peach hides a dimpled stone so I couldn't be pierced too deeply in Birmingham. If anything, I think crying intrigued me. A blonde girl knocked her teeth out on the climbing frame in the park once – I remember it distinctly. She sat there on the tarmac and bawled through bloody gums, and despite my age I remember feeling a young, odd contempt for her. I could feel sad, too, but I didn't cry – why should she? So I didn't help. I went home for tea, leaving her there to wail.

There was no midnight sobbing for me at Pencarreg. I think they hoped for it. I think they listened at my door sometimes, holding their breath, but if so, they always padded away disappointed. At night I'd just stare into the dark, or sleep. In the winter afternoons I'd stand amongst the cows, their heat damp and rising, and wonder where everything could have gone. Where was her silver bell? Where were her birthmark and her voice and her squeaky green-and-white tennis shoes? How could these things just vanish when they had been so real?

I became ill.

I awoke one morning to find my grandmother's face above me. She dabbed my forehead with a flannel. 'You're sick,' she said. 'Try to sleep. You're hot enough to fry an egg on.'

I don't remember much. My eczema worsened. At some point I think I wet the bed. My grandmother swept in and out with chalky drinks that fizzed away on the bedside table, and I grizzled and smacked at her hands. My eyelashes became gluey. In my more lucid moments I'd hear the wind whipping round the house and worry for the cows.

The bathroom tiles were so icy they made my skin prickle. The loo seat was too cold to sit on, so I decided to hover. One afternoon my legs buckled and I crashed to the floor by the bin, so that I lay there on my side, shivering, staring into old cotton buds and clumps of long black hair pulled out of plugholes. My teeth chattered. I mumbled at a dead toothbrush. The inside of the bin was like a whole other world.

Someone found me.

I was picked up carefully and carried to bed. It wasn't a grandparent. I was rambling away, plucking at my pyjamas, and I smelt a new smell that wasn't sheep or fairy cakes. A smoky, soft smell; almost familiar. My bed felt cool when I was laid in it. Dog was pressed into the crook of my arm.

Whoever stood over me was gentle. Through my illness I sensed it. They tucked me in noiselessly, as if they knew exactly what it felt like to have a tight, hot skin and a heartbeat in your ears.

Influenza. It should have been a girl's name – a sultry, hot-eyed girl from somewhere tropical, with flowers in

her hair and swaying hips. The house creaked and whispered. There were secret meetings outside my door, new
voices. I gradually listened to them. My head cleared
slowly, inch by inch, like winter windows.

Reverend Bickley asked after me. He brought me a pink
glass star to hang on my curtain rail – a clever present,
since it brightened my room, shone out next to the ivy,
and I'd gaze at it for hours. It made me think of jelly-
beans. The boy who cleaned out the chicken coop asked
after me, too, as did Mrs Maddox who lived in the pink
cottage at the bottom of our lane – I heard her thick
Welsh accent downstairs: *You'll send her my love, will
you?* My grandmother baked scones for my recovery.
With Cornish cream, she stressed – the best sort. She
didn't believe in starving a fever.

A grey-haired man with caterpillar eyebrows and cold
hands was my first proper visitor. My bed tilted when he
sat on it; a glass rod was pushed under my tongue.

'Ninety-nine. Aspirin, water and rest,' he proclaimed.
'She's over the worst now, Lou.'

This was Dr Matthews. A family friend, I later found
out. He lived in Llanddewi Brefi opposite the church in
a terraced house that was meant to be haunted. He'd
never married. In time I'd put this down to the fact that
he belched into a closed mouth and had hairy ear holes
– a child sees such things. But my grandparents liked him.
Apparently he'd been the first to listen to my heartbeat
eight and a half years earlier, before my mother had set
out for Birmingham, and he'd known my grandfather all
his life. A soft brown photograph on the bookshelf in the
hall confirmed this. Two Welsh boys, one skinny and one
fat, squinting at the camera in a hazy lane with their bicy-
cles. They would pedal all the way to Llandovery just to
spy on the classier girls there, with their pencilled legs
and powdered noses. Jim Matthews had the loudest wolf

whistle in Wales, I was promised – or he used to. This was before the war – before the war, and before the death of my Great-uncle Duncan, whose leg went so black and foul-smelling from a shrapnel wound that it killed him.

He called again the day before New Year's Eve. My temperature had gone, and I was sitting up, reading a comic. Dr Matthews heaved himself through the door. He brought cold air and the smell of leather with him. A grown-up smell.

'Well, this is a little better. How's our patient today?'

'All right.'

He felt my forehead, nodded to himself. 'You've not been very well at all, you know.'

'I know. Influenza.'

'Indeed it was. Lots of it about this time of year. Open your mouth for me?'

I stretched it wide and pushed out my tongue.

'Lovely. And let me feel your neck?'

'What do you think K stands for?' I asked. 'It's in my windowsill.'

Did he pause? 'I don't know,' he murmured. 'Someone's birthday coming up, is it not?'

'Mine. I'll be eight. I'm nearly into double figures.'

'Well' – he hauled himself back up off the bed – 'have a good day, won't you?' He said it as though he didn't think it was possible, and he gave an odd smile when he left, the smile that people only used when they'd heard something sad, when they felt sorry. When they knew there was nothing anyone could do.

My recuperation was a lonely time. It was the weather's fault – or, rather, it was my grandmother's.

'You're staying indoors,' she said.

'But I'm better! You said so! I want to!'

'You've barely eaten for two days,' replied my grandmother, without looking up from the *Western Mail*. 'You're weak.'

'I'm not!'

'You're weak, Evangeline, and you're staying indoors.'

'But . . .'

'Enough. Put your slippers on, or you'll catch your death.'

Arguing with her was useless, but it didn't stop me thinking gloomy things about her. I scowled and slammed doors. I tugged books off shelves on purpose. When she brushed past me I turned stiff as a fence post, and never looked her in the eye. On one occasion she came to kiss me goodnight and I fought her, pushed her away. I still feel ashamed about that. I can still see her standing there, at the end of my bed, slack-jawed, as grey as city ice.

So in the last few days of the year I traipsed through my draughty prison, hunching by windows with my jumpers pulled over my knees, gazing out forlornly at the fields. I sucked the liquorice Mrs Maddox had left me, picked paint off doorframes, took to peering into drawers, opening books and running sticks under furniture to see what might come out. Lonesome socks and pencils and pennies and bookmarks and hairbands and a dead spider were found that way. In the spare bedroom I stumbled across a battered tennis racket, a dusty orange teddy bear and a windbreak for the beach, and on the top of the wardrobe I spied something I knew. A shoebox. Coloured elastic bands. I stood on a chair, clattered the box with a coat hanger, but I still couldn't bring it down.

At night I'd listen to the rain, and once or twice I thought I glimpsed a flash of blonde out there in the huge Welsh dark.

*   *   *

I suppose if my illness had a purpose, though, it was this: my grandfather and I became friends. Unlike my grandmother, he believed fresh air would help me. They'd bicker about it when I was in bed – an argument that, as in all things, my grandmother appeared to win. But when she was in the bath or on the phone my grandfather would pop his head into the kitchen, check the coast was clear, and then whistle softly for me. I knew his call. With my anorak flying behind me, I'd charge out into the rain. We'd gallop around the yard. We'd stamp in puddles and tug wet boughs. We had to do this in silence, of course, and we went to great lengths to ensure my hair didn't get wet, or my face muddy. But this added to it, somehow. These hasty, clandestine moments bordered on magical. It wasn't the fact I made it outdoors that made it special – sometimes I was out there for no more than a minute or two. It was my grandfather's mischief. We were partners. We had our own secret, something to wink about over the teapot.

Was there a photograph taken of us doing this, sneaking out in the rain? No – because who could have taken it? Yet I see us. If I close my eyes I see us exactly – me in my blue anorak, palms upwards, one foot off the ground in mid-run. My grandfather is smiling, too. He wears his brown corduroys, tucked into his boots. There is yet to be any hint of arthritis about him.

It wasn't the first time my grandparents fooled one another, nor would it be the last. But I remember it perfectly. Those were my first happy moments at Pencarreg. I doubt my grandfather ever really realised how much they mattered. After all, to an adult, such a tiny deception is forgettable when placed alongside the ones to do with love.

*   *   *

He was born David Jones, in Pencarreg itself. His mother had heaved him out fifty-six and a half years earlier in the back bedroom with the brown paisley curtains that looked out over the cow field and the lane. My grandfather was the third generation of Joneses to have entered the world within those four grey walls, and just as the house sighed with the thought of whiskery men with dogs at their feet, so the graveyard at St Tysul's is crammed with my ancestors. They jostle for space in the south corner, by the broken back gate and the poplar tree. I found hours could be spent hopping amongst their headstones, picking at bird droppings and tracing their names. Some of the engravings were in another language. I knew the Welsh for *In Loving Memory Of* before anything else.

On New Year's Eve I sat on the stairs, swathed in blankets, and listened. My grandfather had his glasses on – half-moons that perched on the tip of his nose and left a waxy red dent there afterwards. My grandmother was dozing in the sitting room with a mug of cold tea.

'The man who built the house,' he said, 'was Hywel John Jones. Your great-great-great grandfather.'

'Hai-wool?'

'*How*-ell.' I imagined a hat like a steamed pudding and a waistcoat that looked too tight.

The house had been built a little under a century before, when the gold mines at Pumsaint were still working, the war memorial hadn't even been thought of yet, and there were no such things as cars – still horse and cart, which I never saw as such a bad way of life. Hywel had used slate and stone to build the house, and had planted the lime trees all himself. Moreover, he chose the south slope of the valley which, my grandmother often pointed out, had been his biggest mistake.

'Front door faces the hillside,' she'd announce. 'Where's the logic in that, I'd like to know? And the rest of the house faces north. All the wind and rain God chooses to send us, but never much sun.'

She had a habit of sniffing when disgruntled. The time I came back from my first week at Swansea with a stud in the top of my ear made her sniff so hard she had a nosebleed. Maybe that had been the point of me having it – we were rowing incessantly at that time. Only when I came home for good, unimpressed with university and longing for greenness, was there any sort of calm. Fortunate, since it meant we were friends again in time for the sudden heart attack that killed her at Llanybydder horse market the year that followed. My ear went septic and I now have a scar. 'It's a wonder we don't all drown in this place,' she'd mutter.

She had reason enough to complain, I suppose. This house was never very good at bracing the weather. At first I only knew how cold it could be there, and I'd learnt why there was a whole shelf of hot-water bottles in the airing cupboard. But in the heavy April gales things were different. Dark yard water would flood the hall more than once. There were mysterious gaps under the back door, and all the carpenters, sand bags and drainage in the world couldn't help it. Like black magic, water still slunk inside. If rain was forecast overnight, my grandmother would curse, dig out the tarpaulin and old picnic blankets and wedge them under the door just in case.

Each room had a draught excluder, aimed to keep out spiders as well as the wind. In the kitchen it was a walking sock filled with newspaper; in the sitting room it was a long velvety green caterpillar with eyes that moved when I shook them, and a bright blue nose.

'Could the house blow away?' I'd once asked her.

'I wouldn't bet against it,' she replied.

And the heating wasn't quite right. Radiators switched on and off at their will. For a while, not long after the flu, I wondered if something lived in the boiler, and I skirted it warily in case a claw or a tentacle whipped out from it and took me. I'd been in the kitchen, my fist in the biscuit tin, and the boiler made such a deep, gurgly noise that I could do nothing but stop chewing and stare.

'We've had all sorts of men out from Lampeter' – my grandfather shook his head, brushing the dust off the banister with a frown – 'but the problems just keep coming back.'

I considered this. 'Could it be a ghost?'

My grandmother mumbled through from the sitting room that it was probably Hywel himself, too proud of his shambling attempt at a house to let death take him from it. She enjoyed moaning about my grandfather's family. She'd done it before, over the Christmas dinner when the wind slammed into the side of the house the way a mudslide might. But he never seemed to mind. I wondered if that was what happened with marriage – you saw through the bad things, and only saw the good. The way I never noticed bird droppings or mould on a window-pane when there was snow falling beyond it.

So Hywel John Jones made a lopsided, leaky house on the edge of a north-facing mountain, but he also made eight children. There was a primitive, blurred picture of them on the staircase wall – an experiment of some sort, and one of Wales's first. The women had puckered mouths and hands clasped over aprons; the men lounged around them with arms on bales. Each had a story. Hywel Junior, I was told, fought with his father, marched out of the farm, became a missionary in West Africa and never returned home – I had to have missionary explained to me. Carys, the blonde daughter, died from a cough when she was eight years old.

'I'm eight tomorrow.'

'I know,' he replied.

The youngest daughter married a lord and became a

lady, so that she wore diamonds and ate pheasant and rode in carriages, or so I was led to believe.

But my favourite tale of all was that of Wilfred. Wilfred Thomas Jones. It was almost too good to be true. I tingled when I heard it, clutching my milk and not wanting to breathe, as if breath might dissolve it.

'What did he do?'

'He went to America,' he whispered, 'at the start of the century, looking to make his fame and his fortune.'

'As a film star?'

'Land! He was going to buy land! There was lots of it out there, you see – huge lush pastures as far as the eye could see! And do you know what he planned to do?'

'No . . .'

'Start a farm of his own! Out in America!'

'And did he? Did he have cows?'

'No, *cariad,* he did not. Do you know what he did?'

I shook my head, saucer-eyed.

He said that Wilfred tried to rob a bank in Brooklyn and was shot dead by a riled customer. Stories couldn't, surely, come any better than that. Even though it was a tale about breaking the law and a violent death, my grandfather gave me every single detail, and I deeply liked him for it. I crouched on the stairs in awe. Wilfred was, I learnt, a gambler in debt, a whisky drinker, a loud-mouthed man who drew attention in bars and spent money he didn't have on fancy waistcoats and pocket watches. The word for this was *spendthrift*, although my grandmother claimed she had a far better word for such a man. It all sounded super to me. He was shot straight through the heart, my grandfather said, and I pictured a slimy red heart with a hole in the middle you could peep through. Did he die slowly? I wondered. And what did they do with him afterwards?

He had a lot of sweethearts, too. This didn't surprise

me. I'd been raised with the knowledge that men never stayed put. I'd been brought up with the view that they slipped through fingers like chicken feed, and evaded capture like the cottony poplar seeds that would come to cloud the lane every June and early July.

It was Wilfred I decided I liked the most. I had to stand on tiptoes to see him, but there he was, a freckly, beaming young man with chipped front teeth and his thumbs under his braces. Behind Wilfred was a white dog scratching its ear; behind the dog was our back door, and I liked that it hadn't changed in nearly one hundred years. The house must have been busy then, I decided – eight children, two adults, and that white dog.

Another of those children was Samuel Jones, my great-great grandfather. I was disappointed with his picture. He looked like men seemed to in old photographs – bearded and thin-lipped and stern.

'He looks cross,' I sulked. 'And boring.'

'Well, he had a hard time of it. You see our front door?' I hung over the banister to spy it at the end of the hall. 'We have him to thank for that, you know.'

It was a huge, gnarled, varnished thing, with dozens of bolts and chains and too heavy for its hinges, but my grandfather told me that Samuel Jones didn't take risks. His wife died in childbirth at the age of sixteen. After that, it seemed, he was keen to lose nothing again.

Their only child was Henry John Jones. He looked like Father Christmas.

'My father,' he said. He didn't look anything like him. 'He made Pencarreg lamb famous.'

I wasn't quite sure how he did it, but my grandfather seemed very proud all the same. Henry also took in evacuees during the war, and the village admired him for it. My grandfather gave a slow faraway smile and said the farm was a rowdy, amazing place during wartime. 'Three children plus me, stampeding round the house and over the hills, whooping like Indians and finding trouble.'

'What sort of trouble?' Maybe my grandfather robbed banks too.

'Never you mind.' He grinned, tapping my nose.

He'd been seventeen when the war broke out. Whilst his older brother was fighting, he stayed with the farm, and gained three new siblings with Cockney accents. Not long into the new year, I decided that my grandfather had been in love with one of them – not that he would have acted upon it, being the shy man that he was. A pencil drawing of a girl laughing in a raincoat was stuck between the leaves of a dictionary, and so I took it out and wandered through the house, waving it, demanding to know who had drawn it and who she was. When my grandfather spoke about her he used his wistful voice, the voice he only ever used to talk about dead people. My grandmother sniffed when he mentioned her. I never asked him anything else about the dictionary evacuee. I was only eight, but I sensed the subject troubled him. Paths not taken, perhaps. Love, and what could have been.

As for Henry's wife, my great-grandmother, she was ill for most of her life. She looked like a ghost in their photograph. Henry was holding her around the waist, and it was the only photo on the wall of the stairs that had any sort of love in it. How she managed to have children I'll never know, for she was tiny, and doll-like, but she did. They had two boys, but one was dead now.

'Gangrene,' I was quietly informed. 'A nasty way to go, Evie.'

Duncan Jones had been twenty-one and smiley. He'd sung in the church choir and been engaged to a girl from Llanwrda. I imagine his death to have been a lonely thing – in a quiet, yellowy ward with flies at the window and a tired ceiling fan. He must have known he was dying. The stench of his wound must have told him, and the dark way people looked at him. Was he lonely? Calm? Afraid? Did he screw up his eyes and long for Pencarreg, his girl, the view from the ridge? Who knows how we act when our own death looks right at us. He was sent home like a parcel for burial, and his name is etched up on the war memorial. My grandfather laid poppies there every November. Having never had a brother, his sadness meant little to me.

Within a few weeks, one more picture appeared. It's a good one. It still hangs there, on the staircase wall. My mother, no older than eighteen, so not yet in love, but with a bloom to her all the same. She wears a sunhat. It looks like she's in a wood of some sort, because the light suggests it – it comes down in shafts behind her, dusty, as if through a canopy of pines. Her hair is loose. She looks over her shoulder, straight into the camera. On her left arm there is a silver charm bracelet, and the sunlight catches it. She holds the brim of her hat with one hand, as if to keep a breeze from lifting it. She has good, straight teeth.

My grandmother once said to me, *This is how I remember her*. Before the trouble, she meant. Not so much in a sunhat, but, rather, before my father waltzed past the phone box into Cae Tresaint, hands in pockets, with a casual smile. *Before you were conceived*, I could have taken that to mean – and once or twice in my teens I wore that thought like a shroud. But that was self-indulgent. Twisting her words like that wasn't fair, because she never meant them that way. She loved me, I know that. Despite all my faults, she wouldn't have changed me at all. She just meant that my mother changed the day she fell in love – but don't we all? We garner secrets and become misty-eyed. We daydream and find a hidden slyness, and my grandmother lost her grip on her daughter the day my

69

father appeared. It was always going to happen, sooner or later. But in this photo, Bronwen is still unshared. A daughter and a friend; nothing more, as yet.

At midnight, as the old year died, my grandparents wanted me in the sitting room with them, to listen to Big Ben on the radio. But I chose to stay on the stairs. I was nodding with sleep, and crammed with stories of holey organs and African jungles. 'I don't look like any of them,' I said.

My grandfather smiled. 'Still your family, Miss Jones.'

For the first time I was part of something bigger. Suddenly I didn't believe in the stars any more – I didn't have to. I came from Wales, not the night sky. I came from people with dirty fingernails and a whole other language in their mouths. It was a strange, powerful thought. I felt like a bead on a necklace, a leaf on a tree. I felt there were huge invisible hands scooping me into a secret room, where there were others who knew me, where my mother was. The same blood; the same bones. Had they always been waiting? Ancestry – I tried out the word, and liked it.

My grandmother came out after a while. She patted me up to bed, called me the birthday girl.

Just before lights out, I asked, 'What was my dad like? Are there photos of him too?'

She stiffened.

Her eyes blazed.

'We don't talk about him in this house. *Not ever*. Do you understand? You don't say his name. You don't talk to anyone about him – *anyone!* OK? Do you hear me?' She bent down, so close I could feel her breath. '*Do you?*'

I took this to be the tenth rule.

The rain grew harder, spattered against the glass, and the new year came in blustery.

The Tattoo

Men. Very few ever came to our house in Birmingham. The dustmen and the postman didn't count. Mr Willis rarely left home, even before the cancer, and if he did it was to place a fiver on the dogs at Hall Green or have a pint at the Wharf Tavern, not to come round and see us. Old Mr Soames collected for the poppy appeal every November, but ignored us for the rest of the year. There was a newspaper boy who chewed gum, and there were salesmen from time to time – I remember leaning out of her bedroom window and spitting at one who wouldn't leave the doorstep. But that was it. No men called. My mother wasn't interested in anybody new.

Does this explain my intrigue, or my blindness? The fact I wholly failed to notice that another man lived on our farm? It wasn't just the three of us. For several weeks this fact escaped me. I expected no one else, although all the signs were there.

How odd, and wrong, to think of the place without Daniel. It feels more his than mine, in a way, even though there's no Jones blood in him. If there had been, he'd have had the black family hair, the stubborn jaw. As it is, his hair is a light brown that turns blonder in the summer

71

months. Before long I learnt how to pick him out of a crowd by that hair. It curls when it rains, and when it rains, he walks slowly. *It's only water,* he says. That's so like him.

Just as I'd never noticed the owls until my grandfather pointed out their eerie hoots to me – *Ssh! Hear that?* – and then I heard them every night, so Daniel's signs would turn up everywhere once I knew of his existence. I got to know his footprints; I learnt the smell of his cheap rolling tobacco, and even now, if anyone else smokes it, I still breathe, turn, and expect to see him there.

This is a hot September. Not the hottest on record, but we can't be far off. We've not had rain for over five weeks, which is rare. It means the Brych is low, the earth is as cracked as the skin on my heels, and the cattle slash their tails at the flies. Not the best weather to be pregnant in. I wish I could have planned this better, but then, it wasn't planned at all. As the cliché goes, it just happened. Not intended, but certainly no mistake.

My heaviness frustrates me. I feel useless. And with the September sales there's a lot to be done. I'm used to being a skinny, capable creature, with not much to me at all save for the arm muscles that sacks of sheep feed and hay bales bring. But now I can do little except check the henhouse for eggs and feed the dogs. I've become the girl who stands in the yard and bellows *Tea! Delivery! Telephone!* Daniel and the other men are working with their shirts off, and I worry they might burn. A tube of sun cream sits in the porch, and I thrust it at them when they come in for lunch. I'm a redhead, I tell them – don't you think I know what I'm talking about?

This sticky heat means a storm is coming. I know the signs. I have the pulse of a headache at the back of my skull that only ever comes with thunder. The air will soon become strange, bluer, and the dogs will be restless and yet won't bark. Nature readies herself for storms. Given a little more time, the wind will pick up. The scarlet pimpernel will close their buds. I love thunderstorms here – they rumble and flash over the bowl of our valley, and our lime trees sway. The sheep don't like them much – they bleat and move over the hills like a shoal of fish. So quick to panic, and yet so useless in their panicking; there are legends of whole flocks filing off cliffs to their deaths, and I believe them. The more brains are put together, the fewer people think – Rosie's death proved that.

I read a poem once, during my brief spell as a university student, about a first pregnancy. *Cow-heavy*, the poet called herself. Do I feel that way? Cow-like? I lumber a little, I can be a bit unsteady on my feet. But perhaps not so much an animal as a fruit of some kind. I am taut, round – as ripe as a plum, and on the verge of being as messy. Fibrous. So ready that I might split. I remember the seminar, rocking back on two chair legs and dismissing the poem. I was cocky. I told the truth – that a cow is not a cow until she's calved twice. *Heifer-heavy*, I'd suggested, throwing my pencil on the desk. I'd never really wanted to be there. I certainly didn't fit in. And I doubt I was missed by anyone when I left the place at Christmas time with barely a shrug or a backward glance.

Rain would clear the air. My belly is protruding from under my shirt – I see my hard navel, the dark stripe of skin. I even look like a plum, with its shadowy central seam. Is that creature inside me wiping its brow with the back of its hand? Will it hear the thunder, when it comes? What's more, imagine being born in a thunderstorm. All your life you could believe that your arrival had an importance to it – that you were heralded in by a lightning bolt. As if the world – or mid-south Wales, at least – approved.

My introduction to Daniel was not momentous. I'd like to say it had been, that we were accompanied by a thunderclap, but that would be a lie. And a poor one, since there aren't such storms in winter. A shame – I'd love our meeting to have been dramatic. I'd love to have a better answer to the questions, *How did you meet? And when?*

My grandmother had always thought him special. She said that from the moment Daniel walked up the drive at Pencarreg, the year before my birth, she knew.

'Knew what?' I'd asked, desperate.

And she'd just shrugged, said she'd had a good feeling about him, that's all. Women's intuition, she'd offered. It alarmed me to hear her say such a thing – romanticism sat strangely on her. But I could believe her, all the same.

Daniel. How did I ever win him?

As it was, he walked into the kitchen on my eighth birthday with his thick hair and a red woollen jumper. I discovered his cigarette smell.

'Evangeline?' He smiled.

I nodded slowly, my mouth full of cake.

From behind his back came a small, flimsy bunch of early snowdrops – *Galanthus nivalis*.

'Happy birthday,' he said.

There were others. A man with a limp delivered the hay. The vet was a jovial man who named me Miss Blue Eyes and taught me how to blow grass. A spotty boy called Owen cleaned out the chickens every Saturday morning for one pound fifty – or, at least, he would become spotty. He'd develop a smattering of acne on his chin, become tongue-tied with it, and when we were fourteen he sent me a Valentine's card as some sort of joke. I swore at him for it. I tore up the card in front of him, to prove I knew his game. Reverend Bickley, too, made regular appearances, usually going home with my grandmother's best Earl Grey tea swilling in his stomach, and half a dozen warm Pencarreg eggs.

As for farmhands, though, there were only two. Daniel was the one that mattered. He lived with us. Or rather, he lived near us – the long green caravan that rusted amongst the fir trees at the back of the barn was his. He refused our spare room, always, promising he was happy where he was. And that place was cosy enough – a stove, a fridge, cushions, and the sound of rain on the roof. I'd seek refuge there constantly, given time – I'd press myself into his cushions, read his books, drink his tea and listen to his stories. So much began in there.

He used our downstairs bathroom, where the moth lived, so that if I woke early enough I'd find the steam from his shower hanging in the hall. His mail and phone calls came through us; his lap was the only one our tabby cat trusted. Sometimes his laundry would billow on the line at the side of the house, like sails.

And there was Lewis. I liked him a whole lot less. He lived out by the gold mines, in Pumsaint, where legend had it five saints fell asleep as they passed through there and left their indentations in the stones. He was nineteen years old that summer – a strong, solid man. He pulled the necks of our chickens when they were too old to lay. I remember, too, seeing him carry a bale of hay in each hand and being wowed by it. But my grandmother disliked him. 'Never a please or thank you. Manners cost nothing,' she'd mutter, 'cheeky sod.'

My resentment of him was for baser reasons: he was vain. He stroked the hair on his chest lovingly, and wore fierce aftershave. And Lewis had a tattoo on his biceps – a green band of barbed wire on his white Welsh flesh, that led him to wear short sleeves whatever the weather. This tattoo was his trademark. It made him stand out in a crowd, and I could never understand this, because I'd always wanted to blend into the background like a peppered moth on stone. But he liked the attention this tattoo brought with it. It gave him away once – it was from this green band that I recognised him one April, delving into the trousers of a brown-haired girl under the alders by the Brych. She moaned as if injured; he looked pleased with himself. I ran home, feeling sick and frightened. The awful secret I'd almost forgotten had been awoken by him. I learnt to hate that tattoo.

All this was a shame – in truth, he was a good-looking man. Lewis made me think of the geese at the park that honked and preened and swaggered. They could have been lovely if they hadn't tried so hard, if they hadn't believed the pond was theirs for the taking.

He works on a dairy farm now. He came over to me at Llandovery market not long ago, scratched his head and said, *Evie, is it really you?* I was civil enough. He had no idea that my grandfather was dead, and seemed genuinely sorry about it. He gave me a kiss on the cheek and his mobile number, which struck me as a dumb thing to do – I hold no grudges, but he used to be cruel to me. He teased, threw a stone at me once, and when Rosie disappeared he quipped that it should have been me, not her, because I'd be missed less. How could I forget such words? What kind of a man could say them? I took his number, smiled, but it's foolish to think we could ever really be friends. Too much has happened for that.

January gales shook the house. Dark pools appeared in folds of tarpaulin, nettle bushes splayed open, and one afternoon, when I had officially recovered, Daniel and I pulled on our anoraks and walked down into Cae Tresaint to buy my grandmother a bag of tea. We never ran out of tea – this was just a ploy, to get us to know each other better. My grandmother watched us go from the landing window, one hand resting on her chest.

The drains gurgled as we passed them.

We walked in silence for a while.

'Tell me about Birmingham,' he said. 'What do you miss? What were your favourite things?'

No one had asked me this. I frowned. Where to start? I had to filter through pink glass stars and cowpats and Wilfred's face to find city things again, as if I'd packed them away in a basement. What did I miss? Trains. The playground in the park. Television. Mrs Willis, of course, and my bicycle, and the sherbet lemons from the corner shop. I missed fish and chip dinners. Sitting on the top deck of the bus. Even school, a little bit. Were these the right things to miss? I glanced over. He didn't seem shocked by them.

'And there were no cows?'

I saw his smile. 'No cows.'

'Well, it sounds like a good place. I nearly went there once, you know.'

'To Birmingham?'

He nodded. 'When you were born.'

'Why didn't you?'

He shrugged. 'Your mother was a busy girl. She had her hands full. With you, with work, with all sorts. And anyway, I'm not made for cities.' He winked. 'I'm a country boy, at heart, Evie. That's why I came here.'

'To the farm?'

'To the farm, to Wales.'

'You're not from Wales?'

He smiled. 'From the borders – so nearly. Have you heard of the Malvern Hills? Well, that's where I'm from. My family are there.'

'Is it nice?'

'It's lovely.'

'Then why did you come here?'

He considered the question for a while. He ducked under branches, hands in pockets. 'For the clean air, the big spaces. Life here' – he shrugged – 'well, it just seems to fit me better.'

I wondered if I understood. My mother would sometimes press her fist to her forehead in a queue or on the bus and say, *I need air, I can't breathe in this place.* She once told me she missed the sky. I'd been baffled. I'd looked up to check on it.

'Did you like her?'

Daniel looked over. 'Like her? Bronwen? What wasn't there to like? She was kind, bright, funny. Do you know, she could walk on her hands?'

I shook my head.

'She could. For hours on end. Your grandmother says she spent one whole summer upside down.'

I felt we could both see her then, wobbling down the lane with us on her tiny wrists, hair tangled.

Just as I wondered if Daniel looked sad or not, he turned, bemused, and said, 'You miss sherbet lemons? Mr Phipps has them, you know.'

Sure enough Mr Phipps did. In his gloomy village shop opposite the church, he had a row of glass jars on the shelf behind the counter – out of the reach of greedy little hands like mine. I cracked my knuckles eagerly. Aniseed balls, liquorice, chocolate limes, toffee. The jars were cobwebby. Daniel shook his hair dry, ran one hand through it and said, 'A quarter of your finest sherbet lemons, please.'

Mr Phipps looked at me for the first time. And for the first time I looked back. Those eyes, from the start, were resentful. He was a wrinkled man. Skin like bacon. A red, bulbous nose.

He said, 'I suppose so.'

The shop was dusty and thin. It had the air about it of a place that needed washing. I suspected there were mice. I suspected, too, that some of his tins were so old that to eat their contents would have meant a day in bed. His vegetable rack was well known – blackened courgettes, holey apples. There were grubs found in his potatoes sometimes.

Dead flies crisped underfoot. A low electric hum.

Daniel counted his change. I moved tins aside to see him. He talked of the rain, my grandparents, the state of mining. In my nose I felt dust.

'I'd heard about the curls,' said Mr Phipps.

I froze. Whose curls? Mine? Surely mine.

'Had to see them with my own eyes, though. To believe it.'

'She'll be quite a head-turner,' said Daniel. 'Don't you think?'

'What happened,' Mr Phipps drawled, 'to Bronwen? Where's she in all of that?'

A pause. 'We think she has her mother's eyes.'

'Bronwen's were brown.'

'In the shape,' said Daniel, 'of her eyes.'

I heard a coin spin on the counter, and stop.

Mr Phipps leant over the counter. In a voice as thick as tar he said, 'You listen. I'll be watching her. You go home and tell them that. You tell them I've got my eye on her. One foot wrong, do you hear me, now? Just one.'

A silence.

I didn't understand.

I held my breath behind my hand.

'Evie?' Daniel called for me. 'Would you mind waiting outside?' I stepped out into view. His look was a gentle one. 'Just for a moment,' he said.

So I took my sherbet lemons and the bag of tea and hung about in the rain. Mrs Hughes stepped past me in a belted mac. Her shoes tick-tacked down the road.

I saw a thin man come out of a white house, and when he saw me he walked towards me. *Bore da, cariad,* he whispered, raising an invisible hat. *Evangeline, is it not?* He had little green eyes. I felt uneasy; I bunched my lips into a sheepish smile. I wanted to be on my own.

Red hair. People always had views on red hair. My mother called it a gift, but it never felt that way. It felt bad, like a blemish. It meant I was spotted when I didn't want to be. School had been hard just because of it. My hand shot to my hair and gripped it. I thought, *don't curl.*

I wandered over to the war memorial, where fabric poppies drooped in the rain. Great-uncle Duncan's name was there. I nudged it with my shoe, and wondered what he'd be like if he still existed, if he too lived on our farm. Would he like me? Would he show me how to shoot rats and climb trees? I squatted and traced his letters. There were bird droppings and moss, which I tried to pick off. One foot wrong?

I studied my own feet.

Then I looked up.

In the churchyard there was a figure – a figure in a dark-green coat, with a tatty grey scarf wrapped up to his ears. Thin, colourless hair. He was looking straight at me. Head on one side, huge pools for eyes. His hands were held out, as if balancing.

I stepped forwards. I said, 'Hello?'

For one tiny moment I saw it. I saw a shadow, a blur, a mark like a blackberry on the side of his face. By his ear, above his eye. Pinkish, dark. But before I could name it he was gone.

The nettles by the back gate swayed for a second, then were still.

I knew who he was. I knew from the mark. I stood in the rain, gazed at the space where Billy had stood, and knew he would be my secret; that something of importance had just begun.

Daniel sensed my quietness on the way home. He told me that Mr Phipps was just jealous, because he had so little hair of his own. 'And do you know who Olwen was?' he asked.

I shook my head.

'She was the most beautiful woman in the whole of Wales. And do you know something else? She had hair just like you.'

I mumbled.

'It's true! That's the legend! Wild and curly. And everyone thought she was wonderful. Do you believe me?'

'No.'

'Not a word of a lie, Miss Jones. Ask Mrs Maddox, she'll tell you. So you just keep Olwen in mind, now. Never mind what others say. Your hair is a lovely thing, on you.'

As we came into the yard I asked how old he was.

I didn't know what the answer would be. Nor did it strictly matter. It would alter nothing. 'Me? I'm an old man, Evie.'

I knew he was lying. Old people didn't look like he did.

'Almost twenty-four,' he said softly. 'See? Old.'

I watched him shake his boots off, hang his jacket on the hook by Samuel's oak front door, and did the maths by myself. Sixteen years meant nothing to me. All I knew was that Wales seemed a better place now that Daniel was in it.

*   *   *

That night I crouched on the landing in the dark and listened to the voices in the kitchen.

'Damn him,' hissed my grandmother. 'Who the hell does he think he is?'

There was the clink of crockery, the scrape of a chair. Daniel said, 'She didn't hear any of it. I sent her outside.'

'But the nerve of the man! The nerve of saying such things about an eight-year-old! In her state! Is he insane? Is he actually properly insane?! I'll see him tomorrow.'

'There's no need.'

'There's every bloody need. This is my granddaughter we're talking about! Bron's baby, and I won't have that bloody fool say such things about her. I'll be there for when he opens. I'll camp out on his doorstep if need be.'

When the muttering was over I slipped back to bed and curled up around Dog. *Not her fault*. That was the expression I'd heard Daniel say as I trudged out of the shop. But what wasn't? My mother's death? My blue eyes? It was too early to know.

As I sifted this through my head on the brink of sleep, the way my grandmother sifted flour, I heard a noise outside. Not sheep, nor the cattle. Not a dog. What? I stirred in bed. *Billy*, I thought, *is that you?*

The noise came again. Not footsteps, either. Was it even a human sound? I couldn't understand it. All I could think of was the sea, the sound it makes as it breaks onto sand – or, being a landlocked girl who knew nothing of the coast, at least how I imagined the sea to be.

Bonfires

Lined paper, torn from a notepad:

A bad week, in that winter's arrived. Early November, but my breath steams now, and the sheep stay near the feeder all day. The bogs have hardened with the frost. They are white-tipped, almost lovely. I want to step out onto them, but if I sank, what then?

Tonight they'll set fire to the pile of wooden crates and broken chairs that Rev. B has piled up at the back of the church. I'll wear a hat. I'll pour the hot wine as always, smile, stay till the last firework has dropped somewhere beyond the main road. Mum won't come. It reminds her of being young, and she hates that. She hates looking back. Too sad, she says. As a little girl, no one took her to bonfire parties so she had to creep out to them all on her own. A lonely thing to do, I think. No one to talk to. No one to jump at the noise with.

But K will come. All men come to fires, I've noticed this. Bonfire night lures them like moths. The Rev. lights the fireworks, Dad shows the little ones how to toast marshmallows as though he's the same age as them. K will turn up late. He'll keep me waiting. He won't stand right by the fire, but still close enough to be seen. I'll go up to him – when? Before the display? During? Perhaps when everyone else is looking up, I'll look across. I think he'll kiss me tonight.

Reverend Bickley remembers her from this night, from the bonfire party of 1968. It was a good one, by all accounts. There were more fireworks than ever before, and people shook him by the hand over a job well done. Enough money was raised to mend the west window, and a picture of the Reverend made the local paper. I've seen it – he had a good head of hair back then. My mother was his assistant, of sorts. The girl who wandered through the crowds with a jug of spiced wine, who stayed behind to pour water on the embers and pick up dropped cups. I think she must have looked beautiful on such evenings – fire-rosy and dark-eyed. I can see my grandfather perfectly, bent by the fire with a stick in his hand, because this is what we did together every bonfire night – squatting in the heat, turning our marshmallows black. 'Gently does it,' he'd tell me. 'That one's ready now.' He was made to be a grandfather. If my stick caught fire or I lost its load, he'd offer me his. Those ones tasted better, somehow.

Once the shoebox was mine, at nineteen, I asked Reverend Bickley, 'Did my mother disappear that night? Was she funny at all? Strange?'

He looked up at me, steadying an armful of hymn-books with his chin. 'Strange?'

'Distracted. Absent-minded. Only, I think my father was there, wasn't he? I think that's where they first properly met.'

He frowned. 'You're asking me to remember a night that took place twenty years ago, Eve. My brain's not as it was!'

A lot to ask of a man in his seventies with a dead wife, an old heart and a problem with pigeons roosting in the church eaves, but he did recall my father being there. He said he remembered him sitting on a log by the field, all on his own. No vagueness in my mother, he said – at least, no more than usual.

But I think they did kiss then. I have no proof, yet I'm sure. After all, in the same blue ink on the back of my grandmother's shopping list she has written *K* over and over again. Italics, capitals, lower case, all in a gentle, measured hand.

Rosie

Today a postcard came. It's from Gerry – my best school friend, and in truth, my only. He has reached Sydney, and as I sit here, writing this, I can picture him sauntering down by the harbour in the sun, with beads in his hair and his boyish smile. I imagine terraces. I imagine the ferries to be blasting their horns. He asks after me. He has been gone for over half a year now – 'wherever sounds good,' he'd shrugged when I asked him where he was going. Two weeks after I told him about the baby, too – was that deliberate? Should I be cross, that he upped and left? I'm not, although I know the news affected him, and I can understand why – it's the age gap again, the unexpectedness. I know, too, that I miss him. I miss his dry humour, his wise words. These things are hard to get on postcards, or crackling phone lines from the southern hemisphere. But I shouldn't be selfish. I shouldn't mind that he hasn't yet said when he might come home.

Anyway, this is a good sign. It means he's happy. Perhaps he's met a girl – although I doubt a tanned Australian beauty is quite his thing. A barefooted dreamer would be better – someone serene, with whom he could contemplate philosophy in a foreign bar. In his way, I think he's fussy. He's bright and kind, yet Gerry was never lucky with girls. It's as if he has an ideal no girl can meet. He loses interest easily. We are opposites there, it seems.

Gerry is proof that there's life beyond the Brych valley. Cae Tresainters have a tendency to think otherwise. My grandfather always told me that Mrs Jessop had never been further than the eisteddfod at Llangollen. I couldn't believe that – 'not even Swansea?' I'd said.

I might still be here, at Pencarreg, but that's because of the way my heart works. Otherwise, I think I might have moved away long ago. I have, after all, traveller's blood in me. My mother left here when I was tucked up inside her, for a city she'd never been to and knew nothing about save for the fact that my father might, possibly, have gone there. That was enough for her. And he too lived out of the pack on his back. A hitcher's thumb, a cigarette; a map of the world in his head.

Gerry and I would sit up on the ridge by the shepherd's hut on clear evenings and imagine the other places that lay beyond Cardigan Bay. Wales, he said, was just a rainy backwater with too many sheep and too few vowels. He wanted heat and sand, to get away from his parents. He'd talk of Greece, Mexico, Egypt, India – all burnt, fragrant, far-off places. 'Come with me,' he'd say, 'it'd be good.' But we both knew I wouldn't. I had a brown-haired, grey-eyed reason to stay, not to mention a farm to run, whilst Gerry was just fed up of hay fever, of lanes with grass growing down the middle of them, of no nightlife, no job. Plus I think those events troubled him – I think he struggled, always, to shake off the thought of Rosie rotting in a nettle bank. He, like me, had dreams of her blonde hair and arched back as she was tugged into shadows like a doll.

And then there's the burning barn. My scarred wrist. Even now, he won't be in a room with a candle; he still runs spent matches under cold taps.

So he always wanted to leave. Australia, he would tell me, had koalas and kangaroos – words I listened to, and which began a list in my head – and a huge red rock at its centre. He said that rock was ancient, full of secrets. Since I met him on my first day at school, this was his dream – to see Ayers Rock. Even now, those two words make me think of sitting on the tussock grass, drinking cola through straws, picking at our scabby summer knees.

He'll be there soon enough – *two weeks till AR!* he has scribbled at the bottom of his card. But then what? What happens when you arrive at your destination? What does a person do when everything they've wanted comes to be? A question best not asked. Tempting fate, perhaps; pessimistic, certainly. The answer to that should be: you are happy. You have no need to look elsewhere.

With February came the curlews. They winged over the fields in the evening, giving their low whooping noise that made my grandmother quieten. 'A good noise,' she concluded, and then returned to mending my socks.

So too came her birthday. As would always be the case she'd refuse any fuss, and then be delighted when the fuss came. I think she managed to have a happy time. I spent my pocket money on a glittery comb for her hair, and she wore it all day, patting her head to check it was still in place. Daniel produced a bottle of wine, and showed me how to uncork it. Mrs Maddox hauled her soft bulk up to the farm to deliver her a rack of her home-made jams – damson, gooseberry, rhubarb. '*Penblwydd Hapus!*' she announced. I must have looked baffled, since Daniel leant over and said, 'That's happy birthday, to you and me.' Reverend Bickley, too, made an appearance, pressing a ribboned box of toffees into my grandmother's hand. As for my grandfather, he arrived back from the town with something slippery and pungent in a brown paper bag, and the six of us had a good dinner that night – fresh sea bass from Mr MacAvoy in Lampeter, whose son had caught it off the Gower peninsula from his very own boat. I was impressed with fish, although a little dubious about the whiskery bones. Still, it wasn't in batter. It surprised me that you could have fish any other way.

That was the month, too, that Daniel took me to the cattle market in Llandovery for the first time. I remember the shouting, the stench, the clatter of hooves on metal. Men talked over my head; some winked at me. The green-eyed man from Cae Tresaint was there, and ran a hand through my hair as he moved past. I swung on the bars, held my palm to the bullocks' nostrils as they panted in their pens. Daniel was scared of losing me – 'stay close,' he kept telling me, 'because what in the world would we all do without you?' He worried for nothing – I didn't stray far.

And more anonymous flowers arrived. I found a clutch of early daffodils sitting in the porch by the boot scraper. 'Daffs!' my grandmother said, unbothered that they were still green and sealed up like clams. Although there was no label, we assumed they were a birthday present. They took pride of place on the kitchen windowsill. *Narcissus*. It took over a week for the buds to open, but when they did, everyone agreed that they brightened up the whole room.

But when I think of February it's not curlews or the sea bass or even the market that comes straight to mind.

I remember the rain – how it hammered day and night against the windowpanes; how my grandmother left a hay bale outside the back door to act as a dam; how Mrs Maddox came to us for buckets when her porch began leaking – 'I might drown!' she wailed. 'I might!' The main road had new signs on it, warning of floods – *ARAF! LLIF!* – and our tractor helped pull a car out. The chickens stayed inside their shed and the sheepdogs smelt horrid. My grandfather's hair plastered itself down over his forehead, like weed.

And I remember how, by Valentine's Day, the heaving ewes were huddled in the barn, the Brych finally burst her banks, and the mud came.

Mud – such a small word. It looks weak, bashful – what harm can three letters do?

The answer is more than you think. That mud was the start of things.

What sort of mud had I known before now? City mud, the silt of a puddle. Not this. This was invasive, stealthy, as sly as a fat brown snake that inches closer the moment your back is turned. At first I marvelled at it – it was perfect for mud pies, for picking up and throwing, and I caught the back of Lewis's head that way. A perfect shot. He yelled out, and I flung myself down behind the heart-shaped rock, out of sight. He searched, but couldn't find me. I listened to his curses, held my breath, and crouched there until he was gone.

As for Billy, I took to studying all the footprints left in the lane. *Are you there?* I'd whisper into the bushes, hoping to find his red face looking back. But I conceded probably not. I found nothing that could have been his. All I ever came across was a blue silk ribbon in the pit beneath the cattle grid, which I left to rot. This was not the weather for wandering up hillsides in, however mad you were.

And I remember, too, with real clarity, how I got stuck in that mud. It was evening. I stumbled into the cow field and suddenly the ground wouldn't let me go. I panicked. I thought of the bogs by the Tor, the first rule, and felt sure I was going to die there. I didn't want to. I wasn't ready. I felt myself sinking, called out for my mother, and I squirmed and hollered until I was found. My grandmother scoffed as she ran me a bath, said of course I wouldn't have died. But I'd been certain. I'd looked up at the winter sky and said goodbye to it.

The animals, though, had the worst time of all. Sheep were heavy-fleeced and slower to run, so we lost more to fox kill that month. As for the ewes, they began lambing in the barn. They heaved and sweated to the sound of rain on the roof, and I'd sit on a bale and watch them whenever I could. My grandfather and Daniel would peel a bluish film off the newborns and squeeze their noses till they bubbled into life. 'What do you think?' asked my grandfather. But I felt a little sorry for these lambs – what sort of world was this for them, full of mud and rain and sharp teeth? It made sense that some of them died. A few of the stillborns looked nothing like sheep – more like sticky brown birds with snapped wings. These dead ones smelt foul. Daniel placed them in a wheelbarrow and burnt them downwind of the house. Not a good bonfire, though, in such weather.

And my grandfather worried.

He took to pacing at night; I found him standing in the yard, as if listening hard. Instinct, perhaps – the same kind that makes us feel watched though we think we're alone. He threw cattle cobs out with the hay. He did what he could, with hindsight. But just as the rain began lessening, foot rot came.

Interdigital phlegmon. Trench foot for cows. Their hooves fill with black pus; tissues die. The smell is beyond description. I spent three days with my hand clamped over my nose, squinting. And that was the first time I ever heard a man cry – my grandfather, behind the bathroom door. I was puzzled – was mud really something to cry about? What else was there to make him sad? As I hovered by the door all I knew was that men weren't designed for crying. It didn't suit them. They were made, I decided, for other things.

I've only heard a man cry once more, since then. Over a decade later, and my grandfather again, but in the hospital this time, standing under the strip lighting of the waiting room having heard from my own mouth that his wife was gone. *No*, he kept saying, *no*. He felt as frail as a leaf when I held him.

It was a Tuesday. I woke to a drizzle, and to a draught that scooted through the house, flapping papers and curtains. Downstairs I found the front door was wide open, and so I wandered outside in my boots and dressing gown.

'What is it?' I asked.

I was ordered inside. I protested but was snapped at. Daniel swept me into the house, used the phone and left his cigarette smell behind. Lewis swiped at me when I pestered him – 'Leave off! Stupid!' I shifted from foot to foot in the kitchen, not knowing what had happened, or what was to be done.

'Are the cows dying?' I cried.

Strangers came to help us that day – at least, they were strangers to me at that time. The kitchen became an alien place, full of unknown smells, Welsh mutterings and stewed tea. I hung in the doorway, unsure. Men with holes in their jumpers and stubbly chins leant against our walls, sat in my chair, and the cat took refuge under my bed. Dr Matthews was there, the Reverend, Mr Wilkinson, and I recognised the man from the white house with the green eyes – what was his name? How can it be that I've forgotten? *How?* I chose to keep out of their way.

I spent most of the time in the barn with the lambs, or with my chin cupped on windowsills, watching the cattle blunder through baths of formaldehyde, studying the vet's back as he scraped hooves and punctured sores.

My grandfather's face found new wrinkles. He took to running his forefinger slowly along his bottom lip, scrunching up his eyes when he thought he couldn't be seen. I wanted to go to him. I wanted to make things better for him, the way he had helped my flu. But at eight, what could I do?

When Mrs Maddox came into the kitchen, I ran to her. She was warm and plump, and she pulled me into her chest.

'There, there,' she cooed. 'It's all in hand, my lovely. They're being taken to another field. Somewhere drier, lucky things.'

I thought, what other field? We had no others big enough.

So late in the afternoon, when the crowds had dispersed and the vet had gone home, when the smell of infection had lessened and the whole world seemed tired, we knocked the cows down the lane. They trudged, necks swaying, to a gate I'd never noticed before – brambles hid it, and hawthorn.

'Whose is this?' I asked my grandmother.

She sighed. 'Don't know. Never have done. It's not ours, or Mrs Maddox's, but it's empty and it's the only field for miles that isn't a bloody quagmire.'

She was right. It was well drained and unchurned. It sloped down to a line of beech trees – just grass and mole-hills, and a nettle bank down the right-hand side. The cows wandered in. I stood in the rain, unhappy.

Daniel leant heavily on the gate.

'What does this mean?' I asked him.

It meant that my grandfather spent the evening doing

sums and rubbing his eyes with the heels of his hands. It meant that my grandmother took tablets before bed. It meant that I'd be sent to Mrs Maddox's for tea for the next two nights, to keep out of their way, and that zinc would be fed to the cattle for weeks. I'd look out at the old cow field and miss seeing them there. And it meant that the next day, when I was visiting the cows, I would look up and see the derelict barn half hidden by the beech trees. A shadowy, unexpected place, and I vowed to go there one day.

But more than anything else that foot rot meant this: when we made it back to the house, a little before six at night, Rosie Hughes was waiting by our oak front door in her pink waterproof jacket and embroidered jeans, rocking back and forth on her roller skates, with her wide, unquestioning eyes.

Rosemary Anne Hughes – a familiar name round here. A name that would soon adorn posters, notice boards, the front pages of newspapers. A name that would be called through cupped hands all summer. So christened because when she was born prematurely on her living room floor, the scent of rosemary from the family herb border was so strong it was all her exhausted mother was aware of. Mrs Maddox told me that. I had no idea what rosemary smelt like until I sidled past their house one evening and snatched a handful from their bush. It was a spicy, sneezy smell that stayed on my hands for hours. From that moment onwards, whenever we ate roast lamb I thought of her.

   If there was a rich family in our village, it was the Hugheses. They lived in a wide brick house with a gravelled drive and fir trees in a line that hid most of the house from the road. I wasn't sure what Mr Hughes did – nor was anyone – because he was rarely seen, but it involved a suit, a tie and Swansea, and he made enough money to provide Mrs Hughes with diamante brooches and an exercise bike in the front room. He made enough, too, to ensure a selfish divorce settlement that came into place only a year or so after Rosie vanished – hardly a kind act. Cae Tresaint muttered about it. It made my grandmother bitter. She'd tenderise the steaks with a brand-new ferocity, curse, narrow her eyes.

'What is it with men?' she'd hiss at Mrs Maddox. 'Why do they bugger off when the going gets tough? Is it our fault? Are we stupid? Are they all bastards, sooner or later, or just the chosen few?'

Mrs Maddox was not, perhaps, the best person for such a conversation. The late Mr Maddox was a saint, or perceived as such. When his wife played love songs on her piano, he'd sing them. When she ran out of soap he'd leave a new bar of it under her pillow, as a surprise. *The little things*, she would tell me when I was older, and starry with love. *They are the ones to take note of, Evie. Grand gestures are all well and good, but love shows itself in the little things.*

'Just a bad egg, Lou,' she'd reply breezily, sipping her sherry. 'There are a few good ones about, don't forget. Your Dewi, for one. And there isn't a bad bone in Daniel's body. You know that as well as I do. Quite a man, that one. What a catch he'll be for one lucky lady some day.'

Rosie was an only child. She'd had her ears pierced, properly pierced, with little gold hoops, and she had a gold bracelet to match. Welsh gold, of course – from the very ground we walked on. Her hair could have been dyed, it was such a bright blonde. Almost white, in the sunshine, and it made her eyes look even bluer. I didn't like that about her – not just that her hair was so very different from mine, but that her eyes were such a colour. Mine were dim in comparison. Envy sprouted inside me, like a white shoot from a bean.

She drew well. I remember her paintings were pinned up in the assembly hall, and she made her own Christmas cards. I watched her play pooh-sticks once, on the humpbacked bridge in Tregaron, and she chose her twig carefully, as if something vital depended upon it. All the boys wanted to kiss her. Once or twice I'd sidle up to her, dare her to climb a tree or eat a leaf of wild garlic in the hope that she might flounder. But she always refused with a knowing smile. Under her school uniform I once glimpsed white lace, and was entranced by this. What did this lace do? When might I have some? These are the things I remember.

If she hadn't vanished, surely she'd have painted. An artist, perhaps, in a house deep in the Cambrians. Married, no doubt – who would not have wanted to marry her, with such eyes and long blonde hair?

And roller skates – I hate the sound of them. I hate the pull and rush of them, like waves breaking on sand. In Newcastle Emlyn, not long ago, a girl sailed down the street on a pair. I felt like pushing her over, to make the sound stop. How did Rosie ever make it up our lane in them? A question we all asked ourselves. Our only answer was that she must be slyly athletic, with a real hidden strength in her. This was a thought people used to comfort Mrs Hughes, in the first few days, before anyone dared mention the word *abduction*.

But that evening, when the yard smelt of formaldehyde and our feet were mud-shod, she stood on our doorstep very much alive. She had brought a pie. It sat in an old biscuit tin. 'Mother said you might be too tired to cook tonight.'

A generous offer, I conceded that much. My grandmother made weary appreciative noises; I inspected the tin, hoping for a fruit pie, or a crumble.

'How kind of her, Rosie. Please thank her for us. Won't you?'

'How are the cows?'

'Most are fine. We've caught it now, that's the main thing.'

'How are the sheep?'

'Very well. We've some lambs now, if you'd like to see them?'

'And how is Daniel?'

I looked up from the cake tin. I examined how her hair wisped at her ears, her jewellery, her embroidered jeans, how her roller skates were pink with sparkly silver stripes running down the side of them. Twelve seemed old to me.

'He's fine,' I told her. 'Thanks.'

She looked straight at me. I suddenly felt ugly, sore-skinned. 'You're Evangeline, then.'

I took Rosie to the barn to see the lambs. I didn't want to, but my grandmother had flashed me her warning eyes. *Don't be awkward*, they had told me. *Not after today*.

The barn was warm and sour-smelling. Straw and dung wedged under my boots. The ewes ground their jaws and eyed us warily. I pointed out the newest lambs, the twins, the ones we'd had trouble with, the orphan. 'We're bottle-feeding that one,' I said, 'just like a baby.'

I thought Rosie might coo over them. But she just pushed her way through the straw on her roller skates, her hands at her sides.

'Do you like having red hair?' she said.

I shrugged. 'S'all right.'

'Only, not many people have hair like yours. Do they?' She turned round.

'So? No law against it.'

'Oh, I know that! My mum says your hair is distinctive. It means you're headstrong,' she said, 'and' – her eyes widened – 'it means you're heartless.'

I snapped at her. 'Does not!'

'Does too.'

'Who says?'

'Everyone. The whole village. And Daniel. He told me to be careful of redheads.'

'When?'

She tucked a loose strand of hair behind one ear. 'Before you came here. I've known him for ages. Much longer than you. He said redheads were liars. He said to be careful because they took people's hearts and trampled on them.'

Hearts? Trampled on? I thought of gum underfoot, of the straw I now trod on, how it felt to step on a snail. And what about Olwen? What about her wild hair? Daniel had straightened my curls and then let them go. *It's beautiful,* he'd said, *on you.*

'*You're* the liar,' I said, narrow-eyed. '*You* are!'

She surveyed me for a moment, her head on one side. 'No, I'm not. It's true, Evangeline. Ask anyone. Even Billy Macklin knows it.' She smiled. 'And he's *mad.*'

'He's not mad!'

'Have you met him then?' she replied, eyebrows raised.

I longed to say yes. I longed to say yes, I've met him, he's clever and bright and you're the mad one, actually. But I couldn't. A glimpse of him in the rain wasn't enough. That wasn't a meeting, and to say that it was would make me a liar, like her. 'No,' I spat. 'But I will.'

'You won't! No one has. Not for years. He hides away,

but he sees *everything*.' She skated slowly back to me. Bending down to touch a lamb she whispered, 'His head is crushed, you know. All bloody and horrid. *Ugly.*'

Don't speak ill of the dead. Who said that? Is it wrong, therefore, for me to say that I hated her? From the start? That everything about her made me awkward and sad? That I wanted her out of our yard, away from our farm?

'Is Daniel about?' she said. 'Is he in his caravan?'

'No,' I snapped, 'he's not.'

I watched her as she sailed down the lane, back home. Her silvery skates flickered in the gloom. It occurs to me now that somehow, magically, they weren't muddy. How could that happen? Still, they would be found muddy – or, at least one of them would be, given time.

I'd see her again over the next nine weeks – in the village shop, in Lampeter, in the playground at St Bart's when my grandparents finally deemed me recovered enough to be sent there. And I'd see her once in a while in our shady lane, twirling on her roller skates, ballerina-like. But we never had a proper conversation again. That was it. That was all we ever really said to each other – that redheads were evil and Billy was mad. We were never friends, we never mattered to each other. So more than anything else my memory of Rosie is of this night, of our first meeting – of our battered, filthy February yard, under a prison-grey sky with disease in the air, and how brightly she shone amongst it. She glowed. Her perfect skin, her perfect hair, that smile.

Mrs Maddox would one day tell me that white flowers were at their best at night, that I should always pick those for a dinner party table. Hopeful of her – when would I ever have dinner parties? And for whom? But such advice made me think of Rosie. I'd walk past clematis or yarrow and feel her skating next to me. Cow parsley, too, did that, but not jasmine. That was not her flower. It grew on the back wall of the pink cottage, and I wouldn't let her have it. It wasn't hers to have.

Daniel and I still talk of her. Not often, but from time to time we hear the news or read a paper, and her name returns. *Rosie Hughes*. A year ago there were rumours again. Bones had been found deep in the Brechfa Forest by a man walking his dog. I remember Daniel telling me, his hand cool and lovely on my sunburnt arm, and we thought of little else for three whole days. We hoped it was her. We hoped she could be gathered up, brought back to St Tysul's and buried near her mother with flowers on her grave. We fell quiet in the evenings at the thought of it. But the bones weren't even human. A deer, they said, in the end. An easy mistake. Just another false alarm, one more in a long line, two decades after she'd gone.

To me she is twelve, always – on glittering roller skates, blonde, pristine, carrying a pie in a biscuit tin. Something moved between us in the lambing barn that night – more than just terse words and dislike. Some sort of understanding. I don't know what, exactly. But I went to bed feeling strange. As if we were two different creatures, heading in different directions, and the barn that night had been our passing place.

The Preacher

As I stretched he saw my birthmark. I hate it, and told him so. But K held my sides, bent down and kissed me there. They would all disapprove if I told them. But I won't. This is ours. I want to keep it this way.

I meet him tonight, at 8.30.

This is how it goes. Children hate their oddities – fingers are pointed and blunt questions asked. But we don't mind them so much when we're older. As adults, they become idiosyncrasies, quirks, the things that make us different. Take Gerry's puckered vaccination mark, or the scar I now have on my wrist. I wasn't the only one to like my mother's little dipping boat. Two of us have both reached out for that same smooth patch of honeyed skin.

I am five foot ten these days. Tall, for a woman. If I sit on the bottom stair and stretch out my legs, I can touch the kitchen door – a useless skill, but no one else in the house could ever do it. I am pale, so pale in places that my veins are royal blue. I have freckles everywhere, pretty much. Needless to say, I used to loathe them, right through my teens – if only they'd join up, I'd grumble, I might look passable. But now? I have one particular cluster of them on my left shoulder blade that looks, Daniel has claimed, like a tulip. I took some persuading. 'It's true,' he promised me, and when I was asleep he played dot-to-dot to prove it. He was right, in a lopsided way. In the morning I twisted in the mirror to see a blue-biro tulip wilting there.

Something to identify me by, I said, should I ever be dismembered.

The old, empty cow field at the back of the house became a magnet for magpies and rooks. They'd hop over the mud, gathering old hay and branches that our cattle had torn off and left behind. Building their nests, I knew that. There was a rookery over near the pine plantation. When I walked there they cackled above my head.

The better weather meant that I could stay on the ridge for longer. I took old blankets and picnics to the hut, and spent hours cloud-watching, thinking of things. Who did this trampling on hearts that Rosie had purred about? Not me. I wasn't guilty. But then who? Were there other redheads that I hadn't met yet? Unlikely. I remembered Mr Phipps – *I'd heard about the curls*, he'd said. And I thought of Daniel. He was mine, not hers. The shoot in me grew a little more.

I wanted to find Billy Macklin. I wanted to track him down, to touch his face, to prove her wrong. I wanted to talk to him about red-headed men, because didn't he know everything? So she had claimed. Like everyone, he could tell me things – about me, about K. But unlike them, he was a forgotten man. No one saw him, no one was bothered about him, so if I met him who would find out? If I spoke to him about forbidden subjects, how would my grandmother ever know? I knew he'd be my secret. I walked amongst the sheep wondering if they had seen him – a grey-scarfed man with a blackberry mark shambling through their fields at night.

My grandmother sensed a change in me. She blamed the foot rot, I think, since she kept telling me that the cows were fine now, that I had no need to worry. 'You can cry about it,' she urged, 'if you want to. It might make you feel better, you know.'

It was about this time too that I saw the preacher.

I was outside the convenience store in Lampeter. My grandmother was short on washing powder and stoutly refused to visit Mr Phipps. 'That bastard? Over my dead body,' she'd declare. So there she was, shifting in the queue with a carton in her arms. I grew bored. I went to wait outside.

He was standing on the street corner wearing a sandwich board. It read, THE KINGDOM IS AT HAND. No one noticed him, or they pretended not to. He rocked a little, his eyes on the sky. He looked so sad to me, tilting his head back and crying out in a strong Welsh lilt, 'Repent! It's not too late to be saved!'

I would dream of him that night.

I know it is hindsight that makes me write him down. I know he meant little to me at the time. Was he an omen? Do such things exist? All I know is that I added *kingdom* to the list in my head, and that I have never seen that preacher since. Not in twenty-one years of visiting Lampeter have I spotted him again. Just that one afternoon in the spring.

All the same, I'd be lying to you if I said that those words didn't come back to me in the months that followed. After lights out I'd remember them, and they would make me sad.

The Grand Piano

There was nowhere else on earth like Mrs Maddox's pink cottage. It was remarkable. It nestled at the bottom of our lane, with a vegetable patch and a magnolia tree. I've always loved that magnolia tree – it's there, still, and in April it still sheds fleshy white petals, as smooth and huge as dishes. They blow all the way down to the pub front door. They're beautiful. Their scent is worth standing still for.

Mrs Maddox wasn't tidy, or clean. Her hallway comprised of a tartan hat stand and a vase of ostrich plumes. The downstairs loo boasted a grotesque Elvis plate; a broken typewriter served as a prop for the door. Nor was she always practical – she hid her keys in the busy lizzies, left chairs and mugs in the garden overnight and sometimes fell asleep with the front door open. Not that there was much of worth to steal.

Her walls were magical, too – she had Chinese hangings, silky and dream-like, showing spreading trees and neat bridges. Did you go there, I asked her? China, to me, was a quiet, dainty place. She shook her head, explained that Mr Maddox had been the adventurous one. A man in a cream safari suit, perhaps, a broad smile and drink in hand? These were his presents for her, his betrothed, as he came home. 'As if his coming home wasn't present enough,' she sighed.

As for her kitchen, it was a bubbly, sickly-scented laboratory. Her jams and pickles were conjured up here, and these she sold with twee gingham covers in a shop in Lampeter. A sign on the main road, too, advertised her wares – FOR SALE/*AR WERTH* – JAM/*JAM* – and this sign was forgotten after her death four years ago. It required wire cutters and all my strength to remove it. She was well into her nineties by then.

In that kitchen there were jam pans, saucepans, frying pans and milk pans. She boiled strawberries and damsons and sharp seedy blackberries from the bushes at the end of our drive; she stewed apples and pears and rhubarb; she would pay me, in late summer, to scramble through ditches to pick sloes off the blackthorn bushes, which she'd then prick, pickle, and turn into gin. That was potent stuff. Only once do I remember ever seeing my grandmother drunk, and that was after an evening down at the pink cottage. That night I stuck my head out of my bedroom window to hear her babbling in the yard at Daniel, and he was leading her indoors by the elbows, agreeing with her, his soft hair shining out.

Mrs Maddox was a pianist, too, of a sort. In her dining room she kept a grand piano on which she'd croon out wistful tunes in the evening. Cole Porter, I was informed. Sometimes I'd slow down in the lane and listen to her – songs about old-fashioned love, love with cocktails, pearls and evening gloves. Her era, not mine, and one I missed out on. She had a good voice, for her age. 'I was quite the looker,' she assured me. I always struggled to reconcile this lame widow with the dazzling girl she must have been. We believe the old are born so, when we're young.

But I didn't seek her for jam or Cole Porter.

'As Welsh as the dragon, you know,' she claimed to be. This was true, in that there was no legend, no fact, no Welsh lore that she didn't have stored up in her head and labelled. The Rhondda, the Five Nations, *Pobol Y Cwm*, red kites, coracles, the legend of Gellert the faithful dog – they were all there, crammed like berries into the same glass jar.

Moreover, though, she knew Cae Tresaint. She knew its people, and she knew what they did. She was a gossip, quite simply, but the well-meaning kind. She polished up rumours and held them to the light. Some were true – Mr Hughes's infidelity, for instance, was suspected years before the divorce, and only Mrs Hughes was shocked when it was at last revealed. But some rumours had no fact in them at all. That Reverend Bickley had lost his faith? Nonsense, and we all knew it. Through the blurred glass of the church door I'd see him sometimes, head bowed at the altar, talking to no one. 'You're wrong,' I assured her. He wore his dog collar with pride.

So had I had more faith in her theories, I might have asked her straight out about K; but I sensed, too, that if I whispered the letter to her, it would vanish. It would catch the wind like a spider's thread, and would be lost to me. Everyone would watch it skitter through the lanes. Worse still, it might reach my grandmother, and her wrath was to be avoided. *Don't say his name, not to anyone! Do you hear me?* I felt tiptoes and cunning were best.

So a teller of tales, some of them tall, but Mrs Maddox knew things, that was certain. Even my grandmother conceded it. 'A mind like a millpond, she has,' I was told. But what did that mean? That her brain was bottomless, I supposed – full of weeds, pike and bicycle parts. Tales of love and loss and sadness wafted beneath her surface. I pictured a drowned girl, for some reason – her hair in fronds, her skin as white as moonlight, her skirt swollen up around her like a patchwork bell.

With all this in mind, it was Mrs Maddox I decided to see about Billy Macklin and how to find him.

Two weeks after the foot rot. Our cows trudged and chewed in their new, better field. The daffodils were out and the Brych was noisy. Wales had a fresh smell to it – watery, cool – and I set off with a clean jumper, a scrubbed face and a bunch of Pencarreg crocuses wrapped in silver foil. I stepped over leaky snails on her path.

'Evangeline! What a lovely surprise! Come in! Come in!' she cried. 'Would you like some tea?'

I said tea would be nice.

Her sitting room felt more like a greenhouse. Her windows were mossy and bird-squirted; tomato plants grew on a shelf. I shared a sofa with a feathery fern, and a tub of geraniums sat at my feet. I liked the colours, but so many plants made me wary. I thought a bug might mistake me for something flowery and crawl into my hair.

'To what do I owe the pleasure?'

I shrugged. 'Just passing, Mrs Maddox.'

She eyed me over the rim of her teacup. 'Just passing? You pass my little house every day of the year, *blodyn*, and you've not popped in unannounced before.'

A good point. 'Well, I've got a question.'

'Ah.' She smiled. 'I thought as much.' Then she leant closer. 'It's not the facts of life, is it, Evie? Only that's not really my place, you know.'

I slurped my tea. It was rosehip, and tasted sour. 'It's about Mad Billy Macklin.'

She blinked at me. 'Billy? Macklin? Well, there's a name I've not heard in a while. Why do you ask? Why the interest?'

'Because he was kicked in the head by a horse,' I said. 'Wasn't he?'

She straightened her back. 'Indeed he was. Are you being gruesome, Miss Jones? Don't you want happy stories?'

'I just want to know,' I reasoned. 'No one tells me anything round here. It's not like I want to find him, or anything.' And I pouted a little, used my forlorn face and tugged at my fingers. 'I'm just curious, Mrs Maddox. When did it happen?' I mumbled. 'And how?'

She exhaled thoughtfully. Those geraniums smelt, I decided, as poison must. The thought made me shiver. 'Let me see, now. When was it? Years back. Long before you were born. Before your mother left, that's for sure. Ten years, I suppose. Maybe longer. Let me tell you' – she leant forwards, her giant bosom swaying – 'a *terrible* thing, it was! Amazing he didn't die there and then.'

She stirred the tea, tapped the edge of the cup twice with a spoon.

'What happened,' I asked, 'exactly?'

'Well,' she began. 'He was always a bit of a loner. Always. Even when he was just a boy Mr Maddox would see him dawdling on the bridge all on his own. No friends, as far as anyone could tell. He lived with his mother in a house miles from anywhere. There's a back road to Ffarmers' – she waved her hand behind her – 'over there somewhere, and it's the remotest little track in the world! She was a funny one too, that woman. Edgy. Refused to send Billy to school – would you believe, he learnt everything he knows from hearsay and the mobile library? And never answered the front door, apparently. Nor the phone. How anyone was meant to get in touch with her I'll never know. *And* she sent Billy out on her errands in all weather. I remember' – she waggled a finger for emphasis – 'finding him soaked to the bone on the Tregaron road. Absolutely drenched, he was. He can't have been much older than you are now. Sent out to buy milk! In a storm! From a village five miles away! What kind of a childhood is that, I ask you?' She tutted. 'Is your tea sweet enough for you?'

'Does he still live there? In that house?'

Mrs Maddox slurped, smacked her lips. 'Apparently. Though heaven only knows how he manages it. The place became a shambles once his mother died. That was quite a few years back now. Angina, officially – heart trouble. But I think it was the shock that really killed her. Seeing your only child like that . . . Can you imagine? I think it was all too much for her. I think her nerves got the better of her. Anyway, that house has gone to rack and ruin now. Not fit for rats. I doubt he really spends much time there. It's a dingy, nasty place.'

'So where does he go?'

'Billy?' She pulled a face. 'Who's to say? A wanderer, he is. Should think he sleeps rough.'

I watched her cradle her teacup. He slept rough? As if homeless? I knew about homeless people. They camped in subways, slept in doorways with their heads hidden so that they looked like damp, lonely caterpillars. 'But he must live *somewhere!*'

She shrugged brightly, smacked her lips. 'Do you know what squatting is? Well, there are a few empty houses about. Old churches. And think of all the outhouses in a place like this! I'm not sure where he lives now, as such, but if I were Billy, I'd find myself a nice warm place, tucked away, and I'd stay there. That's what I'd do.'

'What does he eat?'

'Couldn't be sure. Maybe he goes through bins at night, that sort of thing. I hear he has money enough, though – he's done some odd jobs for the village in his time – lawn mowing, painting . . . Plus his mother might have been crazy but she wasn't exactly poor.' She puckered her mouth. 'All a bit strange, if you ask me.'

This seemed awful. 'Whose bins?'

'Anyone's. Pubs, perhaps. Cafés. Maybe he begs some-times.'

I suddenly wondered if he picked through our dustbins at night, silently, with careful hands, as if he was a surgeon at work. I'd heard noises out there, after all. Did he take our eggs? It was possible. But then, how would he scramble them? He'd need a fire, a frying pan.

'Anyway,' Mrs Maddox said, shifting in her chair, clearly enjoying herself. 'It was October. I know this because Halloween was coming, and Mr Phipps had this horrible leering pumpkin in his window. Nobody liked it. Honestly, it was an awful thing. Your grandmother and I boycotted his shop. Refused to shop there! Who wants to shop in a place with some creepy evil thing like that in the window?'

It sounded just like Mr Phipps to me.

She drained her tea, placed cup and saucer down on the coffee table. 'It happened at Bryn Mawr. No one was really to blame, you know. Perhaps Billy should have known better. He was seventeen, or thereabouts, but he wasn't the rowdy type. He was a quiet thing, remember. And he liked the horses. Wouldn't ride them but he took them apples and peppermints. Drifting round the stables, keeping himself to himself, when one day he wandered round the back of a mare and *bam!*' She slammed her gnarly fist onto the arm of her chair. Her arms wobbled. 'Just like that!'

My jaw dropped. Who could have seen that coming? Who could have predicted that this would happen to a friendless boy whose mother wasn't normal and who was just minding his own business a few days before Halloween? So many things weren't fair – I already knew that, of course. So many things were cruel and sore and made no sense. Why didn't this happen to a loudmouthed, cocksure, aggressive rugby boy, who had been teasing the horse or showing off to others? Why did it have to happen to Billy, a boy with an unloving mother and no friends at all who was only at Bryn Mawr in the first place because he liked holding out sweets for the horses, patting them? Too many questions, and not new ones. No doubt they were asked by everyone in Cae Tresaint, along with *How is he? Did you see it? What's his head like now?*

Mrs Maddox told me that Billy had been thrown ten feet or more. The noise had been like that of a cricket ball and bat – a hard, clean pop. Not much blood, she said. This surprised me. I had imagined rivers of it, creeping out across the yard. Red puddles in potholes. Straw turning pink.

'And he was friends with your mother, you know.'

I blinked.

'Well, of a sort. A few years older than her, but he followed her everywhere, all moon-eyed, God bless him. Not that he stood a chance.'

'He was friends with Mum?'

She looked at me strangely then, as if sleepy. A hand reached out to me. I looked down at it, its blue veins and age spots. 'Aw, *cariad*. Do you miss her very much?'

What could I have said to that? How do you begin to tell someone? I gave a sheepish smile, a light shrug.

She patted my leg, retrieved her hand, and rose from her chair.

'Well, Billy never recovered from your mother leaving. As near as broke his heart, I should say. Not that she meant to. Probably didn't know he loved her, but it was as clear as day to the rest of us. As plain as the nose on my face! More tea, Miss Jones?'

I shook my head. I didn't like her tea. When she turned her head, I poured it into the geraniums.

*   *   *

114

Her word for Billy Macklin was *simple*. As if the rest of us were complicated. As if by having the accident, Billy had somehow been reduced to the barest, purest of things. All his frills had been taken away, trimmed back like the grubby outer leaves of a cabbage.

Simplicity was, in this respect, viewed as a tragic thing. Mrs Maddox uttered the word as a whisper. It was a word that accompanied a downward glance or a shake of the head. But on the walk home I ran the whole incident over in my mind. It was a sad story, for sure. It made me feel heavy-hearted to think of it. But how did Billy change? He was as solitary before the kick as he had been after. He still crept around the Brych valley on his own. He still had no friends. The accident didn't really rob him of much – a fact that hurts me now. It's almost too much to bear. What kind of life had he had?

After that I listened at night for new noises. Any rustle of the wind made me dart to the window for a glimpse of him sifting through our bins. I'd keep my eyes open for new footprints. I kept a shoelace and a lone leather glove that I found in the lane in the belief that they both belonged to him. I was never obsessive, but I was intrigued. Nor was I ever really afraid. Perhaps the thought of a lumbering, mysterious, shadowy man was enough to worry most children, but for some reason, not me. The sound of a twig snapping underfoot didn't scare me, not then. Not once, when it came to Billy, can I remember wanting to take off and run.

I placed an importance on him from the start. It wasn't just a case of proving Rosie wrong – I knew he was far more important than that. I knew that if there was a little box of secrets I couldn't quite prise open, he was the one with the key.

*   *   *

115

After leaving the pink cottage I went straight to visit our cows. They raised their heads as I passed them, wading through the damp grass towards the line of beeches. My hair snagged on wire as I ducked under it. It smelt of foxes round there.

The barn sat in the next field. Half collapsed, with nettles guarding the door. I didn't explore it at that time – it was getting late, and cold. But I stared, and knew he came here. And I vowed to come back till we met.

I would visit the barn three times before Billy and I encountered each other for the first, proper time. There was a strange allure to the place. My heart would jump at the sudden burr of a wood pigeon in the rafters. Beams of light came down through the dark. I'd circle beady spiders, reluctant to get too close. Everything was dusty. Outside, against the south-facing wall, wild strawberries grew, but these weren't really as I'd hoped. Not ripe yet, but hard little berries that tasted so sour I'd wince. Some were bone-white, as if somehow bled dry.

No one else seemed to go there, yet it wasn't officially out of bounds. So this is where I'd run to, whenever school was discussed. I'd charge through the cattle to the barn and its silence. 'What was it used for?' I casually asked Daniel.

His answer was vague. 'Hay storage, maybe. It's been in that state for as long as I've known it. Be careful, though – it's derelict. I doubt it's very safe.'

The floor was dry earth, and I'd sit there, wait, and write my full name into it with twigs. *Evangeline Jones.* Who do we write such things for – in dust, in wet sand, in windowsills with a kitchen knife? Anyone at all: it's evidence that we've been there. It's proof that we've been and gone, when footprints are not enough. But there were footprints there, too – big ones, wide apart. If I tried to follow them, putting my feet where these others had been,

I found I was lurching. A clumsy gait, the gait of an injured man.

My mother's birthday came on the day that the lambing was finally over. The last lamb was swung into breathing, set up on its legs, and the four of us made the trip up to Tor-y-gwynt, a procession of billowing anoraks and flowers that shed petals in the wind. I carried a rather limp bunch of wood anemones, and celandine on behalf of Mrs Maddox – her legs were too rickety for the climb. My grandmother fought the easterly wind for her head-scarf, but the wind won. At seeing her spotted scarf race out over Wales, I suddenly wanted to laugh. I had to bite my lips together to stop myself. I had to jam my chin down into my coat to hide my smile. I was surprised at it. It was a crisp, unfamiliar thing.

That would have been her twenty-ninth birthday – her own dark-red age, her own last backwards glance before thirty.

Charms

No one has noticed yet, but they will. I can't wear long sleeves forever. The shop? Looked there. Not the church-yard. Not at the Tor, although it could be in the bogs. If so, that's that. Could I blame a magpie? Or my wrists for being too thin? Am in trouble. A lifetime of charms and I've lost them. Where? The barn? Maybe the barn. I hope the barn. K doesn't understand it – he says it's just a bracelet. He says, can't I buy another? But where would I begin? Ballet shoes; a Bible; a horseshoe; a clog; a church with a steeple; a horse; an open umbrella. I remember these, but there were others. Such trouble. Maybe the barn. I hope the barn.

Panicked words. I can relate to this – who can't? Haven't we all lost something of worth? But rather her than me. An ancient charm bracelet – an heirloom on my grand-mother's side. Nearly half a century of marriage and a charm for each year of it – there are neither words nor pennies enough to compensate for losing such a thing, as my mother was aware.

Not that it brought my grandmother's mother much

119

luck. It's a heavy thing. Too many charms on it, perhaps – *too charmed*. They clunk together and catch on wool. And it's too wide, made for a chunky arm. Plus these days, it is blackened in places. If I hold it up to my nose and breathe, I can still smell wood smoke on it. All in all, never meant for wearing, and certainly not any more.

Aberporth

As is the way, when my grandfather died two years ago – from not much more than a bad cold, in the end – there was business to be done. He left a whole room of boxes behind. Nothing was in order. I don't suppose he felt the end was near, else he'd have arranged it all a little better. But then, he was only seventy-six. Not really so old.

There were boxes, envelopes, folders, notepads, phone numbers, reminders, lists of cattle prices, advice on tick removal, and loose sheets of paper bearing words that meant nothing to either of us. It took Daniel and me three weeks to sort it out, putting things into piles, filling old bin bags, storing anything to do with the farm in a red plastic chest marked *Pencarreg*. Three whole weeks – but we managed it in the end. I took his old clothes into town to the charity shop, and felt callous for doing so. But I can't have been the first person to do that. The shop assistant reached for the clothes with a comforting smile, as if she knew exactly where they came from. What else does one do with old jackets, old ties? All clothes in such places are surely just items that the dead leave behind.

On my return from there, feeling lonesome, I found a photograph in the top drawer of my grandfather's bedside table. It was creased, well thumbed, thinly coloured. I carried it to the window where I could see it better. My mother with plaits in her hair and a fringe that needed cutting. An untidy, proper smile, as if she'd been caught laughing. Cupped in both hands was an ice cream – strawberry? I turned the picture to find printed in pencil: *Bee, Aberporth, June '60.*

My grandfather called her Bee. It was her nickname, his private term for her – even Bumble Bee in her toddling days. In this picture, then, she'd have been twelve years and two months old. Not a mother, nor lover, not yet anything but a daughter, and in charge of nothing more than a wayward fringe and a melting pink ice cream.

This is not my favourite photograph, but it's a close second. It's an absolute, unquestionable capturing of joy. Her expression is wonderful. She gives the bright, careless smile that only a child can give. Moreover, I think of my grandfather behind the camera lens, happy, barely greying. I assume my grandmother was paddling somewhere, hair pinned back against the sea breezes, trousers rolled up to the knee.

But we went to Aberporth too, Daniel and I. A long time ago now – twenty-one years, or more. He had rapped brightly on my door on an April morning when Rosie was still living and said, 'Are you busy, madam?'

I shook my head, hopeful.

'Then a trip to the coast, perhaps?'

I was overjoyed. I whirled round my room trying on tops, flattening my hair, my brain awash with sea stories. I'd never been to the coast. I'd only ever heard tales of it – shipwrecks, pirates, mermaids, and (my favourite) giant octopi that sucked boats down and pressed their gigantic, unfathomable eyes against the portholes, checking for life. I knew these were unlikely stories, and fictional, but surely only the most magical of places could inspire these kind of tales.

'No octopi, but there are sea bass,' said Daniel, 'and wrasse and bream. Turbot. Fresh mackerel in the summer. Even blue shark right out at sea.'

We had borrowed the Land Rover for the day. He was wearing a pale yellow shirt that made his arms look tanned, and he had sunglasses, not over his eyes, but pushed up into his hair. It was unusually warm for April. Had we known that this heat would carry on right through the summer, that we'd be craving rain as early as June, we might not even have gone to the sea that day. 'Make the most of it,' my grandmother had said. 'This might be our summer, here and now. For one day only.' I sat in the passenger seat, my socked feet up on the dashboard.

'Blue shark?' I asked, excited. 'Could they eat you?'

He smiled. 'Could give you a nasty nip, perhaps.'

'What else?'

'There are seals.'

'Seals? Really?'

'Have you never seen a seal?' he gasped, in mock surprise.

'You know I haven't!'

'Well, perhaps you'll see one today . . .'

The first cow parsley of the year was coming out. As we drove through the winding back roads around Lampeter, I stretched out my fingers and ran them through the stalks. We'd be dipping under trees and scooting over bridges. Even when I closed my eyes, I could tell when we were passing trees or not, because the light beyond my eyelids went from red, to black, to red again.

Aberporth. I remember seeing the name. The sky was as blue as it could be. Everything glinted – the sea, the car park, the shop windows – and we picked our way gingerly into the sea. 'Too cold for me,' he said, feigning shivers.

We wrote my name, the full version, in the sand with a stick. 'Why couldn't you have been called something shorter?' he asked. I found a dead crab. He talked about home, his family in the Malverns, and he said I'd like it there. We ate ice creams with chocolate flakes on a bench overlooking the beach, and watched the tide come in. It slapped itself over the rocks we'd been standing on minutes before. My name was wiped out except for the long curl of the *g*.

Was that the perfect day? I can't think of a single thing that marred it. There have been perfect days since, of course, but is our first taste of perfection the one that lasts the longest? I think yes. After all, two decades on and I can still feel that sand between my toes. I didn't even get sunburnt, because he bought me a navy-blue fisherman's hat from a stall on the seafront. There were no seals at Aberporth, but there were lots of gulls. I learnt how the sea smelt – not fishy, like I'd imagined it, but so salty it made my tongue water. I saw women look twice at Daniel, but it didn't matter, because he was mine all day long.

So I like the picture of my mother for another, simple reason. I, too, have been happy there. Not at the same time, of course – that strawberry ice cream of hers was made eight years and ten months before me. But we've stood on the same beach, she and I, and smiled. I recognise the hill of white benches that rise up behind her; I know that to her right the Irish Sea unfolds.

We came home not long after five. Mr Phipps saw us scoot past the pink cottage, and I caught his eye. As before, there was sturdy malice in it. His gaze was as soulless as a fish's was, but even he couldn't ruin things. I was sitting with Daniel, Billy was in reach, nothing had yet gone wrong in Wales, and the sun had already turned the tips of my hair a little lighter.

Butterflies

She refers only once to Billy in her shoebox diary. At least, I assume it's him. My mother had an irritating habit of referring to everyone by their initial – a sign, perhaps, that she never imagined anyone else would read these letters but her. I was relieved to find no one called E in them – E was for eggs, elephants, eagles, but first and foremost it stood for Evangeline. I was selfish. I felt it was my letter, as if I had the monopoly on it.

B and his brain! I ask him how he knows so much, but he just shrugs. There I am, coming back from the Tor with a stem of corncockle tucked behind my ear and he points and speaks Latin at me. How does he do it? Has he always? K and I hid from him yesterday. I feel bad about it, even now, but three's a crowd, isn't it? And two is meeting in the old barn and grazing my back on the broken beam. I can't believe these things! I can't believe I'm doing them, but nor do I want to stop! I blush! K can speak Gaelic. He whispers it in my ear. When I ask about Limerick he says he'll take me there.

*   *   *

I chose the early morning to look for Billy. I don't know why. Maybe it seemed the simplest time of day to me – unpeopled, quiet, the hour I'd most expect a lonely man to find solace in. I remember the birdsong. Rabbits watched me as I tripped through the field.

I was right; he was there. Through the blackberry tangle and dappled light I saw him. A slender man in a green waxed coat, sitting on a tree stump; a man with big pale hands that hung between his knees, and a scalp that reflected the sun. He was looking upwards. There were butterflies out – orange tips and cabbage whites – and he watched them. Head on one side, slack-jawed.

I held my breath, transfixed.

This was the man Rosie had called mad? The man Mrs Maddox had shaken her head over? Two butterflies tumbled together. I saw him lift a hand, rub his nose, drop his hand again. How could he be mad? In my head madmen ranted and slobbered, talked to themselves. They did not sit on tree stumps not long after the sun had come up, watching butterflies.

I can still see him there.

And I could still draw the mark on his face, if asked to.

When I moved through the nettles he turned to me. That mark was a strange colour – not red, but not pink. It wasn't as large as I'd remembered. It didn't claim his face like some angry veined mask; it crept from his ear to his eyebrow, and then lost itself up in his hair. It bloomed like an old rose, curled like a beech leaf. There was almost beauty in it.

One dark line curved in its centre. It traced the socket, and looked as if someone had taken a pen and drawn there. The edge of the hoof. The crush. The one place where he'd bled.

His head wasn't dented at all.

I thought, *everyone lies.*

'Are you Billy?'

He kept his head to one side, his mark out of sight. I wanted to say, *you don't have to hide it. It's not as bad as you think it is.* He just looked at me, as if I was something remarkable.

'I'm Evangeline,' I said. 'Jones. From the farm. Over there?'

'I know.'

I flinched. 'How do you know?'

Simple did not mean mad. Simple did not mean stupid, or cruel, or unthinking. 'I just do,' he told me. No scorn. No hidden meaning. Just matter-of-fact.

When I shook his hand it felt as light and dry as tree bark.

I was eight. It never occurred to me that friendships could be dangerous, or that there could be wrong reasons for making them. I just smiled, and joined him on the log. I was glad I'd tracked him down. I knew nothing of betrayal, back then.

St Bartholemew's

We never arranged to meet, as such, Billy and I. It was more a case of luck. When I found myself free from chores, I'd dart down to the derelict barn. He was either there, or he wasn't. That's how it came to be.

And as is the way, I seemed to have more chores than ever in the days that followed. My grandmother had offered my services to the Reverend, and so I spent long afternoons polishing church silver with an egg-smelling lotion and a dirty rag. Mrs Maddox, too, began paying me to get her groceries so Mr Phipps's sourness had to be endured. *That silver's not safe in those hands,* he'd remark. And the green-eyed man waved a five-pound note at me one afternoon – 'to wash my car?' he explained. But I was already fed up and said no. 'Ten pounds, then? Go on – it's filthy!' But I had far better things to do.

Needless to say, I always met Billy in secret. I knew if I were to tell my grandmother about him, she would yelp and strictly forbid it. And what guardian wouldn't? He was a loner in his thirties with a blemished face and mysteriousness – how could I have blamed her? Even I knew this friendship wasn't quite normal. So I didn't tell a soul. If asked, I lied, and I became quite deft at it.

'Where are you off to now?' my grandmother would call from the kitchen window. And I'd fib breezily – *the Brych. The shepherd's hut. The pub to buy some crisps.* If she doubted my word, she never showed it.

I'd steal out of the house with sandwiches or biscuits, and munch away with him under the splintered eaves. He rarely ate, but when he did he ate slowly, studying everything with a raised eyebrow as if what I gave him was odd to him. He liked my grandmother's bread, but not the crusts, so we threw them out for the wood pigeons. 'They're making nests,' he told me.

'Where?'

He gave a slow smile, refused to tell. His knowledge, and his alone.

We met by chance at the gold mines, too, although we had different reasons for being there. 'There's no gold there now,' he assured me, but I was convinced otherwise. I trawled through the mud at the side of the path, believing I'd find a fortune in there. Billy just watched, bemused. Whenever I paused, he'd peer over at me and say, 'So? Anything?'

It's important to describe him. It's important to say that although he was four times my age, maybe more, I never really felt the gap. I viewed him as an equal, right from the start.

Despite the smack in the face, the rest of his skin was unlined. No wrinkles at all. I'd look askance at him in the half-light of the barn and think about this – did he never worry, then, and never laugh? Surely his face should have been weathered. Daniel was much younger, yet he had creases round his eyes from squinting into the sun. Why hadn't Billy? I put it down to good genes now. Lucky him.

His hair was that strange non-colour, somewhere between blond and brown. It was thin hair, too, and he was balding a little on top. I was intrigued by that hair. I was tempted to reach out for it, to see how it felt under my tough palm. After all, thick hair was the only hair I'd known.

He was slow to move, as if he had all the time in the world, which I suppose he had – no job that I knew of, no school. What did he do with his days but wander, keep himself to himself? He was blue-eyed. His hands were big and calloused. And I think, looking back, he must have been puzzled by me. From nowhere I appeared, wild-haired and precocious, wearing boyish clothes and a stubborn face, demanding friendship from him. A familiar sight in some ways.

He wasn't mad. Not even a little. Of course people like to say he was – it's a better story. It appeals to human darkness to say he was a savage wreck of a man. But he was just a quiet, tired, pensive man who had taught himself all that he knew, whose family were gone, who was content to let Cae Tresaint believe what they wanted to. He was far cleverer than most of them, that much is plain. Who else knew that hogweed could blister the skin, that the gargoyle existed, or that a gauze around the sun meant rain was coming? These things he told me, and so much more. I know my flowers because of him. He belonged to Cae Tresaint far more than anyone else did.

Although he shrugged off the comments, I still believe they hurt. No one's armour, however old, is without its chinks. I think he was secretly ashamed of what he was. I think, at heart, he was resentful of the life he had been handed. What could he have been, if things had been different? Beneath the red blur he was not ugly. His smile was an odd, sideways thing, on the verge of being lovely. He took his life to untrodden places and lived his life differently. That was all.

Yes, he had a limp. What no one told me – what not even Mrs Maddox knew – was that it had nothing to do with the kick in the head. He'd fallen and broken his ankle, not long after his mother died. Off a log, he informed me coolly. He had told no one. No painkillers, no bed rest, no plaster cast. It took months, but it healed on its own eventually. Incorrectly – hence the limp. There was that sort of toughness to him.

It's important, too, to say that he was never anything but kind to me. He humoured me. And he looked at me as if I was pretty sometimes. No one else had ever done that before, and I liked it.

Billy was neither mad nor depraved. He was a good man – no matter what Cae Tresainters now believe, no matter the stories they pass on to their children as a warning not to wander too far, and to do as they're told.

Those early meetings were polite and wary. I skirted him, biding my time. But just as I was starting to test him for knowledge, and moving closer to him, our meetings were put on hold as quickly as they'd begun. My timing was poor. Like every April that had gone before it, blackbirds began singing in the evenings again, sticky buds burst out at the end of things, and I had to go to school.

It came at a bad time, of course, but then school always did. I'd grown used to my new lifestyle – days at the market, trips to the Tor, walking over the dusty pews in the church. I had calluses on my hands from swinging on fences. I'd learnt how to whistle for the dogs so that they moved to my command. Plus the lambs were perfect by now – out in the fields, leaping the way lambs were meant to.

For a while I'd hoped that maybe this was how life was in Wales – no school; children were simply left to build dens in bracken and explore. But I knew, in my heart, this wasn't so. I'd seen Rosie in her uniform, had spotted the school bus that rumbled down to the war memorial twice a day. But I kept my fingers crossed. Maybe I'd be an exception. I told Lewis this and he laughed at me. He said I was stupid. I said not as stupid as him.

But one evening, not long after Easter, as I sat on the back wheel of the tractor and watched the pipistrelle bats swoop through the yard, my grandmother called me indoors earlier than usual. I frowned; it wasn't bedtime yet. Then my heart sank. I crept into the sitting room, hovered by the sofa and chewed my nails as they broke the news. Those months full of cartwheels, hidey-holes and nettle rash had been set aside to help me settle, to help me recover, and it was believed I had settled now. I was ready. Time's up, said my grandfather. Back to the grindstone. Back to the real world, *cariad*.

For a while I put up a fight. Two nights later I marched downstairs and told them I already knew all that I needed to. School, I said, was pointless – how would history lessons help me? Or French? Or stupid maths? What did a girl need to know that she couldn't learn from the farm? I tried my best to sound clever. I used the biggest words I knew, and widened my eyes because Mrs Willis had once told me she found that look endearing.

They listened but couldn't be swayed. My grandmother said it was about time I had some company; my grandfather looked up from his *Farmers Weekly* and said that no girl could get through life without being able to recite her twelve-times table, which was sneaky, because he knew I got stuck after elevens. I was angry. I told them that I'd refuse to learn anything, that the germs and head lice and stuffy air would kill me, and then they'd be sorry.

Daniel joined me on the ridge that night, and we stood in silence for a while. He pointed out the stars to me. 'See that?' he pointed. 'That's the Plough. The Big Dipper.'

I sniffed, stared at it. Whenever I see those stars now, hanging above the barn roof or reflected in the water trough, I feel disappointed all over again.

This was a new, strange sorrow. It took me roaming. Unable to find Billy, I went to the pine plantation all on my own, and scuffed through the carpet of needles. I thought I saw the green-eyed man there, dipping through the branches at the end of the path, but the light was strange there, so I could have been wrong.

Then, in my last week of freedom, I travelled further than I'd ever been before. I set out on the road to Llanddewi Brefi without telling anyone, and made it there by mid-afternoon. A sleepy, cosy village – I pressed my face against windows and curled up on the stone bench in the church porch, feeling deeply sorry for myself. I climbed down to the Brefi and watched it clack over its stones. 'Take me with you,' I asked it, and the crows in the trees wailed for me. When it grew dark I reversed the charges in the telephone box and my grandmother scorched down the road to pick me up.

'You have some explaining to do, young lady! Get in the car!'

So I explained by shrugging my shoulders and not eating my tea.

'Wonder where she gets that stubborn streak from,' my grandmother grumbled to Daniel as I made my way to bed. I imagined a smile from him.

The cows offered their own brand of sympathy – treacle breath, shining eyes, and as I came back from them one evening I found Daniel under the limes.

'I don't want to do this,' I told him.

He slowly rolled a cigarette, licked the paper. 'I know. But you have to, Olwen.' He struck a match, told me to look on the bright side. 'At least the uniform for St Bartholemew's isn't so bad,' he said.

'You don't have to wear it,' I replied.

But he was right, of course – things could have been worse. In Birmingham there had been a school where the girls had to wear orange and navy. I'd seen it with my own eyes – a blouse the colour of a fox's brush, a blue skirt, and beige woollen tights that made their legs look like sausages and would have sent my eczema wild. My mother shook her head softly at them. We'd see them trail past our house in the rain or hunch at the bus stop, and they always looked so ashamed. I decided that if I had to wear orange and navy for my new school, I'd have gone on hunger strike. I'd have thrown tantrums or run off to live on my own in the old shepherd's hut. I'd have survived on berries, hay and rainwater. The sheep would have kept me warm. Billy and I could have met in the dead of night and stolen eggs together. At eight, you think these things are possible, that you can live as you choose and survive it.

I wore the blazer that used to be my mother's. It had faded in places, and was far too big for me, and even though it had been hung in the sunshine and whacked with the carpet beater, it still smelt of attics. There was a hole in the left-hand pocket that I could stick my finger through. Inside, on the lining, there was a rash of black ink blobs, as if a wet cat had walked primly across it. My grandmother tried everything, but couldn't get them out.

'An ink fight, I'd imagine,' she sniffed, 'knowing her.'

The rest of my uniform came from clothing sales. All my new jumpers had other girls' names stitched neatly inside, and it was strange to think of someone else's feet in my hockey boots, another bottom inside my blue skirt. My tracksuit top had been sprayed with scent, so it had to be washed twice. Even then it smelt flowery.

I spent my final day of freedom wandering glumly around the farm. I sulked by the rhubarb patch, scuffed amongst the cows. I trekked up to Tor-y-gwynt, where the world felt at its wildest. I hid myself in the deserted barn, stayed there so long that the squirrels forgot I was there, and the pigeons purred.

When I came home that evening, puffed out and with hayseeds in my hair, I found a kitchen full of navy-blue things with yellow piping.

I wiped my nose and stared in disgust.

'Oh, don't be silly, Evangeline. It's fine! And it's not as if you'll be the only one wearing it, will it? Honestly.'

'Yellow? I hate yellow.'

'Of course you don't. Don't make a fuss.'

'Urgh.'

'Oh, behave.'

There was still a flaky patch of eczema at the corner of my mouth, but if I pressed my lips together it couldn't be seen. I practised in the bathroom mirror the night before. My grandmother rolled up her sleeves and took the dressmaking scissors to my hair, trying her best to make it tidy. I complained, but the next day we pulled it back with a wet hairbrush, and fastened it tightly into two navy-blue clips. She looked flushed, exhausted.

'There! Look! Dewi – come and look! A work of art, Evie, that's what it is!' I sneezed from the hairspray and a pin fell out.

When I sidled into the yard, Lewis was lounging by the sheep race with his jacket off. He laughed and gave a wolf whistle, so I stuck out my tongue and showed the middle finger.

Daniel smoothed something off my blazer, brushed my chin and gave me his smile, the one he said he saved for special people. He was wearing a white T-shirt that was too small for him, so that when he lifted his arms I saw the hairs on his stomach. They grew in a line.

'You look quite a lady,' he said.

They insisted on taking a photograph of me before I left for the school bus. I hovered by the back door, where Wilfred had stood a century before, and I gave my cold, sarcastic smile. The picture was pinned to the fridge for a while. There I was, stubborn, tidy, convinced I was ready for anything.

I grew to quite like that photograph. I saw it whenever I went to raid the fridge. It was the only picture they had where my hair looked pretty – the sun had caught it, and one side of it almost looked blonde.

St Bartholemew. I had no idea who he was. I hunched in my bedroom, picking at my feet, rolling his name around in my mouth, and decided that he must have died in some painful yet dignified way, because all saints seemed to do that. After something Mrs Willis once showed me, I'd always pictured them in sacking, eyes cast skyward, with a thin gold ring perched mysteriously above their heads. I wondered if St Bartholemew had worn navy blue with yellow piping; I wondered if there was anyone in the school who could actually spell his name.

It was a strange place for any building, let alone a school. A four-storeyed, dark-stoned place, it sat squarely on the B-road that led to Aberystwyth, and looked menacing in the winter months. My grandfather told me it had once been a house. I'd refused to believe him at first. I found it hard to imagine anyone wanting to live in a draughty, echoing place that was always too cold. I'd wander the corridors after detentions and try to picture how it must have been – with tapestries and brandy, fires burning in the grates – but even then it didn't feel friendly. The ceilings were so high that no one could reach the cobwebs. I saw some huge spiders in there.

It was built by the Morgan-Reeses, a family who made their money two hundred years before from mining, or something to do with it. They weren't liked much. I learnt that they strutted in furs and dined in style whilst their miners were sooty and tired and poor. Genevieve Morgan-Rees broke her neck on the main staircase, or so they said. I loved the whispers of murder that ran round the school, tales from the older girls that Genevieve still glided up and down the corridors with her powdered nose, glittery earrings and lapdog. When the light slanted through the dusty top windows in the late afternoon, I would feel she was standing right by me. I hoped she'd been flung by a lover or pushed from behind, but my grandmother harrumphed at the idea. She said that woman probably just fell after one gin too many, that the miners no doubt saw it as justice.

The family left one by one after that. For years the house sat empty; lichen crawled up the wall and the winter storms cracked the windowpanes. Then a bearded man with a long surname spent his fortune repairing the place. He stuck in blackboards, desks, hung a portrait of himself in the entrance hall, and created St Bartholemew's. Every year, on the last day of the summer term, a leaver would lob an egg at his painting. It was tradition, an unspoken rule that wasn't, as far as I can remember, ever broken. My mother did it, I'm certain. I can picture her, hair loose, arm back. I lobbed one myself when I was eighteen – a blue egg, since we had some Araucana chickens by then.

So in winter it looked like a prison, but in the sunshine people liked it. The stonework glowed in summer evening light. In May the rhododendrons were the colour of the dragon, and they rolled out over the hills. I knew they were just weeds really, running riot with the bracken, but because they were beautiful nobody seemed to mind – isn't that the effect of beauty? They were famous, too, having been talked about in guidebooks. During the half-term holidays the school served cream teas in the canteen for the gardening enthusiasts who drove miles for a glimpse.

What's more, between two of the many tall chimney-pots, a pair of jackdaws nested every year. At first the school didn't want them there; they put spikes on the roof and little metal hats over the chimneypots, but the birds came back all the same. Each spring, when the chicks hatched, there'd be a small article in the local paper, next to a photograph of Mrs Ifans trying her best not to look bug-eyed. I liked the jackdaws. Their cries could be heard from the science labs, and their droppings splattered on roof tiles, windowsills and freshly shampooed heads.

I caught the school bus there. A rattling, dark green thing, it smelt of teenagers – of baby talc, antiseptic, feet, cheap aftershave, of minty gum being worked between teeth. Cigarette smells too, sometimes. There were clods of mud on the steps from football boots, and on rainy afternoons the bus steamed inside with wet bodies. It could be a lonely place. Strands of hair hung over the armrests. Lip balms and drink cans raced over the bus floor every time it braked.

On my first day, I sat on the bus and felt sad. All I could think of was the farm, and what I might be missing out on. April had unfurled into a warm, promising month, and I felt the ridge was the best place in the world in such weather. Deer had been spotted tiptoeing there. I'd wanted Billy to take me to his shambling old family house, or to show me where the red kites lived, and wouldn't today be the perfect day for it? I stayed miserable. I tugged the loose threads on my blazer. Kites began with K. I tucked the thought away inside me.

The entrance hall was cold and smelt of polish. I remember the walls were turquoise, and the infamous staircase curled round in front of me. The new pupil's list declared me as *Jones, E*, and I had to stretch up when I reported to the woman with the mole behind the reception desk. She didn't smile. Neither did I.

'Wait in the corner,' she said.

The first days at places make no sense – they are jumbled, distorted, and as I watched the other pupils file past the window I noticed how big they were, how real, how grounded. They knew what each bell meant. They knew where each heavy door led to. They knew a whole other language.

'*Melyngoch*!' A boy with straining buttons pointed through the glass at me. He blew a mocking kiss.

I showed two fingers back.

He laughed fatly, stumbled on.

'Ignore them,' said a voice.

I turned to find a pair of anxious eyes beneath brown scarecrow hair. Pale eyes with long lashes. Why should his lashes be so thick and long, when mine were short and red?

'What was he saying?' I asked. 'I'm not Welsh.'

'I know,' he said. 'You're from Birmingham.'

'What did he say?'

'It's your hair. They're calling you ginger.'

'That's all?' I could do more damage than that.

*   *   *

140

This was Geraint – but I could call him Gerry, if I wanted. And whilst Mrs Jones – no relation – assigned a bespectacled girl with a blocked nose to look after me in my first week, it was Gerry who told me the important things.

Don't lend out your rubber or it won't come back.

Don't stick out your bum at the water fountain.

Our school's haunted, you know.

Don't eat the cabbage.

See him? Joe Vickery? He's got someone else's kidney.

I couldn't believe it. 'He can't have!' I cried. 'How could he?'

'He has. Everybody knows it. He's got the kidney of a dead boy. Ask him if you don't believe me.' I didn't ask, it seemed wrong to. But to have someone else's organ sitting there, pulsing under your skin? It was an incredible thought.

Gerry was brainy. His work came back on the second day with stars on, and he was always asking me about Birmingham. He wanted to know about our coal mines and the double-decker buses and curries. He asked me about the IRA bombs and rush hour. So I'd tell him. We'd hunch together on the steps at lunch time and I'd bring out the stories I'd kept safely tucked away – the rats under the garden shed, the things I'd seen under the railway bridge, how we'd wander up and down the High Street on a Saturday with our eyes peeled, looking for red-headed men. I felt special, talking about the city. Others listened to me, too. I thickened my accent; I spiced up my tales.

'How did your mum die?' He asked me this on Wednesday, as we wandered round the playground, our mouths coping with gobstoppers.

I shrugged. 'She just did.'

'My dad said he heard it was suicide.'

'Well, you can tell your dad it wasn't. Your dad's wrong. There was something wrong with her heart.'

'What was wrong with it?'

I pouted. 'Not sure. It was just weak. It wasn't built like everyone else's.'

'So it was a heart attack?'

'No. Only old people have heart attacks. It just stopped working.'

He considered this. 'Do you miss her?'

Why did people ask me this? A stupid question. I looked down at her blazer. I wanted to say that she smelt of jasmine, that she used to present my tea to me with a fanfare, as if that food was magic. But instead I just said, 'Sometimes.'

In return, he told me that his parents hit each other.

'Never on the face,' he said, 'because people find out that way.'

So by the end of my first week there, I felt that our secrets had been pressed together, twisted into the same shape, and that they couldn't be peeled apart again.

My first Friday. It's infamous now.

It was lunch time.

Gerry was playing football so I went to lunch on my own. I filed into the room and picked up my metal tray.

The canteen smelt of boiled vegetables. It was as noisy and steamy as a swimming pool. I sat on my own. I felt hot, tired, fed up. I couldn't leave my plastic seat until I'd eaten everything, but I didn't want it – I hadn't yet learnt that food could be mashed up and hidden under cutlery, or how sprouts could be flung under the table with a spoon.

I sat there for nearly an hour. It was cheese pie – I remember that because I found out it was easy to pick up and throw.

The girl was older than me – older, and twice my size. She wore lipstick. She had rolled up her skirt to show off her knees. I watched her sway to my table, place both hands in front of me and lean over. Her perfume was strong. The polish on her fingers was chipped. I was confused. Did I know her? A table of boys was watching me.

'Those scabs on your mouth? You a leper?'

In the playground in Birmingham years before, a boy from the other class had made fun of my eczema. I'd bitten him. I'd sunk my milk teeth into his chunky arm. He'd yelled, swiped at me. But I'd done enough. A red dented half-circle swelled up on his arm, and turned the colour of a bruised banana. I got into serious trouble for it. There were letters home, no playtime for me for a fortnight, and the boy had a plaster for nearly a week. But it was worth it. I thought I'd been so clever. He'd mocked my skin and I'd damaged his skin back. Violence had worked that time.

'I'm talking to you! Are you deaf? *Byddar?* I said, are you a leper?'

Then there was the time in winter, when my skin was at its worst, and a woman in the Bull Ring had covered her mouth and nose as she passed me. As if I was contagious. I'd followed her round like an imp after that, breathing at her, tugging her sleeves, and she'd shrunk from me in horror, which only made me want to chase her more. My mother pulled me away and kept me pinned to her side for the day. I'd hated that woman in the Bull Ring. I'd wanted to bite her too.

'I heard,' the girl purred, 'that you're half thieving Irish bastard anyway. As well' – she smiled – 'as a leper.'

I lunged for her. I snatched at her hair, pulled out fistfuls. My chewed nails scratched at her face. She flailed, slapped, but from nowhere my fist came, and I slammed it into her chest. I punched the way I'd been taught to,

143

with my thumb wrapped over my fingers, my elbow driving it up, and I shouted out as I hit her. She wheezed. My water glass fell and smashed, my cutlery rang out on the floor. Chairs were pushed back as I smacked her again. Her face was red and sweaty. She tried to clamber away, but I grabbed her jumper. I managed to scoop up some cheese pie and push it into her hair, before my shoulders were seized and I was dragged off. I was yelling at her, and she was shaking. *Take it back,* I was shouting, *take it back*. The whole canteen was roaring.

As I stumbled back, breathless, I saw Rosie's face in the corner of the canteen – pale, expressionless, more beautiful than anyone else. And I saw, too, that she was the only person there who wasn't afraid.

I sat in the headmistress's office and swung my legs. She gave me an hour-long talk, two thousand lines, a fortnight of detentions, took away my playtime for a month, wrote a strongly worded letter to my grandparents and told me that, since it was my first week, she'd give me one more chance. But only one, she warned.

'I don't care what you've been through, Miss Jones, but I will not tolerate that behaviour again! Do you understand me? It will not do!'

She wore rectangular glasses. One eye didn't move much – it had a gluey look about it, and spent its time gazing over my shoulder, as if rumour had it there were two of me. I nodded dutifully. She had eyebrows like snail trails that met in the middle.

On the bus ride home, I found that the fight had torn a second hole in my pocket. For the rest of my days at St Bart's, I lost a lot of money that way.

* * *

That fight had repercussions. Gerry told me, years later, when we were in our late teens, that he'd seen it through the canteen window. I'd had no idea. He said he'd thought me vulnerable till then. I'd blinked at him, laughed, and wondered how he could ever have thought that. *Vulnerable?* I asked him. *Why?*

But his view of me wholly changed that day, he said. For better or worse, I don't know, I didn't enquire. But I knew he hated violence. He'd seen it at home, now he'd seen it at school. Did my fists make him anxious? Or was he amazed to see a girl fighting back like that, a blur of limbs and hairpins? At any rate, we're still friends. The lesson we both learnt was that all it takes is one event to see a person differently.

As for Daniel, even when I was eight, his view mattered. I wanted him to really like me. Whatever I did, at the back of my mind tapped the thought, *will he approve at all?* I certainly thought that, after the fight, and feared I might lose him because of it. All I could think of on the bus home was, *don't hate me.*

But after our first kiss, two years ago, the only question that mattered was: when did I stop being childish to him? When did I become a woman? When did he first see me, as I am now?

One lazy Sunday morning not so long ago I turned to him and asked him. I said, 'Daniel? At what point did I stop being eight to you?'

I don't think I'd expected a definite answer, but one came.

'When you came back from university,' he replied. 'You wandered up the drive with all your bags. Your hair was past your shoulders then – you remember? Eve, you have no idea . . .'

Of course I remember. I remember my aching back and the drizzle, and the throb of my piercing in the top of my ear. I'd left university because of him. I'd learnt that I didn't want to be anywhere he wasn't, that I physically couldn't stand it. I was eighteen; he was in his early thirties. I came up the lane and found him standing there, under the limes, wearing blue.

The Trout Hotel

On a softened beer mat for porter ale:
The Trout Hotel, Llandysul, 12th February.
'It is too late to start / For destinations not of the heart.'

A poem? Wouldn't that be like her, the romantic soul, to turn to poetry once in love? And if so, was this a line she herself discovered, or was it something my father offered her, which she scribbled down as he went to the jukebox, or the bar? Her handwriting, for sure. The mat smells of stale beer and cigarettes, even now. I once thought I'd detected jasmine, but I must have imagined it. I pick it up, hold it to my nose and breathe – it's not there now. My baby and I cannot smell jasmine. There's nothing flowery about a beer mat that's been kept in a box for twenty-nine years.

Did they stay the night there, at the Trout Hotel? If so, whose initiative? Under white sheets in a brown-walled room.

Sunburn

Everyone heard of my fight.

Like all bad news, it pushed its way under doors. My grandparents weren't pleased. 'We're raising a thug,' hissed my grandmother, hands on hips and hair tangled. I tried to reason with her. I told her the punches were all deserved, that that girl had been bullying me. Wilfred, I told her, would have done the same thing. But such protests were to no avail. My punishment was to be in bed, lights out, by eight o' clock for a fortnight – a cruel sentence in such good weather. Even midges stayed out longer than me. I sulked. I thought of Billy, sitting there on his own. I was yet to really find out anything from him, and I minded that. A knock on my door and I'd shout, *I don't care! Leave me alone!* My grandmother muttered to Daniel that if this was a taste of what was to come in my teens, she'd be dead through her nerves by sixty-five.

Mr Phipps was more self-righteous than ever before when he heard I'd been using my fists. *You've proved me right,* he said. He sneered at me whenever we met – that bulbous nose of his would wrinkle and his lips would curl. 'Didn't I tell you?' he asked Mrs Hughes. 'Didn't I?'

'Yes, you did,' she replied sagely.

'This is just the start of it, I'm sure. Bad blood . . .'

'No doubt!'

'It's just a matter of time before she causes more trouble. Mark my words. *Mark them.*'

How do I know this? Gerry overheard them. He felt it his duty to report back – *Because you're my best friend*, he said with a shrug. Sweet Gerry. He was more girlish than me, in a way. There I was, wild-haired, square-jawed, unrivalled at climbing trees and vaulting gates – and there was Gerry: slight, even delicate, with eyes like puddles and a complete inability to run. His legs would flail, so that he looked like a panicking crane fly. In all our races I won. I'd crow about it, too – 'You're *so* slow,' I'd tell him. What could he do but agree?

He's never been my best friend. Is that unkind? It's the truth. Of course we're closer now, having lived through the same trouble. That summer, its heat and fire and worry, bonded us, in a way. But back then, I just saw him as someone to chase, to steal the Reverend's pears with. And he invented some games that seriously impressed me – peeking up Mrs Hughes's skirt, teasing Mrs Jessop's scraggy old hound till it barked itself hoarse and she came storming out of the shop, waving her fists and jabbering with anger. Plus he helped me to cheat in Welsh lessons by wafting his paper to let the ink dry, and tilting the answers my way. Valuable, in that respect.

In return, I showed him the shepherd's hut. I offered him the view, the peat bogs, the Tor. I think his wanderlust was born on our ridge. He'd stand with his arms out, swallowing mouthfuls of air, smiling. He loved that. In the evenings he'd look at me with gratitude. Up there, he felt freedom, or a child's version of it.

As for Daniel, news of the fight made him try to hide a smile. He took me down to the Brych one evening and listened gravely to my grievances. I told him how unfair

150

it was, how the whole school had been watching me so what else could I have done? 'Just walk away next time,' he told me.

Walk away? That felt easier said than done – how was anyone supposed to walk away from such taunts? But he looked lovely on that river bank, all sun-flushed and earthy, and his eyes were as grey and soft as pigeon wings, and I felt happy just by sitting there, and looking up at him, so I said yes, yes, I promised to walk away next time. *Yes*. 'I won't use my fists,' I said. 'Never.'

A promise I kept. To this day, I haven't hit anyone else. But what if I had done? What if I'd taken that promise and broken it six weeks later? Snapped it over my leg like a branch? Left scratches or bite marks to be explained away?

What if . . . ? A question we ask to hurt ourselves.

May rolled in with a gauze of flies. They bothered the cows by nestling round their eyes, and wasps found their way everywhere. They crawled over the flowers on gravestones, and the White Hart garden buzzed constantly. I was stung by one. I'd seen it drowning in the dog bowl, and so had dipped my thumb in to save it. It pressed its sting right into the pad, and I screamed for my mother. My thumb swelled like a plum. What sort of justice was that? I trapped wasps from that day onwards. If I could crush them, I did.

The men began working with their shirts off, but despite the heat, Billy still wore his green waxed jacket. I'd spot him up at the Tor sometimes, his hands grabbing the air as he skirted bogs, that coat flapping at his sides. When I met him in the lane one evening, a few minutes before my curfew began, I asked him about it.

'Aren't you hot in that?' I asked.

He considered me as if this was a trick question. Perhaps

he thought I might throw a punch at him if he got it wrong. 'No.'

I shrugged. 'All right. If you say so.'

And he'd dug a frail purple flower out of his pocket. 'Pansies,' he told me, 'for thoughts.' And I'd see his slow smile and watch him walking back down the lane, out of sight.

This is how he was known. Waxed jackets in a heat wave; an unreadable glance and a two-toned face. He gathered flowers as if they belonged to him – as if they were things he'd owned, then lost. *There you are*, he'd say, reaching down into the grass.

A few days later, in the gloom of the derelict barn, eating the fruit I'd sneaked under my shirt, I asked him why he came to the barn. I was meant to be at school. I was in my uniform, my shoes kicked off and my socks unpeeled. That evening I would forge a note from my grandfather. *Evie has been poorly.* I was sure I could manage it well enough.

'If you have a house, why bother coming here?'

He'd caught the sun on his scalp – proof that summer had already arrived. Despite the light I could see its redness. I knew how it felt to burn like that. I knew if I pressed there his skin would turn white for a second or two. Would he too become freckly now?

'Here?'

'Uh-huh. Why?'

He sat against a beam, his knees bent and his arms resting out on them. 'It's peaceful. No one else comes here.'

'How did you find it?'

'Just came across it.'

I sunk my teeth into an apple. 'When?'

A suspicious glance. 'Ages ago.'

'Only I had no idea it was here. I just saw it, through the trees. Who owns it? Do you know?'

Billy shook his head. After a time he shifted a little and said, 'So, you've hit someone.'

Not a question but a statement. How did he know that? How could Billy have caught hold of such news so quickly, when no one ever saw him to speak to? I slapped the dust with my hand. I hadn't wanted him to know. 'She deserved it.'

Did he smile in the dark? If so, only the ghost of one. 'You'll have no friends.'

'What? Like you?'

No response.

'Because you don't have any. Do you? Do you have any friends?'

'Happy as I am,' he said.

I didn't believe that. Everyone had to have friends. I knew I didn't have many, I never had done, but I'd had my mother, and now I had my grandparents and Daniel. I had enough. But to have no one? Not even one person to talk to? Even I wouldn't want that. That would be real, awful loneliness.

'You can't be happy! You can't be! Don't you miss people?'

I felt his mood darken. His hand retrieved something silvery from his left pocket; he studied it. It seemed best to say nothing for a while.

Eventually I broke the silence by saying, 'You've burnt your head. Did you know that? It's pink.'

He sighed.

'Not there! There.' I pointed to his crown. 'Should I bring some cream? We have some cream at the farm. I need to use it. I'd burn a lot otherwise. It's my skin. I have Celtic colouring.'

'Of course you do. Look who your father was.'

He stood, brushed himself down. I knew I'd offended him. I felt I'd pushed him away into a faraway place only

153

Billy could go to. He inched out of the barn into the light. I couldn't let him walk away. I couldn't afford to. 'Billy!' I called. 'Listen! I'll be your friend! If you want!'

He said nothing.

'Where are you going?' But he didn't look back. 'I'll come again soon!' I promised. I hoped he'd heard me. He was already halfway through the field by then, limping through the cows, hands in pockets, head bowed.

I did come back – with sun cream and liquorice and bottles of orangeade I'd spent my savings on. And he would be back there, too. He would study me with his huge blue eyes, and he might twirl a lone buttercup between his finger and thumb, but he didn't say much. I was bursting with questions – *Did your head hurt? Can you remember it? Who was K? Who? What else do you know? What about trampled hearts?* But I was wise enough to take it slowly. He wasn't a man to be hurried, or else I knew I'd lose him – he'd vanish off into nettles again, and become nothing more than a rumour, a weaving track through the grass.

One more thing: some more flowers turned up on our porch at this time. Not pansies or buttercups, but huge stalks of cow parsley – the pollen made my eyes run. No one could understand it. I was blamed for a while – *For God's sake! Is this some joke? Evangeline?* But those flowers were nothing to do with me.

In time my grandfather would tell the police about it, in the belief it was sinister, that surely it meant something bad. But they were as baffled as we were. A secret admirer? they suggested. My grandmother scoffed, but not unkindly.

'Aren't I getting a bit old for that?' she said.

Swimming

Is that why we give flowers? To express admiration? Sometimes. But there are other reasons. A symbol of love, or of commiseration. A way of saying thank you. A mark of respect. Proof we like someone, and want them to smile. And we put flowers on graves to say *Look, we still think of you. You've left a space behind.*

The fourteenth day of May.

The hottest day of the year so far, or so the papers said. Our cattle stomped their feet in the dust; our sheep were sheared. I saw my first ever mole that morning. From the landing window I saw earth being thrown around under the sycamore tree, and ran outside to find it. Seeking water, my grandfather supposed. It seemed such a vulnerable thing.

We swam in the afternoon, Daniel and I. He said my grandparents could manage without him for an hour so I wedged a towel under my arm and set out after him, along the blackberry track and through the sheep. It was heavy, sticky-fingered weather. Our legs disturbed crane flies in the longer grasses, and they rose drowsily, like lost

155

balloons. I was too hot to catch them. I just tripped after Daniel, his white shirt darker at the base of his spine.

The lake was as round as a penny and just as bronze. I lolled in the shallows, watching Daniel drift out into the darker water. Pike lived in the lake, they said, and perch. I'd heard, too, that these lakes were deep things, huge bowls of black water that had been there for centuries. Anything could hide there. Daniel glided on his back in the distance, and I thought, *Don't go so far. Come back now, come back.*

I remember that afternoon because I sat in the water for so long that my fingertips shrivelled like apple cores. As Daniel lay on his back on the grass with his cigarette, I managed to skim my first stone. And the midges began biting my scalp on the walk home, so I wrapped my towel round my head and walked with my arms out for balance. He smiled at me for that.

That afternoon was the last time anyone saw Rosie. She beamed at Reverend Bickley as she sailed past the church on her roller skates, just before four o' clock. I was examining the shale for gold then. If she was taken, as it's now believed she must have been, it was as I squinted over the water to watch Daniel swim. The arc of his arms, his quietness. I remember, too, that I didn't miss my mother that day.

BOOK TWO

Ghosts

At night my baby stirs. With the heat of the house I cannot sleep, so I lie in the dark, wide-eyed. My baby won't sleep either. As if it knows I am troubled, it pushes a tiny foot against my stomach wall. *I'm sorry,* I want to tell it. *I'm sorry I'm not sleeping, and I'm sorry it's so hot.* I run my fingertips up and down my bump, the way I'd trace a spine. I wonder what it knows. Easy to say nothing at all, because it's a foetus, it's unborn. But as I hear my own breathing and the foxes barking, I believe this child is all-knowing. It feels wise to me. As if by being inside me, it sees it all.

Mrs Hughes killed herself in the end. She stocked up on sleeping pills and aspirin and laid herself down on her silk bedcover with two bottles of vodka and Rosie's baby album. Her husband had remarried by then. He didn't attend the funeral. He didn't even send flowers.

I'm afraid. It is not like me, it is nothing like me, to admit this. But I am, I can't help it. What I feel for this creature – for this tight bundle that presses its fists into my ribs, that gives me heartburn, swollen legs, that made me crave vinegar by the tablespoon for two months, that has no name yet, no face, no anything – what I feel is too much to take, already. I knew nothing till now. Till now, I had no idea of what fear was like. What did I feel when an unwanted hand moved down my eight-year-old back, and under? A weak, clumsy version of this. What I felt at nineteen as I drove to the hospital after my grandmother collapsed at the market was stronger – that was a definite fear because I didn't want her to die, I wasn't ready for it, and I didn't want to have to turn round to my grandfather in the hospital waiting room, look into his eyes and tell him that she was gone. Yes, that was fear. I was afraid then. And I feel fearful, too, whenever Daniel's late. The thought flickers through me like a twilight bat – *what would I do? What would I become?* My breath falters with that.

My grandfather told me, having been widowed, that nothing is joyful again. Happiness returns, he said – laughing comes back to you, and the world is still good, and you smile again at things. But real joy leaves. Everything lacks from then on, he said. Mrs Hughes learnt that well enough.

But above all else, more than anything, I am scared I'll lose this. That I'll let it down. That my back will be turned at the one time it matters, the one time it needs me, and my child will be gone. My little kicking deer. My second heartbeat. How did my grandmother bear it? How did she not dissolve, go mad?

I wish I could speak to her now. Only now can I understand it. I'd like to thank her, because I don't think I ever did.

She was a remarkable woman. I now know that her life was weighed down with unfathomable sadness, so much more than anyone realised. Yet she still sang under her breath and remembered everyone's birthdays.

No wonder Reverend Bickley was privately, hopelessly in love with her. He's in love with her still, although she's long gone. He leaves lilies on her grave, and shy, dry, mournful kisses on my cheek when he goes, because my cheek is the next best thing.

My grandmother wasn't born in Wales. She was a Cornish girl, raised in a battered village on the north coast where the windowpanes were sticky with sea spray and the weathervanes never stayed still.

'Ghosts,' she claimed, 'lived in our house. Old smugglers. I heard them creaking downstairs at night.' I'd study her face, never quite sure if she should be believed or not.

She was unruly, hot-headed, even then. Her father was a headmaster, and although I never once saw his picture I imagined him often enough to feel that I had – beaky, pale, sweeping through empty streets with books against his chest and his black coat snapping at his heels. He slashed a cane against teenage legs, but his one and only daughter ran unchecked. She answered back; she stood in the surf with her clothes on; she questioned the vicar and sauntered home after dark.

'But I was never beaten,' she told me, 'not once. I was locked up instead – any time he felt like it. Said it would do me good.'

'And did it?'

'No,' she replied, 'it did not.'

As for Mrs Fenwick, she was bedridden and never left the house. I couldn't think of anything worse. All that coastline and no way to explore it.

'Fat, plain fat. Even before I was born she was a big woman. They had separate bedrooms, my parents. He had the attic room, with the sea view, and she just kept herself at the back of the house.' I saw her become glassy-eyed, far away. 'All my life, she just lay in the dark.'

'All your life?'

'Ashamed to be seen.'

'Even by you?'

'Particularly by me. If I went into her room she'd curse me. She'd tell me to get out of her sight.'

That was an image I couldn't shake off – of a warm, fleshy creature, sprawling in a gloomy back room, smelling of old sweat and talcum powder, lumbering further under the blankets when her daughter came in. I said I didn't understand it – why did she let herself get so big? Why did they marry at all? How did she make it to the bathroom? I said Mr and Mrs Fenwick sounded more than a little mismatched.

'Maybe,' whispered my grandmother. 'But then love comes in all shapes and sizes. He gave her that charm bracelet, remember? A charm for every married year. Proof of his love, that was.'

So a teenaged Louisa Fenwick waltzed into pubs and smoked Woodbines and learnt how to lower herself from her windowsill by her fingertips so that she could race off at night to meet soldiers on leave. She sat on the very edge of cliff tops. She rolled up her skirts and drank gin in the dunes. This I learnt from my grandfather. He said she cavorted. *Cavorted* – a good word, although back then I had no idea what it meant.

Given time, I found out this meant she'd had a lover.

A secret lover, of course – these were the days when women were demure, crossed their legs and saved themselves. But then, my grandmother rarely heeded tradition. I should have guessed she had such secrets in her.

She confessed to me when I was fifteen – over her third glass of sherry on a rainy evening. 'A scar under his left eye,' she said, 'like a crescent moon. And he was a fisherman, Evangeline. Proper boats, netting, lines, pots – everything. He'd set off from Padstow, and I'd stand there, watch him go, and imagine what it would be like if he never came back.'

162

Could any story fit a novel better? How romantic. My grandmother on the jetty, one hand holding her hair back, the other keeping her coat wrapped round her. Or maybe raised in a wistful goodbye. 'And did he?' I asked. 'Come back?'

'With sea bass, or even lobster.' She sipped her sherry. 'We could catch sea bass just offshore in the summer. You've missed something,' she added, 'not living by the sea.'

Why did this discovery trouble me? Because I'd always assumed that my grandfather had been the love of my grandmother's life. I'd always assumed that, at the close of the day, he was the only man she thought of. Maybe he was. After all, she married him. But at fifteen my heart was hungrier than ever. I was ready for love, I craved it, and I went to bed that evening with my head full of a fisherman. I lay awake, picturing him – a face lined from squinting, an oily smell, his hand on the back of my grandmother's head as he kissed her. Such thoughts left me with an ache under my ribs. Not so much for my grandfather – surely he knew there'd been another; there must have been physical signs, at least, in the Pencarreg marriage bed. But I ached for *her*. A huge pain unfurled itself inside me without warning. What had gone wrong? Why didn't they marry? Didn't he love her enough?

The truth was that he died. I only learnt this after she too had gone. I found a newspaper clipping folded in half and tucked into a girlish paperback. Missing, presumed drowned, it read. His fishing boat was found rocking gently with a belly full of water and no crew. My grandmother was just seventeen. Still a child, really. I see her mouth stretched wide at the news, and her hands clamped on her temples. I see her screaming her heart out at night, whilst her parents pretended not to hear. The boat had been called the *Louisa*. I don't suppose such love happens twice in your life.

I don't know how much my grandfather knew of all this. There's no doubt he was loved, but it must have been a different kind of love. After all, he was a very different kind of man. He was quiet. He never strayed far. He entered a kiss bashfully, as if entering an unknown room. And it was the Welsh land that was his livelihood, a less treacherous thing, on the whole, than the sea.

'Where did you meet Granddad, then? If you lived in Cornwall?'

My grandmother smiled quietly, rolled the last drop of sherry round the sides of her glass. 'Here. In Wales. I came to live with my aunt for a while. Whilst they buried my mother.'

A huge soft mound in the churchyard. 'How?'

'At a village fete. I was twenty-two; an old maid – well, of sorts. He bought me three goes at the coconut shy.'

They were engaged three weeks later. She said that he asked her to marry him on the leafy path above the gold mines, and that when he stood back up he had one wet knee. That was the story I preferred. I wanted to hear about love that worked, not love that was lost in a storm. I wanted to believe that affections were that simple, that smooth-edged. No one lied, no one's heart got broken.

But the question has always lain in the pit of my stomach, like an adder in long grass: what would have happened if the fisherman had lived? If there had never been that sudden storm fifty years ago, looming out of the Atlantic with no warning, no slapping black waves to precede it? My grandmother would have married him – in a squat Cornish church under a sky of gulls. My mother would not have been born. Nor me. This baby in my belly would not exist. And Billy Macklin would not have shuffled through the midnight lanes of Cae Tresaint, not whispered to himself, not recited the names of the flowers he passed – *Campanula rotundifolia, Clematis Vitalba, Viola tricolor.* His head and heart would still be intact.

Still, it doesn't pay to think like that. What good does it do?

What matters is that my grandmother had more loss in her life than she should have done. That's all.

K

Of course everything changed when Rosie disappeared – but not overnight. It's easy to look back and believe that panic seized Cae Tresaint, that doors were suddenly bolted, fields disallowed, curfews imposed. It would make a better story, perhaps, if I talked of the sinister places – of how Tor-y-gwynt watched us, of shady lanes, of peat bogs, of the old gold mines that felt dank, even in dry weather. These were eerie places, certainly; and Welsh lore is full of shadows. But the changes were slow in coming. They crept on. They soaked up into our lives as slowly as damp on a wall.

Despite Rosie's disappearance, the dragonflies still came. Gerry and I would ignore homework and gallop down the Brych with nets to catch them. Some were huge, electric-blue, and would rattle under the alders before spinning away. We rarely caught any. They'd hover, eyeing us. They seemed to know our game.

Some evenings I would join Daniel on the steps of his caravan and talk to him about school or the farm or him. He always sat downwind of me, so that his smoke never came my way, although I sometimes wished it would because I'd grown to like the smell. If there were stars out he'd try to name them – I suspected he made names up, sometimes, and would challenge him about them. 'All true,' he'd assure me; 'I was raised knowing them. My father had a telescope, you know.' Those were good evenings, and I could have sat on those metal steps for ever. I was always downhearted when I heard my grandmother call out for me from the porch, telling me it was getting late, and that tomorrow was another school day.

And Lewis was busier than usual. He had acquired a new girlfriend, an older woman from town who was, my grandmother drily informed me, a bottle-blonde. I wasn't sure what this meant, but knew such a thing wasn't advisable. We'd look out of the landing window together to see her stepping over the cowpats in unsuitable shoes, and although my grandmother said nothing I could tell what she thought of her. What was her name? It escapes me. But she provided me with my first, proper glimpse of breasts. She dropped the straps of her dress in the empty cow field as I hid behind the dog cage, and I was transfixed. I was meant to have *them?* Maybe she knew I'd been watching, since she would wink at me from then on. She lasted longer than most of Lewis's girlfriends – three weeks or so. But she left abruptly, when the village became too tense, too hot, too dark a place to be. I was glad that she didn't feel Lewis to be worth the trouble. He was sour about that. All she left behind for him – and me – was the memory of her bleached hair and low-slung chest.

And Carreg Cennen castle. I remember, too, we had a school trip there at this time. It surprises me now, to think of it. Did the thought of abduction not cross anyone's mind? That children clambering through the countryside might not be so wise just then? Perhaps St Bart's believed in maintaining a sense of normality. Perhaps they just refused to accept the worst. Or perhaps it was just too early to worry so much – after all, Rosie's home life had not been so perfect, and runaways happened every once in a while. But whatever the reason we still went to Carreg Cennen, and I liked it. It was an amazing, breezy, ancient place. An army of navy and yellow descended on the ruins and walkways. I stood on the battlements with my hair loose, with the Black Mountains behind me, feeling like the queen of the world. I loved the castle's height. I loved staring out over Carmarthenshire and pretending I owned it all, that I was ruler over everything I surveyed. We were miles inland, yet I still believed I could smell the sea from there.

Billy seemed edgy in this warmer weather. All through the winter months, through the rain and the mud and the whipping wind, the lanes and the hillside had been his, he said. He'd shared them with no one – who else would walk to the Tor in a gale? 'Wouldn't see anyone,' he remarked, 'for weeks.' But now there were others. Red kites had nested near Cors Caron bogs, and each day more walkers appeared. Binoculars winked up on the ridge; Mr Phipps sold out of postcards. My shepherd's hut lost its appeal, since hikers rustled past with their ruddy cheeks and woolly socks, disturbing me. So I turned to the old barn. I'd lie in its cool with Billy and hear the clink of something being turned in his pocket. I assumed it was money – I always did.

'I'm sure no one will come here,' I told him. 'Why would they? It's just a barn.'

With his eyes shut he said, 'Because she's skated here.'

I jumped at the news. 'What? *Here?* To the barn? *Our* barn?'

'Just in the lane. I've seen her there. Going up to your farm. Which means they'll come here eventually, have a look round.'

I breathed, sank back against an old beam. She'd never been *here* – only the lane. *All mine.* 'Billy, where will you go, when they do?'

'Not far. I wouldn't want to go far.'

'Have you been to the sea?'

He smiled, shook his head.

'It's nice. I'd go there, if I were you.'

But it was not quite consolation enough. He still seemed anxious, and my presence could make him jump.

I found him dozing under the eaves one afternoon. I crept up on him in my school uniform, crouched down close to his face, and studied his mark. The skin was shinier there. If I held my breath, leant closer still, I could see the *dot dot dot* where the stitches had been. I almost touched it. I wanted to feel its waxiness, its bumps. But I woke him. Somehow he sensed me, heard my heartbeat or smelt my new, young sweat, and he jumped, stumbled, ran to the corner shouting *What? What?*

'Sorry,' I said.

It was ten minutes before he felt ready enough to come back into the light and sit with me.

Sometimes I'd ask him about his head. He wasn't always forthcoming – often he'd turn his face away from me, or just growl, *Leave it. I don't want to talk about it.* When he was in these moods I'd let him be. I didn't want to upset him.

But other times he was softer. As I followed him through the pine plantation after school one day I asked him, 'Do you remember it happening?'

He shook his head. 'Not really. I couldn't see in this eye. It took me months,' he said, 'to see properly again.'

'You were blind?!' No one had told me that.

'Half,' he corrected me. 'But my eye got better. See?'

'Did it hurt?'

I imagined the answer to be yes, yes it did, and that sometimes his head still ached as if broken all over again. I imagined his heartbeat to race through his skull at night, and that his skin there prickled if you touched it. What did rain feel like on that damaged skin? Had he ever bumped it on a low beam, and if so, who had he cried out for? His mother? Someone else? But he just shrugged at me.

'Not so much. It was afterwards.'

'Afterwards?'

'When I had to look at this,' he said pointing. 'For the first time.'

Imagine it: feeling your way to a mirror after the accident and seeing a whole other person. Seeing this reddish bloom take over one side of your face. *It may fade a little,* say the doctors. Your friends, if you had any, might say, *It's not as bad as you think.*

The first real change, as I recall, came from my grandmother. Even that was subtle. It was nothing more than a creased forehead, for the first day or so. She would look up the staircase at me with crushed eyebrows and pale lips. Then, instead of talking to the hens when she went to gather any eggs, she took to doing it in silence, and then she began to forget about the eggs altogether. It became my pre-school task, to open the little wooden door in the mornings and grope into the dark. It smelt musty in there, but there was tiny joy in finding a warm egg in the straw. Laid just for me, or so it felt. I liked how each one fitted snugly into the well of my hand.

One night I heard her pad down to the bathroom, turn

the tap on and lock the door. She slowed down a little. When I set off for the bus I'd glance back over my shoulder to find her watching me walk down the lane. Why? Sometimes I waved, sometimes not. It was as if she was waiting for someone to come, rather than waiting for me to leave. I worried a little for her.

And suddenly I was able to get away with less. She banned gobstoppers and chewing gum from the house, and gave no reason as to why. I ran down the stairs with scissors once and was pounced on for it. Like a kestrel diving on prey she would tug baling twine out of my hand, believing it could hurt me somehow. I was nonplussed. My whereabouts now mattered – *Where exactly on the ridge?* she'd demand, one eye closed in suspicion – and one evening I came home late from school to find her electric with rage.

'Where the hell have you been?'

I frowned. Two hours late was nothing to worry about, not to me. 'The churchyard,' I replied, 'with Gerry.' A lie, of course. I'd been in the barn learning that my mother once had a water fight in our lane with Billy, before he was kicked in the head – buckets, squeals, and her wet skirt slapping. 'I'm not that late anyway,' I shrugged.

She smacked me on the bottom with her oven gloves, and I was outraged. I screamed, *I'm eight! You can't hit me!* Her response was a second smack, and I screeched, slammed doors and stormed out to find Daniel. I sank into the grass by his caravan and whinged. He listened, smoked, and said little. His mind, I think, was on other things.

And she began spending less and less time at Pencarreg. I'd traipse in to find a quiet house and a note on the kitchen table: *Gone to the H's – ham in fridge for tea. Love G xx.* She would cook casseroles for Mrs Hughes and ferry them round to the red-bricked house; she phoned her in the evenings in a soothing voice. I shrugged this off as a passing phase, and had no idea that this relationship would last for the next four years, until the suicide. Perhaps it would be too much to say that Mrs Hughes and my grandmother became friends – they hardly laughed together, or went on outings. I don't think Christmas cards were exchanged or secrets swapped. But they became acquaintances. After all, if anyone had a right to visit Mrs Hughes, my grandmother did. She was the only other woman in Pencarreg who knew what it was like to walk into your daughter's room once your daughter was gone. Books open on their pages; cold mugs of tea; snagged hair ties; socks pulled off in a hurry so that they were still inside out and on the floor, looking back at you.

I couldn't say who benefited the most from these meetings in the early days. I have pictured them both, hunched on armchairs in the immaculate Hughes sitting room, watching the clock and picking their fingernails. I imagine policewomen making tea. She was good-hearted, my grandmother, certainly, and I have no doubt she felt deeply, incredibly sorry for this woman whose daughter could be anywhere, and in any state. But secretly I think she sought her own comfort. I think she went to the red-bricked house because at last there was another person who knew what losing a child felt like. Loss is a solitary thing.

Perhaps I read too much into this. But doesn't it make sense? Mrs Hughes's grief was immeasurable, unbearable, but it served as a bridge for my grandmother. She crossed it with stews and home-made soups, finally able to look into the eyes of another mother, who might not be a mother any more.

There's a question in itself – ex-wife; ex-lover. Can you be an ex-parent at all?

*   *   *

There were leaflets. There still are, if you keep your eyes open. Rosie looks dated these days, a little faded, as if over the years her smile has lost its shine. I look at that picture now and instead of seeing a preening, assured, clever older girl, I just see a child. I see a blonde, naïve twelve-year-old, and think, *I'm lucky. It could have been me.* Rosie is a dusty name, a faded snapshot, and I am here, I am breathing, with my first grey hairs and a scarred left wrist, bracing myself for thirty. Could it? Have been me? Was I nearly taken, too?

I first saw a leaflet as I clambered off the school bus. One blew up against my foot. *MISSING*, it read. *Rosemary Anne Hughes, Aged 12.* I had to concede it was a good picture of her. Was she at a birthday party? Her dress had a frilled collar, and a thin pink paper curl hung over her shoulder, as if someone had thrown streamers out over the room. She wore her earrings, and her hair was plaited, tied with a blue silk ribbon. I never knew her middle name was Anne. I never knew that she was five foot two, that she had a scar from a chest operation as a baby, or that she was last seen in a tartan skirt, white cotton blouse and pink roller skates. She smiled out at me. *You don't know very much,* her blue eyes seemed to say. I wasn't yet sorry that she'd gone.

At school, we believed the worst. But don't children do that? News of Rosie's disappearance gathered speed and raced through the corridors like a lit fuse. Everyone whispered her name, and everyone had their own stories. She had gone to Cardiff to be famous; she'd been locked up in a loony bin; in a wild romantic gesture she had raced away with an older lover; a crazy man had found her and chopped her into pieces. The latter was by far the favourite option, until it became the most likely.

Were we too young to understand rape? Almost. Sex still had a blurriness to it – I knew the basics, but not the details. Like a branch at a window, the word pattered against me. And I felt it a word best not said. Rape, to me, meant fists and dirt and alleyways. It meant bruises, closed doors, shame, sadness, and I was sure that if I said the word I would be punished for it. Still, it was uttered at St Bart's. Not by the girls – we somehow knew better, as if we already sensed deep in the core of us that this was a thing we, as females, had far more reason to fear. But behind hands, boys said it. Rape. *Trais rhywiol.* They had no idea what they were talking about.

I dared to ask Daniel, though. Not in those summer months – later, when the police had retreated and the blackberry season had been and gone. I knocked on his caravan door, seated myself amongst his books and cushions and his jumpers that smelt of bonfires, and I said, *What is rape, exactly?* He shifted in his seat. He leant his head back against the wall and looked tired.

I remember his answer word for word – because it was, I now see, a perfect answer. *The corruption of a lovely thing,* he said. When I pressed him further, he gave in, and offered me another, simpler explanation. He used technical terms, and looked sorry as he said them. I listened hard. Knowledge crept into me, like light from under a blind. *A lovely thing* – was it? It sounded so strange to me. I walked out of his caravan that day with different eyes.

Joe Vickery, too, caused a stir. He said he'd seen Rosie thumbing a lift up on the main road – a claim that would get him into trouble with the police before the week was out. No one really believed Joe, anyway. A boy with someone else's kidney wasn't to be trusted. Besides, everyone knew hitchhiking was a foolish thing. *Asking for trouble* was the term.

* * *

175

Whether it was because he had better things to do, or because his kidney didn't allow the strain, Joe never came up our lane. We weren't friends. We had no reason to be. Save for one or two exceptions, boys were of no interest to me; to all of St Bart's I was the bad-tempered new girl with an adult scowl and a touch of eczema once in a while. We bore a mutual indifference. I might see him in the shop, on the bus, or scuffing outside church once or twice. I even saw him in Llandovery cattle market once, which was strange, because he had no reason to be there, but we neatly avoided each other's gaze. He never came up to the farm.

So I was confused when, two days after Rosie's last sighting, he appeared in our sheep field.

I was on the ridge. I'd spent a morning looking for Billy but he was not to be found, so I'd taken myself and a book up into the wind. It was a good wind, too, that day – brisk, grass-scented. After an hour or two of basking, I looked up to see Joe approaching.

'Why are you here?' I demanded.

He didn't answer. He just sat down next to me and looked out over the view.

I stared, appalled. Wasn't this trespassing? I told him as much, but still no answer. I wondered if he might say something profound. His hitchhiking claims were yet to be disproved.

I wondered if he was telling the truth, after all.

Maybe he was going to turn to me and say, *I saw it*. Maybe he had chosen me to confide in. Maybe he knew exactly where she was, or who had taken her, and he wanted to tell me about it. No doubt he loved Rosie – all the boys did. But why tell me? I waited. I tugged at my fingers and held my breath.

'Well? Joe?'

He reached for my book, immersed himself in it.

176

'Give!' And I snatched it back. 'Why are you here? Tell me!'

But he said nothing at all.

He just leant forward so that he blocked out the sun, our noses touched and his teeth knocked against mine. That kiss was a hurried, light, unexpected thing. For a second – less than a second – I let him. I saw the creases in his eyelids. Then I flinched, pushed him back. 'What are you doing? You're crazy! Get off me! Get off!'

He stumbled to his feet and shot off down the field without looking back. I watched him go, scrubbed my mouth with my knuckles and quickly understood it. This had been a dare. A challenge. He had slunk up here, kissed me and raced off again. Somewhere a clot of boys would be waiting for his report. *Did she fight you? What was it like? How bad?*

Or I considered the possibility he might have singled me out – to practise on. I must have seemed the obvious choice. The pretty girls of St Bart's wouldn't look at Joe twice, let alone kiss him. I was the only real option. Not so crazy then, after all.

Either way, as I watched him run back through the sheep, I said the word out loud. *Kiss.* An alluring, beckoning word. I announced to the wind that that too began with a K.

Kisses open doors, I've noticed. That one gesture can unlock secrets, ease open feelings. It can't be prevented – these kisses just *are*. It's how they work. They break into basements you never knew you had.

But kisses can close doors, too – a kiss goodbye, a consolation prize – and in a sense I think these are the better kind. They're safer. Less risky. You know where you stand with a closing kiss. You can turn from them,

177

inhale, smile to yourself and move on: such kisses make you stronger. And such kisses are my speciality. I'd throw them out to boys and then walk away. Until Daniel, I scarcely knew the other kind.

The other kind are not safe. They expose you. They put you at the mercy of the person kissing back. These are the kisses that Hollywood opts for – the knee tremblers, the heart stoppers, the kisses that lead you to say things you might soon regret. You step into the spotlight for them as if to say, *Here. For better or worse, this is me*.

Such is my philosophy. And Joe's kiss, for all its clumsiness and speed, and in spite of his shameless reasons for giving it, was a turning point. It was an unlocking. It opened up part of me. Something new revealed itself, because I sat on the ridge and realised I was no longer prepared to wait, to bide my time, and nor did I care any more about the tenth rule, about not talking about the past – I would break that rule. I would stamp on it like a shard of glass or an eggshell. I would tug it open. With a fling of my hair I stood up, and knew what I had to do.

I came home late for tea that night because I ran to find Billy. I tore through the sheep like a runaway, my mouth still tingling from where Joe's lips had been, briefly.

He wasn't in the barn, or the cow field, so I scrambled through the back lanes calling his name. I met the green-eyed man on a track to the bluebell woods who smiled and said, *Who are you looking for?* But I didn't say. I just sidled past him and dropped over a fence.

I found Billy by St Tysul's. He was chewing his fingers, sweating with the heat. He seemed distracted. 'What does *K* stand for?' I asked.

I reeled off my list to him, the list I'd built in my head over six long months – kettles, kangaroos, kitchens, kidneys, kites, kingcups, kingdoms, kisses and keys. I told him about the letter in my windowsill, the way people turned their heads when I mentioned it, and I told him about the tenth rule, the fat full stop, how I might be eight years old but I wasn't stupid. I thought of damaged hearts and having bad blood. *Bad blood* – as if a blackness would seep out of me should I ever be sliced by a knife. 'What does it mean?'

Beyond the church I saw policemen wiping their brows.

'Billy!' I tugged at his coat.

Without shifting his gaze he said, 'Kieran. OK?'

I thought, *who?*

'You're just like him.'

I blinked.

Billy wiped his mouth with the back of his hand. He looked at me.

'You should be careful,' he said.

I left him then. I ran for the sake of running, leaping over bracken and dodging through our cows, all the time thinking *Kieran*. A pop and a whisper; not a name to be hurried. *Kie-ran*. Did the name fit into a space perfectly? Was I imagining, like a fool, that his name was familiar somehow? I wanted to stand up on the Tor and call it; I wanted to write it in dust, on walls in red paint. I wanted to run to my windowsill, trace that carved letter, because I deserved to now. I stayed out till it was dark. I could almost see myself as I ran into the yard, my knowledge streaming out behind me like bubbles, pink and blue and silver, a diver coming up for air.

Moonlight

It's official: this is forbidden. What do you know about him? was Mum's argument. How would I have replied? That I know where he's ticklish; that his freckles are nearly everywhere. Imagine her face! So what now? K laughed when I told him. He said in my ear that we'll meet at night instead – like in books! Without a moon I don't even see him. He's just hands and mouth. He brought wine last night, and I nearly woke the dogs up by tripping in the porch.

In the shoebox there are more than just scraps of paper. There are objects – things I can only assume had a hidden, private meaning to them. *Love tokens*, as Mrs Maddox might say. I've poured them out over the carpet before. With a mug of tea or a pre-pregnancy whisky I've moved through them carefully, holding up the ones I like. They make me both happy and wistful. Like a mouse, she hoarded these objects. She tucked herself around them, kept them warm. Kept them in the musty dark under her Birmingham bed.

There is, indeed, a wine cork in there – sour-smelling,

crumbly to the touch. And a dried daisychain. A pebble with a white vein; three hardened cigarette ends; an owl feather; one single blade of grass, which puzzled me – what sort of memory can that possibly hold? A crisped cuckoo flower, or lady's smock, or *Cardamine pratensis* had dried itself onto the side of the shoebox, and can't be peeled off. An eggshell – a blackbird's? A receipt for three pounds four shillings; a piece of gold foil, on the back of which, in a slanting, hurried hand that is not my mother's, is written *7pm!*

These are of no value to me, as such. I don't know most of their stories. I am left to guess, that's all. But to her they meant something. They spurred her on, I suppose. On her bad days, when Birmingham was overcast and the adverts in the *Evening News* asking for Kieran Green were yet to bring in a single call, I imagine that this box was a comfort, of sorts. The scent of her best year.

Did it ever really occur to her he might not wish to be found? It must have done – she was a dreamer, for sure, but everyone fears the worst sometimes. She must have felt it in the deepest part of her, like the grit in the pearl. Yet she carried on. Perhaps this shoebox and the mere sight of me was enough to make red-headed men matter again. On seeing one, she stiffened. I remember the signs. The push onto the tips of her toes, the held breath, the quickened pace, the letting go of my hand.

The Broken Rib

So strange, the importance we place on a name. Would I be the same person if my mother had plucked a different collection of letters out of the air for me, a plainer apple off the tree? Does an eccentric name lead to a wayward life? Alternatively, was my grandfather – a man bestowed with a saintly Welsh name – destined to be sturdy, lawful, nationalistic, and a quiet believer in God? Who knows. All I know is that a name should be chosen wisely – we have it all our lives. It hangs over us till death, like our own private weather. And even when we do die, it carries on existing. In fact, the name is the only part of us that really does – letters on a headstone; a plaque on a bench. Too morose?

No one calls me Evie any more. The name has been packed in a box and stored away with other childish things. Age changes a name for practical reasons. Evangeline was too long to begin with. As for Evie, it served its purpose but lost its tail when I hit my teens. I felt it too girly, too misleading – a pink-ribboned, hopscotch name. As a snake sheds its old skin, I emerged as Eve – stronger, plainer, more capable. Eve can spit, win an argument, talk with the men at the markets; Eve can shear sheep on her own, and quickly; Eve can be a good mother. It's a better name, on the whole – although it has a strange elegance to it that I know sits poorly on me.

Kieran. No mouth can say the word harshly. It's gentle. It's a name to raise a glass to.

Enough.

As I write I can hear Daniel downstairs in the kitchen, and the kettle boiling. He's whistling between his teeth – a trademark of his. Sometimes he doesn't even know he's doing it. He can give a real, long, ear-piercing whistle, too – fingers in the mouth, head back. I have always been impressed by that. It's a skill I never truly mastered, in spite of trying the whole of one summer. Once, though, just once, I managed it. A sudden shriek burst out of me, and echoed off the hillside. I was overjoyed; Daniel applauded. I've not given up hope of repeating it. When we manage something once, we always believe we will be able to do it again.

See? *Daniel*. Even the lions like him.

Back to being eight.

One afternoon two policemen came and knocked on my Great-great grandfather Samuel's oak front door.

It was expected, of course. My grandmother hardly seemed surprised when she pulled the door open and found them standing there, hands clasped in front of them, expectant. After all, they'd visited everyone else already: Gerry had kept me posted. He was an inconspicuous sort – weedy and quiet, no one noticed him ducking through the village with one ear to the ground. He knew that they'd talked to Reverend Bickley for hours, that they were stopping traffic on the main road with pictures of Rosie. Plus Gerry knew the police well enough. He even knew one officer by name, since he'd been woken at night by their blue silent light and a knock on the door more than once. Such was the life of a boy with violent parents. I could feel genuinely sorry for him.

Door to door, was the official term. Like salesmen, only they had nothing to sell. Mrs Maddox had phoned us in advance – 'They're coming your way, Lou! Get ready!' – and from that moment onwards I thought of the locusts we'd studied at school, how huge clouds of them swarmed into towns and ruined crops so that people went hungry and died. I felt the police were something to prepare for. Cupboards should be stocked, windows shut. I held my breath and watched from our cattle grid for them.

As in all things, Pencarreg was last on the list. And as with all visitors, the policemen were out of breath when they finally made it here.

'Didn't drive?' remarked my grandmother coldly. 'It's further than you think – isn't it?'

They weren't as I'd hoped they'd be. Only one wore a uniform. The other stood before us like any normal man might – grey trousers, old white shirt with a wilting collar and cuffs turned back. He smelt. It was the smell of hot man – musty, strong, almost animal. He had a gingery moustache that made me think of brooms. His lower lids were droopy. He gave a tight, professional smile – lips tucked together, teeth hidden.

'Good afternoon. We're –'

'I know who you are,' she said. 'I'll put the kettle on.'

I followed them into the kitchen, sliding over the flagstones in my socks. Both men were tall, but the second man was younger – much younger. I decided he was Daniel's age, maybe even less. His hair was neat, very blond. Straw-yellow.

The older policeman noticed me in the doorway. His eyes froze, the way eyes here tended to. 'This must be . . . ?'

'Yep,' said my grandmother. 'Well done. This is Evangeline. Evie, meet Inspector Gregory.'

'Chief,' he said, 'Inspector.'

'Chief now, is it? Goodness.'

I glanced over at her. Why her sourness? She threw teabags into the pot. 'You know him?' I asked.

The chink of china. 'From times gone by. Listen, run and get the boys will you? Try the sheep race. Tell them all the police are here.' She added drily, 'Just a few routine questions . . .'

I was reluctant to leave – what eight-year-old wouldn't be? So I darted to the sheep race in double-quick time. The gravel from the yard dug through my socks.

'Granddad!' I yelled. 'The police are here!'

Three heads looked up at me.

As I could have predicted, I was banished from the house by my grandparents. This was adult business, they told me; I should wait outside till they had gone. Go up to the rhubarb patch, my grandmother had said, and no further. But the rhubarb patch held nothing for me. I considered my options. Was the kitchen window open? In such weather it had to be. I sneaked outside and nestled deep into the crispy hydrangea bush. Not the best of hiding places – but pretty good for eavesdropping.

The older policeman said, 'We'd just like to know the last time you saw Rosemary. Where and when. If that's not too much trouble.'

There was a pause. Even I thought for a second or two – when had I seen her? At school, I supposed. Drifting through the playground. Perfect hair.

I heard Lewis grumble, said he hadn't a clue.

My grandfather offered the foot rot, when she'd appeared in our yard with a pie. About three months ago. 'But I haven't seen her since then.'

But my grandmother had seen her – in the lane, under our limes. 'Last week.'

'Can you remember when, exactly?'

I imagined her blowing over the surface of her tea, beady-eyed. 'Yes. Thursday. Afternoon. Three-ish. I drove past her. On my way to see Dr Matthews. Headaches, if you must know.'

I thought, Thursday? But that was a school day. Rosie had been skipping class?

'Just in the lane, you say?'

'Is there an echo? Next question?'

A throat was cleared. 'Do you know why she was in the lane, Mrs Jones? As you've said yourself, it's a long climb.'

'A long skate, you mean.'

'She was wearing her skates?'

She gave a tut. 'And the tiniest skirt.'

For a while there was silence. I heard a pen on paper. Why was Rosie in the lane? What was there to come up for? Not me. I trampled on hearts. I was untrustworthy. So for whom? I think I knew the answer before it was given me. I think I knew exactly.

'Listen,' began my favourite voice. 'I . . .'

'She had a crush on Daniel,' my grandmother said. 'That's why. That's why she was in the lane and why she was flashing her pants. That's why she simpered like a fool whenever she saw him.'

My heart turned over.

'Is this true, sir?'

Through the window, through the papery blue hydrangea heads I heard Daniel say yes. Yes, he supposed it was true. Yes, she had seemed . . . eager? Attentive? For months, now. But needless to say, he'd discouraged her from the start. He tried his best to be brisk, he said. He'd busy himself if he heard her coming up the lane, for what else can you do? How can you quench childish infatuation? 'I'm sure,' he said, 'it would have passed in time. Just a phase.'

187

'A bloody long one,' my grandmother muttered.

If I had chosen to stand up then, if I'd given up my hiding place, risked a telling off, if I'd turned and looked straight into the kitchen I'm sure I'd have seen them all nodding their heads, like puppets. It made sense, after all. He was lovely. He was brown-haired and soft-eyed, his smile was easy, and Rosie looked so much older than her age. Why wouldn't she like him? How could she not? And if I loved a man, why shouldn't another?

I suddenly thought, *the flowers.*

She's been leaving the flowers.

'But just so you know, and before you ask,' snapped my grandmother, 'he was with Evie that day.'

'Lou, there's no need . . .'

'On the fourteenth. They went swimming, up at the lake. They were there all afternoon. Evie'll tell you. Go and question her, if you want. That's fine by me. She's only outside. Do you want me to call her? Would that help with your enquiries?'

'Not necessary. As yet. But thank you.' A chair was pushed back. 'That'll do for now, Mrs Jones.'

From my hydrangea bush I watched the policemen go. They walked wearily. Both hooked their jackets over their shoulders, one swatted the midges away. I thought, what a sad job, looking for dead people. Did they have good homes to go back to?

I shut my eyes, leant back against the bricks. The heat of the day was in them.

'Incredible,' said my grandmother. 'The same man! Do you remember him? Dear God. If he can't find a six-foot red-headed Irishman with bloody knuckles and a bag full of cash how the hell's he going to find a little twelve-year-old?'

A clatter of china as she threw the cups in the sink.

Daniel. I would lie for him if I had to, would do anything. Even if he had not been with me, if he had not been swimming through the still waters of the forest lake at the time Rosie was snatched, I'd never have told them so. I'd have woven a beautiful lie. I'd have put my hand on the Bible and sworn, blue-eyed, without hesitation.

He just said to her, 'Lou, you never know.'

He's right – we never do. The coincidences, the ironies, the twists of fate.

This bears no real relation to Rosie's disappearance whatsoever, and what was still to come that summer. But that young, blond policeman would reappear later in my life. I was almost sixteen; he was in his late twenties. I met him in a pub in Tregaron and we took it from there. He didn't seem to recognise me – why should he, all those years on? But I recognised him. I gave a false name. And I lied about my age, of course: what we did was illegal, since I was too young for it by a month. It was easy enough to fool him – I've always looked older than I am. I wasn't far off my five foot ten by then; I already had frown lines and a nonchalant air. A weathered, sullen look.

So there you have it. I remember being both relieved and a little sad afterwards. I remember the push of his broken rib.

She loved Daniel. Not the revelation I'd wanted. I picked away quietly at these three words. At night this knowledge troubled me, throbbed under the sheets like nettle rash, and when I woke up in the mornings I knew there was some dark, awful reason to feel sad. She had skated up to our farm some nights – perhaps to peep through his windows, perhaps hoping he was not yet asleep. She'd spun round him in the street. She'd believed he might love her back, and I hated to think of it. I hated to imagine her white fingers tapping on the caravan door, her laying flowers down in our porch after dark. As she skated home from Pencarreg, had she ever paused in the lane to hear Mrs Maddox playing Cole Porter, cocked her head to one side and believed those songs were meant for her? The thought made me grit my teeth. It made me stare at the space he left behind when he walked out of a room.

I've known him for ages, she'd said.

Mrs Maddox must have known. If my grandmother had noticed this one-way love, then surely she had done, too. After all, those roller skates were not silent things and Rosie had had to pass the pink cottage every time she came to the farm. I felt Mrs Maddox would hear the sound in her sleep and nod sagely into the dark. She would have worked it out. She would have added this knowledge to her collection, as if dropping a new marble into a leather drawstring bag.

As I trudged home after school I saw her working in her garden. Sleeves rolled up, sunhat on. The skin under her arms swung like pendulums. 'Evie!' she called out. 'Over here!'

We drank lime cordial on her wrought-iron chairs by the magnolia tree. Wasps were picking their way round our glasses, and I flicked at them. I refused to be stung again.

'Did the police come to see you yesterday?'

'Yes,' I said. 'But they didn't talk to me.'

'They might yet, *blodyn*.'

'But I don't know anything.'

'You might know something without knowing that you know it,' she reasoned. We drank our cordial. She murmured, 'This is a terrible thing.'

I let her think for a while, and shift in her chair. Then I said, 'Did she love Daniel? I heard she did.'

Mrs Maddox looked over at me. 'Love? That's a strong word, Evie.'

I thought, *I know*.

'Well, she liked him, I know that much. I think everyone knows. Rosie was hardly subtle about it. You know she used to come up to the farm, just to see him?'

I nodded.

'Perhaps she just thought it was love. Or perhaps it really *was* love, although she didn't really know him, did she?'

'Didn't she?'

Mrs Maddox scoffed. 'No! Barely passed the time of day! And how can you love a stranger? *Besotted*, I'd say she was. But not love. No, no.'

I felt relieved. I drank, breathed in her honeysuckle and thought of him – how he hummed in the shower; how he'd had his appendix out; how he had no sugar in his tea but two in coffee; how he mimicked my accent and called me Olwen and knew the names of stars. When he sneezed he pressed his face into his upper arm. He always answered the phone with a bright *hell-o?* He was no stranger, to me. *I* knew him. 'He doesn't know anything, either.'

She looked shocked for a moment. 'Daniel? Of course not! Wasn't he up at the lake with you, anyway?'

I said yes.

'Well, then. But let me tell you, Evie, someone does.'

'Someone does what?'

'*Know!* Something! There has to be a tongue in this place that's been telling lies . . .'

Through my curls I stared at her. The heat had left beads of sweat on her upper lip. Someone we knew? Telling lies? The thought was like nothing I'd ever known. It knocked the breath out of me. As I looked at her I felt a chill rising up from my stomach, as if I was wading out into the penny-brown lake again, and the water was closing in around me. *Who?*

'Think about it. Don't you think I'd have noticed if a strange man had been lurking about? Don't you think he'd have been spotted? And wherever she is, she's well hidden. Local knowledge. Even the police have admitted it.' She shook her head. 'It's got to be one of our own.'

'Maybe she fell.'

'Fell where? We'd have found her by now.'

'Run away?'

She shook her head. 'It's been nearly a week, my lovely – a week! – and not one sighting of her. Wouldn't she have taken bags? Food? Money? Wouldn't she have been spotted with all her prettiness?'

I thought, yes. No doubt about it.

Someone we knew.

It was then that Mrs Maddox leant forward. She put down her glass and took me by the wrists. Suddenly her eyes were darker. They sparkled in a strange way, a way I had not seen before. Fear? It glimmered in her like a candle in a cave. 'Evie,' she whispered. 'You be careful. Promise me? *Promise?* It might happen again. There's just no telling. Do you understand me? You look over your shoulder. You trust no one. Don't go too far, or stay out too late. Promise me? Do you?'

The walk home was slow and thundery. The shadows by the Brych seemed mother-shaped.

Hearts

Dr Matthews is retired now. At eighty, he spends his pension in the Red Lion in Llanddewi Brefi and on trips to vintage car rallies, and he keeps his trusty stethoscope in a frame above his fireplace. The same stethoscope for fifty-four years, he reminds me proudly. 'Quite an old friend, you know. And think of all the heartbeats!'

It *is* quite a thought – healthy hearts, diseased hearts, dying hearts; lonely ones, impassioned ones, bruised ones, broken ones, little unborn ones that are yet to know the big wide world. That cold disc of metal has heard a lot of lives. Dr Matthews knows my own heart well enough – from its pre-birth state, to my flu, to mumps when I was thirteen and my neck was so swollen all I could eat was tinned peaches for a week. Sometimes he lets me listen to its gurgles and thuds, and every time he says with a sparkle in his eye, *That's a strong ticker, if ever I heard one*. So far, he's been right. It beats, it's not broken – although, like all hearts, it has had its knocks over the years.

Yesterday I met him in the teashop in Tregaron, overlooking the square. We meet there fortnightly, and I think he enjoys it. I tell him how I'm progressing; he nods, advises, and still feels like a doctor, affecting lives. I like meeting him, too. Above all else, he makes me think of my grandfather. The dictionary evacuee had been called Laura, he informed me – a coy thing, pretty, who spoke in hurried whispers.

And we reminisce. He played his own small part in the search for Rosie Hughes. We had no television at Pencarreg but I've been told he was often interviewed. Articulate and respectable, his opinion was asked for – medical and otherwise. And he spent long hours with Mrs Hughes, watching her, sedating her. Had her heart sounded like a hollow drum?

Yesterday he told me I looked radiant. I replied that he lied.

'Not so! You have a bloom about you, Miss Jones,' he declared. 'Like a rose!'

I shook my head. Roses don't have puffy eyes from lack of sleep, dry skin or varicose veins. But he leant forward, clasped my hand in his, and whispered, 'Like a rose!'

He has always claimed, always, for as long as I've known him, that an expectant woman is the most beautiful thing in the world. Is this a symptom of never having been a father himself? Is this his sadness talking? I asked him in the teashop. I found myself putting my head on one side and saying, 'Jim, how come you've never married?'

The smile he gave me was resigned, wistful. 'Not everyone finds the right person, Eve. What can be done? Besides, I'm too stuck in my ways for any such business now.'

Still, he said my mother had the same bloom to her when she was carrying me. He remembers her as he saw her for the very last time – in a green V-necked jumper two sizes too big, treading warily over the cattle grid with bare feet. She left for good the next day. I suppose that bloom of hers was more excitement than anything else. She was going to a new country to find her Irishman. When he listened to her heart, was it racing?

I paid for the tea and his slice of bara brith, and gave him a kiss.

'Like a rose,' he told me knowingly, before going on his way.

He thinks I should leave the farm.

Not that he's said as much, but he talks to me as if our days of seeing each other, face to face, are numbered. The thought makes him sad, I think. Not because he'll lose me, but because he sees Pencarreg as belonging to the Joneses. It has always been his best friend's farm; its dust has only ever come from one family. I belong there; I am the last of the Joneses, for now. He sees this, and so my leaving Wales would sadden him. The end of an era. But all the same, he thinks I should go.

Across the red gingham tablecloth and our pot of tea, despite my wrinkles and height and bump, he feels he's looking at the eight-year-old again. I know it. He searches my face for a glimpse of her, and finds her – the pout, the awkward scratch of the hair, the scar on my left wrist that the fire left behind. He listened to my heart after that, too. I was still blackened and wheezy, still lost with grief. He brought pungent cream for my burn and orange stargazer lilies for my windowsill. My grandmother didn't leave my side for a week, and when I was better she took my face in her hands and said, *What were you thinking? Evie, what would I have done?*

So why does he think I should leave? If I'm still a Jones, still a little girl in his eyes?

It's simple. He knows I'm still troubled. He somehow knows that I still jolt awake at night, that I hear the word *Hughes* and feel uneasy. He still sees my sadness, even though I claim to have let it go, but he's right, it's there.

195

Move on, his eyes whisper, *for the sake of the little one.*
Leave Rosemary and Billy behind.

Maybe he's right. Perhaps the time has come to move –
the farm is crumbling, I can feel it, and the money is less
and less. But where to? Not a city, or even town; not to
his family in the Malvern Hills, for we both still want a
Welsh home. We heard a nightjar two evenings ago –
where else might we get that? And nowhere too sheltered,
for either of us: he likes his clean air and big skies; I want
views, sheep and dog roses for the kitchen table. I want
our child to grow up knowing strong winds and stickle-
back. The real colours of autumn.

I have lived away from Pencarreg once before – or tried
to. At eighteen, to please my grandparents, I went to
university. A world of blocked showers, burnt toast, warm
beer and a meagre student loan which I spent in a grotty
pub where other students didn't go. I turned up to lectures
late and left early. I got pierced through the top of my
ear. I remember wandering the streets of Swansea on
autumnal afternoons, hands in pockets, rediscovering city
life – how it feels to step on chip wrappers; how unfriendly
big crowds are; how the sound of a train horn carries.
I'd stand still and shut my eyes. The wind was gritty. The
Willises, I knew, were a long time dead.

I hated it. I only ever felt lonely there. I embarked on
a clumsy relationship with a graduate in an attempt to
fill the gaps but it felt wrong, and sordid. *This girl isn't
me*, I kept saying. Why couldn't I handle separation with
my mother's grace? The graduate professed love but it
was pointless. As with everything else there it felt fake, I
didn't want it, I made it fail. I missed green spaces. I
missed bonfires and ditches. This wasn't home, Daniel
wasn't there, and by November I knew I couldn't stay.

Not such a city girl, then, after all.

I caught the train back to Llandovery then hitched the rest of the way. Daniel was the first person I saw as I trudged up the lane with my rucksack. He stood as he was, a coil of wire round his arm. Under the limes we smiled at each other.

Later he would say, *The farm was quiet without you.*

There is no single seminar desk at that university that doesn't have his name carved into its wood, no loo door that doesn't bear the letter *D*. In one term I covered the place with him. It's his.

Anyway, my point is this. If I leave, I leave with him. No question.

Don't let him go, my mother had said. She would have been proud of me.

The first search of our sheep fields took place on a Sunday – a beautiful, blue-sky Sunday full of dragonflies and pimpernel. The swallows were back from Africa, and I opened my curtains to find Daniel in the yard, watching them.

The men wore short-sleeved shirts. Some even went bare-chested. Lewis wore a baseball cap, jeans and nothing else, so that the whole world could glimpse his tattoo. I saw him shout orders in the yard – he stood on a bale to do it. Our yard was a busy place – the whole of Cae Tresaint was there, pretty much: my grandfather, Daniel, Lewis, the green-eyed man, the boy who cleaned the chicken coop, the vet, Dr Matthews, the limping man who delivered the hay, Gerry's father with his fists, Reverend Bickley. And there were journalists – my grandmother ferried tea out to them, one eye on the hills. Chief Inspector Gregory, too, was there – he kept to the shade, and when the men all set off up the field he brought up the rear. When he caught my stare he looked away – why was that? Bad memories, perhaps. His shirt was wet on his back.

I'd argued with my grandmother the night before. I was too young to go on the search, she'd announced. I was to stay at the farm, to keep an eye on things. Keep an eye on what, I'd demanded? And anyway, wasn't Rosie a friend, of sorts? Couldn't I dip into places an adult couldn't? We pawed the dust around each other, narrowed our eyes. I fumed in bed that night.

But she was a headstrong woman, my grandmother. When she made up her mind she kept to it – a dubious quality, and one I think she passed on. Maybe that's why we fought so often, she and I. We would lock horns over many things, in the years to come. But that day, as I watched the line of men moving up over the fields like a line of birds, I knew I'd lost. I sulked. They were like wild geese, perhaps, with my grandfather leading the way. There would be pictures of them in the national papers the next day – Wales looked lovely in it.

I understand her reasoning now. She was worried Rosie would actually be found – worse, that I would find her. She feared me tripping through the bracken to find a softened Rosie under my feet, humming with flies like a windfall pear.

At the time this logic escaped me. But I didn't brood for too long. I knew our land. I knew that if there were a body, or part of one, to be found up there, I'd have stumbled across it by now.

'How tall?' I asked.

'Taller than me,' was the reply.

I was lying on the floor of the barn on my stomach, chin cupped in my hands, my ankles knocking together in the air behind me. 'And his hair?'

198

Billy said it had been mine exactly – tight coils, copper-red.

'But not the same length?'

A shake of the head. 'Shorter.'

He sat in the doorway, splitting leaves of grass into two. In the sunlight I could see his mark perfectly, and wondered if it had faded over the years. Could it have been scarlet once? Could it have been the same colour as Kieran's hair, and caught the light like that? Billy looked sideways at me.

'You're not searching?' I asked. 'Me neither. I'm not allowed. Too young, apparently.'

'Where are they looking?' he asked.

I noticed a scab on my elbow, tested it. 'Our land. The shepherd's hut, the bogs. The Tor, I think. Don't worry, I'm pretty sure they're not coming here.' I looked up from my elbow. 'How well did you know him?'

'At Tor-y-gwynt?'

'Uh-huh.'

'Is everyone there?'

'Think so. All the men, anyway.'

'So everyone but you and me?'

I considered this. 'No, actually. Mr Phipps wasn't there, either.'

Billy looked away from me then, so whatever his expression was I couldn't quite see it. But I heard his sigh. It was a short, hard thing. Almost contemptuous.

I said, 'What? Don't you like him either?'

He didn't reply for a time. He just rubbed the heel of his hand over his forehead, as if erasing a secret sign. 'Not surprised, that's all. Not the helping kind.'

'He's sworn at me. Did I tell you that?'

He looked over. 'Sworn?'

'Yep.'

He muttered to himself.

'Why Birmingham, do you suppose?' I asked him. 'Why there?'

He made a noise as if tired of this. 'Kieran had friends there. Or so he said.'

'He told you that?'

'Not me. Bronwen.'

'She told you?'

'So she went to look for him there. Didn't come back, not even for Christmases. When she told me about you,' he said, 'she put my hand on her stomach.'

I flicked off the scab, stood up, said goodbye and left him there. It had been a good day. At the top of the cow field I looked back through the herd to see him still sitting there, in the sun, watching me go.

That night the sheepdogs woke us.

I snapped out of my dream to hear them barking in the yard outside. When had they done this? Not once in five months. Something noisy must have troubled them. 'Granddad!' I called. 'The dogs!'

He was already up, tying the cord of his dressing gown, flicking on lights as he clambered down the stairs. 'Anyone there?' he bellowed.

He checked every room. Then he took an airgun out from under the stairs and unlocked the front door. My grandmother took a bread knife. I followed them. I stood on the porch, and then stepped into the yard.

'Who is it? Who's out there?'

No one, it seemed. Daniel joined us from his caravan in his jeans. He checked the barn and the sheep race. He shone a torch round the yard. The dogs whined, weaved inside their cage. 'Nothing,' he called back to us.

'At all?' asked my grandmother.

He shook his head. 'Lou, there's no one here.'

Gradually everyone returned to bed. One by one the lights were turned out, and when I climbed back under my sheets my bed was still warm. I felt nervy, alert. There was somebody out there. I was sure of it.

A few minutes later a dog gave one last burst of barks. I sat upright. Through the wall I heard my grandmother groan in her sleep, *For God's sake, shut up!*

I looked out of my window, believed I heard footsteps, but saw nothing but my own face looking back at me.

An unfair relationship, if you think about it. Those dogs worked for us. They were quick, agile, glossy creatures who darted up hills for us, barked for us, defended us. They would have laid down their lives for us, if need be. And us? What did we do in return? We saw them as labourers. We used them. When they growled at a noise in the dark we reprimanded them for it.

And even I failed to thank them in the morning, when a little bunch of feverfew was found on the doorstep – proof they were right to bark like that. And that Rosie had not been the leaver of flowers; they were somebody else's work.

Feathers

It rained today, and I had no jumper. Sheltered in church porch. Mr P saw me. He came out and asked me if I was waiting for anyone special. He spat out the word. He's so bitter! How old is he? Forty-ish? Old enough to know better, anyway. Even when he smiles I shiver. He tells me bad things about K, always. As if I'd actually listen to him! To him! Perhaps I should feel sad for Mr P. Perhaps I should take him up on his offer of a drink, or dinner, and listen to his woes . . . Perhaps not!

In the rain K's hair looks like feathers. I love that.

This is what people write about.

Blood

So Mr Phipps was not the helping kind. Billy hadn't shocked me with that news – I already knew it to be true. Mrs Maddox had once turned up at the shop a minute after five and he'd refused to open up for her – not exactly neighbourly. Christmas was ignored by him. He scowled at the carol singers and never put lights up, or a wreath on his front door. And when a local girl disappeared, and abduction was suspected, he refused to help look for her. What kind of person does that? Who else would shrug off the thought of child murder, as if it were old news?

Plus he was cruel to my friend – my shy, tired, damaged friend. I think more than anything else, that's what I hated him for.

The next day I went to the shop and found it empty. It was cool inside, cool and dark, and I stood on the doorstep, holding my breath. There was no sound. No Mr Phipps to be seen.

I stepped quietly into the room. It was eerie – dust drifted on shafts of sunlight, and a fly knocked itself against the glass. I watched it for a second or two. It would die here. By the thwack of a book if not through exhaustion, and I wondered if it knew that. They were such ugly, stupid things. They glutted on cowpats and flew into flames on the hob.

I crept to the counter, peered over it. He wasn't there. Nor was he at the back of the shop, stocking shelves. I frowned. Then where? I made my way down the aisle, watchful.

I could hear nothing but the fly.

'Well, well.'

He stood in the doorway, a cardboard box in his arms. It was hard to see his face, because the light was behind him, but I could guess the expression well enough. Head to one side, eyes narrowed.

'I'm here to buy an ice pop,' I said.

He considered me. 'You've got one minute,' he replied.

We busied ourselves in silence. He unpacked the box whilst I sifted through the freezer. My hands grew numb.

'Fifty pence,' he said.

I counted out my change in pennies.

'Sunburnt, are we?'

I frowned at him, checked my arms for pinkness. 'No.'

He took my money. He dropped it into the till, slammed the drawer shut. 'You look it.'

'I'm not.'

'Hm!'

'Why do you hate me?'

This was clever of me, although I didn't know it. Bluntness has power. It can throw people off balance. It can drop their jaws and make them gasp for air. Had Mr Phipps been a normal, feeling person he would have buckled at the question. He would have grown flustered, would have said, *What? Hate you? Me?*

But he didn't. He just said, 'You don't know?'

'I wouldn't ask if I did, would I?'

He leant forward over the counter so that my face was full of his broken veins, his broken nose, his wet lips, his bristles, his mouthy smell, and he said, 'Kieran Green was the worst thing that ever happened to Cae Tresaint. And to Bronwen – look what he led her to! How was she happy? And you stand there with his face and his words and ask me why I don't like you in my shop? After what he's done? Get out.'

'What?'

'Get out.'

'Why? What have I done?'

'You're pushing your luck.'

I went to the door.

Perhaps I imagined the next bit. But as I stepped out into the street I was certain I heard Mr Phipps mutter, *Shame it wasn't you.*

I turned.

He had his back to me. I stood there, staring at his damp shirt, his bald patch. Had I heard right? Did he really say that? A bitterness surged inside me. It burst up like the Brych over rocks. He seemed to sense my glare then, because he tensed. Had he meant me to hear? Had he thought me gone? His hands slowed. His head half turned. Was this fear? But how could he be afraid of an eight-year-old with an ice pop, in grass-stained T-shirt and shorts?

Such a coward, that man. Everything he ever did was underhand, and sly, and spineless. I'm not a violent person, certainly not now, but as I write this I still believe he deserved all that came to him. He deserved the damage Kieran caused him – the broken nose, the humiliation. He deserved, to a point, the calculated revenge I vowed to carry out on him, and would, within the next few days.

*　　*　　*

Where is Mr Phipps now? I don't care. I imagine a block of retirement homes in a dreary southern town. The ground-floor flat – no light, no visitors. I imagine him looking at the phone and wondering, perhaps for the first time in his life, why it doesn't ring. I don't mean to sound callous – and I wouldn't wish loneliness on anyone, least of all on the old. But he was cruel. He was never sorry. I blame him for almost everything.

He took Billy from me. He made my grandmother cry. He may as well have taken my wrist and held it in the flames himself, because that fire was his fault – *his*. He would have enjoyed it, too, no doubt – *Feel that? Kieran's daughter? Do you?* It was his decision. He struck the match and I know it.

For years I hated him. I have never hated anyone with the strength or the commitment or hunger with which I would grow to hate Mr Phipps. I would spit against his shop. I would badmouth him to everyone, glower at him, steal from him whenever I could. That loathing has weakened now – I know better than to hate, because it's pointless and it's tiring. *Let bygones be bygones*, my grandfather would say. So I just pity Mr Phipps these days. I think he is a sad, lost man with an empty soul and an axe to grind. Probably a madness to him. And no doubt a broken heart too, somewhere along the line.

As I set off home through the curling Rosie leaflets and the sticky air, I turned back to study the shop. I thought, *watch out*. I would defend myself, I would punish him. Not as I'd punished the girl in the canteen because I'd promised Daniel I would never fight again – no fists allowed, I'd vowed to him, and I would never break a promise to him. But I knew I'd think of a way.

I was so buried in my plotting that I failed to hear footsteps follow me up the hill. Only at the cattle grid did I sense something. But I turned to find an empty lane and our still lime trees, nothing more.

That night I couldn't sleep.

I crossed the landing to the bathroom and sneaked on the light. Our mirror was small and cracked in the top corner. It was flecked with white from when I brushed my teeth, and I'd left sticky thumbprints on it. Not that I tended to look in the mirror too often. It served no purpose. Mirror or no mirror, my hair was still unbrush-able, and my skin was still sore.

But that night I turned slowly from side to side, inspecting myself. I looked not so much at the obvious things, but more at the subtle. I pressed my fingers against my cheekbones, pulled down my lower lip to see the blue veins in my gums. I felt how strong I was in some places, how snappable elsewhere. I studied the shape of my eyebrows, their thickness, the height of my forehead, whether my ears stuck out or not.

How often have you looked at your reflection for a glimpse of someone else? On the whole we don't do it. But I did then. Everything I didn't recognise I suddenly knew was his – the deep groove between nose and upper lip; the broad hands; the prominent collarbone. And the height, of course – since my arrival at Pencarreg I had grown three inches. As had my hair. When wet it reached past my shoulders.

The only other time I showed any real interest in the mirror was two and a half years later.

I'd begun to feel ill at lunch time. I'd been standing in the dinner queue, my metal tray in one hand, when I suddenly

209

realised that my stomach was tightening. I assumed it was hunger. But by home time the pain had got worse. I sat on the bus with my knees tucked up under my chin. Would I throw up? Was I dying? Was there a cancer growing inside me, unfolding like some strange purple rose?

As I stripped off my clothes for a bath that evening I found blood. I stumbled backwards, lowered myself down onto the loo. Not cancer. At least I didn't think so. But what? Then a vague idea came to me. I wrapped my arms round my waist and tried to remember what it was that I'd heard. That this was a girl thing. That this would happen again and again. I dabbed at myself cautiously, and felt sad.

Believe it or not, I managed to hide this secret from my grandparents for the next five months. I made my own wads from loo roll, kitchen towel, even old holey socks that were deemed lifeless and thrown to one side. I was resourceful, and shrewd. I tiptoed to the bathroom and learnt how to hush the sound of the lock; I stole my secret bundles out to the dustbins instead of using my own bedroom bin. But I suppose my concealment really only worked because my grandparents didn't expect it. I had no chest at all. I was hipless, skinny, and I must have looked far from ready for such an event. But then, I *was* far from ready – I was just eleven, still a child. And if I look back now, I find it crazy, even terrifying, to think my body could have reproduced at that age.

But, still, I managed. I wore dark trousers once a month and perfected standing on the loo seat to reach the aspirin cupboard. But I'd be lying if I said it didn't affect me. I took to looking at Gerry differently. I remembered Rosie; I felt oddly wise. I'd have moments when I longed to tell someone about it, to tug on a sleeve and whisper in an ear, but who was there to tell? It was my mother's mystery to explain. Three years on, and I thought I'd learnt not to miss her better.

When the time came, however, my grandmother did a good job. She took me out to Lampeter and treated me to hot chocolate with marshmallows and a bag of *women's things* from the chemist. I was only offered the most basic explanation at first. Think of it as an old friend, she explained: a bit of a nuisance at times, but wouldn't we be lost without it? I struggled with the concept of cramps as being friendly. But there wasn't much else I could do.

For the record, my chest remained as flat as a pancake until about three months ago. It has taken pregnancy to give me any sort of figure – ironic, of course, since it robs most women of theirs. I had a few token bras as a teenager but there wasn't much point to them. Sometimes I was ashamed. Sometimes I wished a man would find more than two pink, apologetic nipples underneath my top. But, at the same time, at least I could run for the bus. And there was nothing to get in the way when I fired an air gun or swung into trees.

Nothing to hurt when I flung myself down into bracken to hide from the hands that had, I'm sure, hurt Rosie, and would try to hurt me, given time.

The next day a roller skate was found on the Tor, under a strip of moss that had fallen back to show its hidden treasure. The search had missed it. Or perhaps it had been hidden there once the search had been done. The village rattled like a wasp in an upturned jar.

'Dear God,' said my grandmother, cupping her head in her hands. She clutched me that night, as if I was the one who'd been lost.

As for Mrs Maddox, she beckoned to me as I passed her pink cottage, and whispered, *Not long now. Trust me. They'll catch the bastard before the week is out.*

Sea View

*Caught the bus without paying to Aberystwyth. There's
a phone box to the left of the pier I now know the inside
of. Late March, so no tourists. I showed him the blue
town house on the seafront that I like, and he said, I'll
buy it for you then, when I'm rich.*

Late March? The end of an era, for them.

Headache

Where would I hide a body? If I found one lying in my arms, and I wanted to conceal it, what would I do? I've thought about it. It became a game for a while, for Gerry and me. We'd get bored in class and whisper to each other. We'd scribble down theories in ink, slide them to each other like blueprints. Proof that if you knew the area, and had a sly brain, concealing a body would probably not be so hard.

The bogs. There are a lot of them. Even in hot weather they would be slick enough to close up around a body before long. And their airlessness would preserve it. Rosie, to this day, after twenty-one years, might still be intact, still peach-skinned and lovely, peat clotted in her hair.

There are lakes here of unknown depth. No one has measured them. No one has dived down to see just how black or cold those waters are, but everyone knows they aren't shallow. Roll her up, tie her down, drop her in a lake a few miles away – Llyn Berwyn or Llyn Gynon. Use enough bricks to ensure she will not float back up again to brush the legs of swimmers.

And then there are forests no one walks in, the closed mines, huge stretches of land that only the sheep tread across. The road to the Teifi Pools goes on for ever – my car rocks along a track for miles, through whipped yellow tussock grass and boulders. It's a desolate place. The wind is always strong there. I've felt my own loneliness emerge by those pools; I've seen it flit over the water like an unknown bird. Tuck Rosie under a rock and leave her, for only the flock to find.

So perhaps we shouldn't be surprised. Perhaps we shouldn't blame Chief Inspector Gregory and his team for not solving this, for not finding her, because this place has secret pockets and hidden doors. I spoke to my grandfather about it. I curled up against him on the sofa one night and said, 'Where do you think she is?' He had no answer. We sat in silence for a while, and I felt glad to be there, in our sitting room, in the warm and dry.

It was a question I posed to Billy, too.

He was picking wild strawberries off the plant that huddled by the barn, and I watched him, my knees tucked up into my chest. The heat of the day had been fierce. I was aware of a dampness under my arms, and I plucked at my uniform sleeves. Still he wore his wax jacket. His hands shook a little as he picked. Some of the berries were still white, knot-hard, and these he left. Only the red ones were of interest. He passed some to me. 'Eat them,' he said. And I did.

'But it's odd,' I told him, 'don't you think? She must have been on our land, if her skate was there. But I didn't see her. We had to walk past the Tor, Daniel and me, when we came back from swimming. We went right by it. And there was no one there. Don't you think it's odd?'

He murmured back to me. 'Could have been put there.'

'A long climb,' I said, 'just to hide a skate.' And I shrugged at him. 'Plus there are better places.'

We took our cache away from the barn, into the shade of the beeches. The place smelt foxy. These wild strawberries were quite a find. They were lovely. I savoured them.

'Was it both skates,' asked Billy, 'or just one?'

I shook my head. 'Just one. But why the Tor, do you think?'

'It's strange up there.'

'Strange how?'

He offered me the story about the farm worker from Caio who was up there for three days and became ill. I had heard the tale before, but I'd never learnt just how ill. He had threatened his girlfriend with a shotgun, said Billy. He'd pressed the barrel into her throat. I could picture her, up against a wall and pleading.

'Really? Is that true?'

'Like I told you, it's strange.'

He told me, too, that many years before he was born, before Cae Tresaint really even existed, people *did things* up there. What things? He meant meetings. He meant that shady unchristian people took themselves up to the Tor and held quiet ceremonies in the wind. I was enraptured. I thought of cloaks billowing, of long beards. Was this some sort of magic? 'Did they make offerings?'

He shook his head. 'Doubt it.'

'Then what did they do?'

I decided they probably chanted, held hands, and just enjoyed the view.

And it was meant to be a sad place. Tor-y-gwynt was so called because the wind there was incredible. But that wind, to the God-fearing ear, sounded like the wail of a wounded thing. I, too, would hear the sound. On a blustery night I'd push open my bedroom window and listen to the moaning coming from the Tor. I'd wonder if Wilfred or Hywel John or Great-uncle Duncan ever stopped in the yard to heed that call, if they believed it a sign of some sort.

'And now' – he shrugged – 'the roller skate. It's the Tor. It's . . .'

'But,' I reasoned, '*you* go there.'

His chewing slowed. He looked right at me.

It was then that he told me the best story of all. Whenever I smell foxes I think of that day, under the beeches, when I learnt how I was made.

On a breezy morning nearly a decade before, Billy said he woke to a painful head. It throbbed. It hurt to move his eyes, and whenever this happened he took himself up to the ridge. He said he wanted brisk, clean air. He wanted to stay up there for a while, hauling in the air and looking seaward. *It helps*, he told me, running his fingertips over his blackberry mark.

It was April – just. The lambs were out. Yellow wagtails, he said, were lingering by the rhubarb patch – nesting there, no doubt. A good day. Bright, promising.

'Did the wind help your head?' I asked.

When he reached the ridge he went to the shepherd's hut and sat back against it, the way he always did. But he said there were others up there. He could hear them. He stood back up and looked around for them.

'Who were they?' I asked. 'Hikers?'

He shook his head. Bronwen and Kieran. They were over at the Tor, lying behind the biggest of the rocks. The far side, he said – well hidden. No one from the village could see them there. 'But *I* could.'

'What were they doing? Why were they hidden?'

Such a childish question.

It goes without saying what they were up to.

It was a day of buzzards. Three wheeled above the Tor.

Billy couldn't get any closer to the couple because they'd spot him, and then what? Kieran would be angry. Bronwen would look . . . what? Disappointed, he said. He didn't want to see her disappointed. So he stayed in the hut for a while.

Billy's headache didn't really go. Normally the air up there did the trick, he explained. But not that time. It didn't work. He took his sore head back down the field, and felt ill for two days. Under the shade of the beeches I nodded; I supposed a kick in the head would do that.

I kissed him for telling me that. It surprised even me. I pushed myself up and gave him a light, childish kiss right on his blackberry mark. For me, that kiss was a thank you – a closing kiss, if anything. But not for Billy. I think it must have been years since he was last kissed like that, if ever, and I think it opened something in him. An attic door creaked ajar. He looked at me. His gaze was measured, calm – anything but mad.

It was July by now.

Luck

She writes,

Today he surprised me – not for the first time. He appeared in the lane, and took me to the Tor. A six-pack in his rucksack, cigarettes to share. Even a rug! I've learnt his smell. It's more than earth and tobacco. There's a softer scent there – soap? I don't know. It's strongest on his collarbone, and in his hair. The Tor is his place now. I'll always see it and think of his collarbone. I'm lucky! Who else has that?

Was she lucky? Debatable. The popular answer would be no – who can call reckless love that? She became a distracted girl with a child and a frown, a brown bottle of sleeping pills and a terraced house by a train track. I've heard her referred to as *Poor Bronwen*. She'd have hated that.

But then I think of Dr Matthews. I think of the old wives' tales, the clichés. Would she have been poorer still if she hadn't met Kieran Green? This is the question – a broken heart or an untouched one? Which is better? Maybe Mr Phipps was right – that that Irishman was the worst of all things. Or maybe *she* was right – she *was* lucky. Maybe to be haunted by an old love isn't so bad – at least it means you've had one. Maybe to look at Tor-y-gwynt and to remember an afternoon with him, a warm rug and a six-pack of beer is the very epitome of luck.

I, at any rate, should count myself lucky. The date of this entry is *1st April 1969*. She has written it in red pen and underlined it twice.

1st April. Count on nine months exactly.

Clouds, lambs, buzzards, and I was conceived that day.

I think of it. I've walked to the Tor and pictured them there, lying on the west side, half hidden from view. Whenever I go there I stand against the granite and hold back my hair. I wonder how much the view has changed since they were here, since I was made. I suspect not a lot. It looks as it's always done.

See? My mother, too, approved of love outdoors. It's not just me. And I had formed my opinion long before I ever knew of hers. Perhaps that's a trait of country girls. But then, I remember well enough a time in Birmingham, all those years ago, when I ran home from the train tracks with my mittens flying on their strings, jabbering with stories of limp, wet balloons. City girls, too, then, choose the outdoor life sometimes. Except isn't a Welsh hilltop better than a railway tunnel full of litter and diesel smells? Isn't the wind the best accompaniment of all?

If my child ever turns to me as a teenager, or older still, and says, *Mum, where was I made?* my answer will be less romantic. I'll say, it was in a bed back in Wales, late at night, and it was a simple affair. The farm was quiet, there was a frost outside, and afterwards he slept. Neither of us mentioned the obvious, when the morning came. It went unspoken, yet I think we both knew. I remember leaning against the bars of a sheep pen in the market the following day and knowing – *knowing* – it was no longer just me standing there. Under my fleeced coat and holey jumper, beneath the striped shirt Daniel had lent me, I was suddenly aware of a dark little room that now had a person living in it.

When I told him he didn't say *whose?* Or *are you sure?* He just ran his hands up into my hair and said, *We're going to be good at this.*

Lies

My resentment of Mr Phipps grew with the heat. At night, as we slept under sheets with our windows half open, I would mutter to myself. My curtains lifted with a slight night breeze and I thought of him, awake, pacing his house, hating me. Making plans. *Two can play that game*, I thought. I brewed my anger, boiled it down into thick, potent form. I felt it sit in me like tar.

July meant there were no days off for anyone at Pencarreg for a while. Despite the police and the journalists and the sun-bleached pictures of Rosie on telegraph poles, it was still sheep-dipping time. The sheep race echoed and clattered and smelt sour, and Daniel could always be found there. He'd push the sheep under with a pole, and they'd emerge the other side, indignant at him, bleating.

My grandfather told me to stay away – chemicals, rule number three.

'The fumes are bad for you, Evie. Go and see if your grandmother needs any help.'

'She's with Mrs Hughes.'

'Then haven't you got any homework to do?'

I thought, of a sort. Daniel glanced up at me, gave me

a bemused look. 'Anyway – how can this be fun? Watching dipping? You're a funny one, Miss Jones.'

So I spent time with Billy – or tried to. He was quieter than ever. I put this down to the heat. It made sense to me that such weather could hurt a delicate head. So I'd let him sit in the barn, and I would talk without expecting answers. I told him about Mr Phipps. I flashed my hatred of him at Billy, the way a pirate might offer a peek at his treasure, but all he did was listen.

'He's hiding something. I'm sure of it.'

Billy always had his eyes on me. Sometimes he studied my forehead when I talked to him, or my mouth. At one point he leant over and placed his hand gently on my hair. As if feeling for warmth, or blessing me. I hadn't expected it, but I didn't mind it at all.

School tests began. I struggled with them. It was no surprise, I suppose – I had missed a term through bereavement, and although I was coping with English and geography, everything else was still hard. It didn't help that I'd barely revised. I'd been distracted by too many things. As had most of the school, I suppose, and I think the marking was lenient that year, all things considered. But I secretly longed to do well. I had private dreams of being top of the class. I wanted red ticks in margins and gold stars, like Gerry. He was incredible. His work drifted back to him with a glow about it. I'd look at him in class and smile. He was lovely in a lot of ways. I didn't do him justice.

My worst subject was maths. It always was, and always would be. Numbers jumbled their way in my head, and I'd lose my patience. The test was terrible. I left questions unanswered. I stared at the paper and thought of other things. I left the room before the end because it just seemed pointless to stay.

After school that afternoon I decided to ignore my grandmother's curfews and laws, and stayed on the bus a stop later.

This was something I'd never done. I tucked myself against a yellow curtain and watched the war memorial and the police van slip away. It was an odd feeling. Was this how real explorers felt? I knew my grandmother would have one eye on the lane, awaiting my return, but I didn't care. I wasn't ready to go home. I wanted an hour or two away from the village, away from the worry and clutter. I wanted a swim. I wanted to set off into the penny-brown lake and duck under, to leave maths and Rosie and Mr Phipps floating on the surface like oil. To go somewhere all on my own.

After Cae Tresaint the bus headed towards Llanddewi Brefi, and I jumped off at a stop on the far side of the pine plantation, on a lonely stretch of road. The driver – a thin woman who chewed gum – eyed me. 'This isn't your stop,' she remarked. I said I was meeting a friend just over the hill.

'Do your parents know?'

I nodded.

'How are you getting home?'

'I'll be dropped back. It's all arranged.'

'OK. Well, watch yourself. See you tomorrow.'

The bus hissed at me as it moved off. As I watched it, a boy I didn't know peered out of the rear window at me. He wore braces on his teeth. I stuck up my middle finger, hitched up my rucksack and headed off into the woods.

I've never really liked that place. It's Forestry Commission land: amid the acres of dense, silent pine trees there are sudden patches of emptiness, where trees have been felled

227

and the air is sweet with sawdust. Those spaces feel ghostly. There are bulldozers there, tyre tracks, neatly stacked logs that prove men work there, and often. But when have I ever seen them? When have I even heard them?

I expected the lake to be busy. I knew some of the older kids came here after school sometimes, that they splashed and dared and groped each other, that they rolled long cigarettes. I knew, too, that travellers parked here overnight in summer months: black grass told of their fires. And Bryn Mawr horses had been tied to trees before now, left to tug at bracken as their riders ate lunch on the shore. All this I knew. And I assumed they'd be there. After all, it was unimaginably hot. I'd never really sweated before. There was a new smell to me – *developing early*, my grandmother had suggested behind closed doors. As if I'd been blurry till now.

But the lake was quiet. I emerged out of the pine trees to find it almost deserted. No children, no travellers. On the far shore a man was walking his dog; in the distance someone was swimming slowly, sleek-haired and white-armed, sometimes diving out of view and then drifting back up elsewhere. Man or woman? I couldn't tell. A solitary hiker was making his way down the hill.

I undressed at the place where Daniel and I had been. I kicked off my shoes and socks. My hair had been pinned back but I loosened it. It was full of knots and dry as straw. I had one more glance round before peeling off my school dress and then wrapping my arms round my chest to hide my little pink buds. Hardly anyone there, yet I still felt watched. The place had never been so still.

The water was ice cool. I waded out up to my stomach. That was the worst part – half hot, half cold – so I held my breath, dropped my arms and splashed under. I emerged with a splutter, then vanished again. Underwater was a good place to be – my heartbeat was down there, and a huge silence. My skin looked bone white. I'd resurface to heat and light. I floated on my back for a while, like a star.

I have never swum there again. I am not superstitious, but I don't trust that water. Not any more. I have swum there twice only, but both times I came home to bad news.

I clambered out of the lake, towelled myself down with my dress and then pulled it back on. That meant that I ran home with it clinging to me, feeling and looking like a chequered second skin.

What did I find? Daniel – on the bench by the porch, holding a tea towel to his mouth.

My heart cried. I ran to him. 'What is it? What happened? Was it the sheep dip?'

He smiled, shook his head. 'A man's fist, Evie. That's what.'

He unpeeled the tea towel to show me a cut on his bottom lip, comma-shaped, still bleeding a little and haloed by the start of a bruise.

Why do men fight? Boredom. Wounded pride. Occasionally in self-defence. In this case the heat and the beer were blamed. Rosie's sapphire eyes watched the whole thing: her leaflets were strung outside the White Hart like washing, rising and falling when a car drove past.

The fight had happened in the pub garden, under rusty umbrellas and parched hanging baskets. My grandfather, too, had been there. After an afternoon of sheep dipping he'd gone down there for a beer with Daniel. This wasn't like him – he didn't drink much – and my grandmother later berated him for it. She declared a hot sun and a cold pint didn't mix. 'You should have known better, Dewi. For God's sake. Exactly how old are you?'

Perhaps it was inevitable. Cooked brains and frayed tempers, alcohol and a few sharp words – accusations were made in the pub that afternoon. Who had been there? Mr Wilkinson from the stables; Dr Matthews; Gerry's dad; and Lewis, too, which was no surprise. He spent his earnings there, it seemed. Perhaps he fancied the barmaid. That would have been just like him.

Everyone was challenged – *Who*, asked Lewis, *is skulking round the place with a filthy fucking heart?* I can see it exactly – Lewis leaning across the table, finger jabbing the air. Nineteen years old, drunk and acting like God. Shirt off, tattoo showing. *So what's your alibi?* It was only a matter of time.

Mr Wilkinson threw the first punch.

Not a brawl, as such. I'm not even sure that that punch caused any damage – more a warning shot than a proper reprimand. I don't think much happened besides a few poorly thrown fists and the odd spilt beer. No one was really sober or talented enough to cause real damage. But Daniel had tried to calm things. He had tried to catch their fists with his, and been punished for it.

'Who?' I asked. 'Was it Lewis?'

'It doesn't matter who it was. It was an accident.'

'Was it Mr Phipps?'

Daniel studied me. 'Mr Phipps? He wasn't there. Or at least, not till later. Word spread, I suppose. Trust him to stick his oar in.'

'His oar? What did he say?'

He dabbed at his lip. It was still bleeding a little, and he examined the tea towel. 'Nonsense. As usual. Blaming Billy Macklin, of all people. No proof, no reasoning, no anything. Who's to say Billy even lives round here any more? This place is going crazy, Evie.' He suddenly looked me up and down. 'Where have you been? It's past seven.'

I stood in the yard in my wet uniform and felt my anger tighten itself, fist-like.

Someone we know, Mrs Maddox had said. *One of our own.* I slammed doors shut in the farmhouse; I felt my rage steaming inside me, a pan close to the boil. Gerry and I spent less and less time together – I was poor company, I suppose, with a head full of plotting and a heart full of rage. I never really listened to him. Even when he came into school with a bruise like a butterfly on the underside of his arm I said nothing. I just simmered in class, on the bus, in the shepherd's hut. I even took myself into St Tysul's and sat there in the cool half-dark. It was a good place for thinking, I discovered. It was there that I decided what I would do for revenge.

Did I genuinely think that Mr Phipps had taken, hurt, killed Rosemary Hughes? It's an immense, incredible accusation. It's a strike I would never dare make at anyone, because mud sticks, as my grandmother would say. And it's on the whitest walls that it shows up the most: he might have been a savage, miserable, twisted man with bad breath and a reddened face, but he'd committed no real crime. He was innocent of abduction, at least, and yet I would accuse him of it. I would shine a torch on his name and say, *There! That's him!*

Age *is* an excuse, of sorts. I knew no better. I was unaware of just what a man might do to a twelve-year-old girl. No. I did not think he had taken her. I did not think Mr Phipps was capable of anything more than mean words. But mean words can be enough.

I told the police it was him. *So you know what it's like to be glanced at, mistrusted. So you know.*

* * *

231

I did not seek them out. I did not run to the Chief Inspector when I saw him next, tug at his arm and say, *I have news*. I waited for them to return – as we all knew they would. They had no clues, no ideas. Word was they were grasping at straws.

Two days after my swim and the fight at the pub, as Daniel's lip was healing, I returned from school to find him leaning against the sheep gate with a cigarette in his hand. Chief Inspector Gregory was with him. He too was smoking, holding it between his finger and thumb as if throwing a dart.

'Good afternoon, Evangeline.'

My heart was pumping. 'Hi.'

Daniel smiled at me with his eyes. 'Nothing to worry about, Olwen. He's just here for a few more questions. And a cup of tea.'

I stared at the policeman through my hair. 'Do you want to talk to me?'

'If that's OK with you.'

Daniel stayed near us. He leant over the fence, rolled back his shoulder as if his bones were stiff. I could see him out of the corner of my eye.

'Evangeline, do you know a William Macklin? Have you heard about him?'

I lie well. I always have.

'Who?'

'Billy Macklin. Your neighbour, Mrs' – he consulted his notes – 'Maddox says you asked her about him. A few months back. True?'

'Oh ... *Billy* Macklin. I just wanted to hear the story. You know – about the horse, and stuff. That's all.'

He nodded. 'OK. But you've not met him?'

He surveyed me keenly. I clasped my hands behind my back, swayed a little in a girlish, innocent way. 'Nope,' I said. 'I don't know where to find him, or anything.' I smiled winsomely. 'Isn't he just made up?'

'Well, no, he's real enough. We need to track him down. His house is empty, derelict, so if you hear anything . . .'

'Why? Do you think he did it?'

'*It?*'

'Killed Rosie.'

Chief Inspector Gregory flipped his notepad closed and pushed it into his pocket. 'We have no body as yet, Miss Jones. We just want to talk to him. He's the type to know something. That's all.'

I thought, *liar*.

Takes one to know one.

As he moved off across the yard I glanced over at Daniel. He was gazing up at the Tor.

I looked away. I didn't want our eyes to meet, in case those dove-grey eyes undid me, and my plot skittered out of me over the yard, like birdseed. I could hide nothing. I was scared my lie was glinting in me, that he would see it, that he might never love me then.

'Chief Inspector Gregory!'

I caught him up in the lane by the cow field. He was surprised to see me, and crunched his eyebrows into a frown.

'I think you should talk to Mr Phipps. Who runs the shop. I think he knows something.'

The policeman leant into me. He searched my face, and said, 'Why do you think this, Evie?'

'He's . . . said things.'

'What sort of things? Evangeline?'

I looked him straight in the eyes and said, 'He said I should be next. He didn't go on the search for her. I just . . .' – I gave a timid shrug – '. . . don't trust him. He's

233

creepy. He looks at me weirdly . . . Up and down. He tried to kiss me once.'

There was the lie. Right there. An opening kiss, or a closing? Both, I supposed. 'He kissed you? Are you sure?'

I nodded. 'But don't tell anyone? Please? Or I'll get into trouble. He told me it was our secret.'

After a moment, he touched me on the shoulder and said, 'Thank you. You've done the right thing in telling me.'

I watched him leave, walking down through the stripes of light that the tunnel of alders left on the lane. I felt satisfied. I had no concept of the damage such lies could do, or of the ball I'd set in motion.

Oranges

Pencil on A4:

Is it? Am I? Too early to tell, and I mustn't worry, because I know me, and I know that if I worry it will take even longer to arrive. My body works that way. But when have I ever been this late?

April showers. The broken gutter means I can't sleep. The weather keeps him busy, so no K for three days now – three!

I need to talk to him. Because what if I am? I must be. I must. Do I look different? Do I feel different? No, I feel the same, I've looked in the mirror, and nothing is bigger than usual, and nothing is sore. No sickness, either – but when is that meant to happen? After one month, or two?

I have to see Dr M. It's time.

Would we give it an Irish name?

It has no rules, of course. Morning sickness comes when it chooses. Only a week or so after conceiving I became ill. Oranges, for some reason, made it worse. Just the smell, and I'd have to run to the loo.

But then, what a thing for the body to deal with. No wonder it gets flustered. Since birth, before birth, it has been learning – when to bleed, when to heal, how to act when hungry or tired or cold or under stress. It has been finding out what it needs to be healthy, what hurts it, what it's allergic to. Rhythms have been learnt, and patterns set down. The body maps out a little more of its country every minute, every day, until it can say *this is me: I am this way.*

Then two joined cells plant themselves, and everything changes. The future has a different meaning to it.

Bindweed

Am I haunted by the lie? Every day. To think I claimed such a thing, and so brazenly – it astounds me still. It's the standard against which all subsequent untruths have been set, and it pales them all. *That man? He killed someone.* Is there a worse thing to say? And I was so good at it. Such a deft liar. My word was never openly doubted; I was instantly believed.

But then, I had to be. I was a young skinny girl who could look rabbit-eyed and anxious when she chose to; Mr Phipps was a strong man with no friends, a temper and a secretive air. It must have seemed possible. In policemen's minds a light must have sparked at the thought.

They took him away for further questioning. They opened the car door for him and told him to mind his head. Mr Phipps's shop had never been closed on a weekday before – not once – so when people tried his door and found it locked gossip was quicker than ever to fly. Mrs Maddox rang us up with the news. I peered down through the banisters at the top of my grandfather's head as he answered the phone. *My God*, he said. *Are you sure?*

I don't remember feeling guilt, not then. I just felt thrilled, alive, and I galloped to the old barn praying that Billy would be there. I hoped for him. I longed to take him by the arms and tell him that the man we both disliked so much was now gone. Would he smile? I wasn't sure I'd ever seen him give a proper, wide smile before.

And he was there. He was breathing hard, as if he'd had to run there, but I asked no questions since I had too much to say.

'It was him! Mr Phipps!' And I rattled out words like gunfire. He listened the way only Billy could – frozen, with eyes like peat lakes.

'Well? What are you thinking?'

I suppose now he was thinking how some things never change. I suppose he was looking at me and feeling wistful. Feuds run in the blood, perhaps. Perhaps hatred can be like height or freckles or a cancerous gene – it, too, can be handed down from parent to child. Our strength of feeling – is that, too, inherited? My mother's heart may have broken in a bath, but it was also a strong, immense, ungovernable thing – did she pass it to me? Did my father give more than red hair?

It was Billy who took hold of arms, not me. His fingers wrapped round my unscarred wrists and he said, *You be careful.*

I blinked his warning away. Why was there a need to be careful? Wasn't the worst of it done?

Picture this, he said.

Eight months before my birth, and late at night. A red-headed man pads down from Bryn Mawr, a bag slung over one arm. He moves neatly, quietly. Only half a moon, but it's enough to see by. This matters – there are no streetlights. He whistles under his breath. He comes into the square, looks to his left. The store is dark, sleeping.

Kieran slows. Perhaps he pulls on his bottom lip as he's thinking. Perhaps he runs a hand from the back of his head forwards, over the curls. Above the shops the lights are out. The curtains are drawn. He scans the street to check no one's about, and smiles.

He works quickly. He forces the window with his elbow – one quick push. The glass fractures, but doesn't fall. He's clever. He picks at it, pulls out enough shards to push his hand through; he must have done this before. He reaches the door latch. One last glance behind him, but Cae Tresaint is silent. It must be three, perhaps four in the morning. No one is about.

In the shop he slips behind the counter and takes all the tobacco and whisky he can. He uses plastic bags. He cracks open the seal of a bottle and drinks as he works. He breaks into the till with a penknife – not a lot of money, but enough. Enough for what? To treat himself. To prove a point. To teach the owner a lesson, to punish him for Irish taunts, the scowls. To leave his mark – his thumbprint in clay, his name drawn in the sand.

Kieran stuffs his pockets, lights a cigarette. He pauses for a second, sucking down the smoke. He's proud of his work.

A light comes on. From the landing. The sound of foot on stair and a voice shouting, *What the hell . . . ?* Kieran jumps the counter. He darts to the door, but a hand grabs his shoulder. Cecil Phipps stands behind him, devil-eyed, livid, clutching Kieran's collar in his fist. He curses. He calls Kieran low, foul names. He snarls up into his face like a bulldog. For a moment Cecil Phipps thinks he has won. He pulls back his wet lips to smile.

Picture this. A punch, as fast as a buzzard's dive. A firecracker out of the dark that smashes the shopkeeper's nose. His head snaps back. His face bursts. He gasps, lets go of the collar and bends at the waist. Blood drips through his fingers onto the floor tiles, making dark pools the police will soon have to step over. He stumbles back into his stock.

Kieran flits out across the square, up towards the main road. The cigarette still rests in the side of his mouth. He flexes his knuckles, which are split and sore. But he smiles at them, shakes his head a little.

Does he glance up the lane as he passes it? Does he slow for a second as he thinks of the farm at the top? Yes. Briefly. Because he is not a bad man. He has a heart, he has feelings, and he stands for a moment in the dark and feels sorry. Maybe he thinks of dark hair spread on a pillow. Maybe he almost changes his mind. But he is young, too young, his knuckles throb, and lights are flicking on behind him, and if he had a choice he doesn't now.

He hitchhikes on the main road. Later, a lorry driver will come forward to the police, saying he dropped Kieran at Llandovery station and no, he didn't seem like a bad type, nor did he say where he was bound.

Billy was the only witness. He'd been unable to sleep, had looked up to see Kieran stealing down the lane that night and had followed him.

'Who else have you told this to?' I breathed.

'No one,' he said.

I was incredulous. No one? It made no sense to me. Billy hadn't really liked my father much. That much I had already gathered. Wasn't it clear to everyone that Billy loved my mother, that he wanted to be in Kieran's place? Mrs Maddox had been in no doubt about that. So why not tell the police this? Why not walk to the police station and say, *I saw it all; it was definitely him.*

240

My theory, now, is this: Billy was just too decent. Unlike me, he didn't wage wars or exact revenge. Such slyness wasn't his way. And perhaps he knew, too, that my mother would not have thanked him if his words had led to Kieran's arrest. Better to let it be. Better to watch him make his way past the red telephone box, leaving nothing but cigarette smoke behind.

Billy picked bindweed for me as I left. *Convolvulus arvensis*, he said – frail, lovely pink-and-white flowers, only faintly scented when I held them right up to my nose. I carried them faithfully back through the cow field, and stuck them in a sherry glass of water when I got home. But the flowers had closed themselves up by then. Bindweed does that. Once picked, it doesn't last long. I sloshed out the glass and binned the flowers. They would still be wilting there the next evening, just twenty-four hours later, when I came home punished for telling such lies, when I felt like a different girl.

The Stile

Not a nightmare as such, because I don't wake up terrified. My dreams of the fire frighten me more. But sometimes in my sleep I hear legs rustle through bracken again and I'm back there – shafts of light, the stench of the stagnant pond. *Hello*, he said, *Evangeline.*

Daniel has woken to my mumblings. He doesn't understand them. I'm indistinct, and like a night nurse he just rearranges the blankets and waits till I'm quiet again. I have never told him. I thought, aged eight, it was my fault somehow. My punishment for telling lies about Mr Phipps, for disobeying basic rules, for having red hair, for walking the long way home, and I thought if I told Daniel about that pushing, unsealing hand he'd tell me off or back away. I thought I might change in his eyes, and all would be lost. So I said nothing. And it's too late to tell him now, because wouldn't he say, *Why didn't you tell me before? Eve? Why not?* And something between us would be gone.

In some ways there is nothing to tell. I was not grabbed, or tugged; I wasn't pulled into shadows and no hand was clamped over my mouth. No knife to my throat, no whispered threats. No stealthy stranger beckoned me into bushes on the pretence of looking for a stray dog. No sweets were offered. No flashing. I saw no part of him I shouldn't have done. I lost no buttons, gained no bruises, and I wandered home with no real proof of it at all. Just memory, and the slightest kind of soreness. It was over in a matter of seconds. It was brief, and light, and if I had been another girl, in another village, who knew nothing of missing children it might never have dawned on me that what this man was doing was wrong.

Late in the day. All afternoon I had sat in the grounds of St Tysul's with my library book, my back against Great-grandfather Henry. The weathervane was still and the gargoyle was on guard for me. I could see the street and the shop from there. A good view.

The white television vans had packed up and gone. Eight weeks since she'd vanished. Old news now. Half forgotten.

I'm not sure why I took the long way home – down the path at the side of the vestry, through the back lanes, past the rookery and the festering pond and then up under the alders towards the back of the pub. But I did. Scuffing through the dust, book under my arm. I rarely walked that way.

Nor can I remember exactly what made me turn round by the stile. A snapped twig? A footfall? Or did I just know he was there, hands in pockets? Did I sense it? Feel him on my skin?

He sauntered towards me, smiling. As if he knew I'd be there.

'Hello, Evangeline,' he said.

He asked me how my grandparents were. If the farm was doing well. 'Sheep to market soon?' He smiled. I nodded and made my way to the stile. I wanted to be over it and gone. It was late. I was in trouble. My grandmother would be waiting, biting her nails.

I had one hand on the fence. My book clamped to my side.

He said, 'Do you need a hand there?'

I never said yes.

I never said yes.

He put his right hand on my back, on my shoulder blades. Then, as I raised a leg to climb over the stile, he slid that hand down. I felt it move along my back, over the hollow at the base of my spine, and onwards. It came to rest between my legs. He lifted me a little. His breath was hot on my arm.

That right hand pushed. I felt it. His fingers hardened, curled.

I dropped down beyond the stile. I spun round.

His eyes were on me. Bottle green, cat green, weed green, acid green. Green for *go! Go! Run now! Run away!* He was climbing over to join me and I didn't want him to.

I sprinted up the lane away from him. I didn't look round, but somehow I knew that those eyes were watching me go, watching me run through the bushes in my outgrown T-shirt and outgrown shorts.

Rabbits fled from their evening grazing.

I ran home thinking, *Why did you have to go?*

So that was it. That was what happened. You might say, not much. Perhaps my mind has worsened it. But two decades on, and I can still feel his hand there. Like a kiss I never asked for, his fingers had opened me.

* * *

I know this is not proof enough. That act, though terrible, does not constitute abduction. A quiet feel in a back lane is not the same – not nearly the same – as the taking, hiding, killing of a girl. Nowhere near. And it may well be that the man with green eyes, though guilty of touching me where I knew no man should touch, is wholly innocent of the disappearance of Rosemary Hughes. I recognise that. I understand it. One should never presume.

But what a coincidence. That, too, must be taken into account. What an eerie, suspicious, unimaginable coincidence that the same small, close village should harbour two men – two! – who think and do such unspeakable things. Is that not incredible? Or am I naïve? Less than one hundred people lived in Cae Tresaint back then and yet two of them wanted girls. What are the chances of that? Just how slim are those odds?

I should have fought him. I should have broken my promise to Daniel and lashed out. A scratch, a bite – anything that he'd have needed answers for, that the police would have raised an eyebrow at. *I tripped over a tree root. I walked into a branch – ffol!* Would things be any different if I had? Would Rosie be buried in St Tysul's? Would her mother be alive?

I stumbled home to my grandmother's anger. The kitchen was airless with it. She took me by the elbows and asked me what I was thinking, what I was trying to do to her. I let her shout. I let her shake me like a sorry rag doll. I barely heard her – my brain and heart and stomach were gone. I felt numb, drugged, dying.

'Anything could have happened to you!' she screamed. 'I nearly called the police! Do you hear me, Missy? The police! *Why* do you keep breaking rules? *Why?*'

I learnt that evening that Mr Phipps had been released

without charge. He'd had an alibi, in the end. Mrs Jessop had thrown up her hands and announced that yes, she had seen him in the afternoon of Rosie's last sighting – cleaning the shop window with vinegar and newspaper. So it couldn't have been him. *You've got the wrong man, Chief Inspector.*

I went to bed with a pain in my stomach. It made me curl up under the sheets, tuck myself around Dog. I tried to remember my old Birmingham bedroom, my old city life, but all I could see was two green eyes. Two green eyes, how I'd seen him in the pine forest, at the markets, how I'd nearly washed his car; how he'd raised an invisible hat at me six months before, outside the shop in the drizzle. *Evangeline, is it not?*

Despite the heat I shut the window that night.

I was wrong: Rosie and I shared two things, not one. We claimed to love the same man, yes. But I believe we also knew the same white hand. The same fingers had pushed at us; the same eyes had looked us up and down. The difference being I was let go of. I was not prize enough, not worth the risk of being caught.

Love

There are pears from the Reverend in our fruit bowl. As I write this I see them. Beautiful – yellow stippled with brown, light-bulb shaped and shiny. They need eating – when I press the skin with my fingers a dent stays there. I know that if I bit into one of these pears right now, its flesh would be an incredible white. Juicy, grainy on the tongue. Pears are the awkward, big-bottomed fruit. I feel they sit in my hand self-consciously. My grandfather used to eat the entire thing, seeds and all, leaving nothing behind but the stalk, and I'd believe a tiny pear tree might start to grow inside him. 'Maybe,' he'd say with a wink. 'I'll keep you posted, *cariad*.'

I never told anyone about what happened at the stile. I felt at fault. I shouldn't have been there. I shouldn't have done so many wayward things. Only recently have I been able to walk down to that stile again. It was last winter, a few days after I learnt I was expecting a child. I sat there in the cold, blowing on my hands, and made my peace with the place. I walked away happy, feeling strong.

And I went to the police that day. Two decades on, a

tiny new life in me, and I finally told someone about the man with green eyes. All that I knew, which wasn't really so much. But I did it. I did it, and walked back outside into the street to find it was snowing. At last, I'd taken my secret and passed it over. Theirs to deal with, now.

Gerry once said to me, in a clumsy, drunken haze, that everything came back to love. I disputed this. I said that made the world sound perfect when surely it was anything but. He just shook his head at me. 'I think,' he said, 'that it's why we do things. Full stop.'

He never accepted the abduction theory. He refused to. In our teenage years we'd be walking through lanes or hitching lifts together on the main road and he would suddenly freeze, hold his fist into his stomach as if it hurt there. Or he might flinch at a blackbird in the bushes. He wanted to believe Rosie had fooled us all, that she had run away for the sake of love and was happy, flushed, breathing somewhere. So idealistic. I lost my temper with him sometimes. There was one evening, not long before I left for Swansea, when I nearly told him about that stray hand. *Explain that*, I wanted to shout at him. *Where was the love in that? Can't you see that you're wrong?* But instead, I just scoffed at his naivety. We rowed. I stormed out of the White Hart and he followed me up to the farm. He was clumsy, slurring his speech, but I had cooled down on the walk home and I understood him well enough. As with them all, he loved Rosie. I was sure of it. With every step he wondered what he was walking on. When I led him inside he took hold of my hair and fell against me. My grandparents let him sleep on the sofa that night.

But perhaps he's right, in some ways. Love, he mumbled into my collarbone, was a funny sort of thing. And isn't it? The things it makes us do. And the things we feel love for – it has no logic to it. Love is as varied and unpre-dictable as the rain is: it comes in constant summer drizzles, or sudden, unforeseen storms that make rivers burst their banks and Cornish fishing boats rock and spill and lose their crew in the Atlantic. It patters into you, or it washes you clean of your senses. It can drip or come in a downpour. It is strange, manipulative. So perhaps Gerry was half correct – it *is* a funny thing.

Mrs Maddox, in her little pink house, was the woman to talk to about love. She knew all its faces. I remember turning to her in the autumn that followed, needy and flustered and so tired after that summer, and how she took my face in her gnarly hands.

'Some things just happen, Evie! They aren't meant to make sense! My darling Mr Maddox died the day before our anniversary – the day before! – out in the garden, weeding under the magnolia tree. I just looked out of the window and saw him lying there. And I *knew*. I just *knew* he was gone. I don't know why he died, or why he had to die that day, and I spent years trying to understand it – years! But the truth is,' she whispered, 'things *happen*. We just have to put our heads down and get on with it. Do you understand what I'm saying, Evie? Do you?'

Did I? I thought so. Don't fight what's gone. Don't look for reasons, because that serves no purpose and it ruins things. Move on.

I nodded. Some things just *are*.

'Good girl,' she said.

So can an eight-year-old be in love? That's a question. Who's to say? Love is such a small, simple word at that age. It trips off the tongue. We have no idea of the power it has, of its jagged edges or the price that comes with it. So easy to mock a girl of that age for claiming to be in love – but I did claim it. Everything returned to him. I'd see his caravan light shining through the trees from my bedroom window, and find real comfort in it. No one ever asked me how I felt about him, but had they done I'd have nodded seriously. *Yes. I love Daniel. So?*

Not that it was love at first sight – I don't believe in that. But just as my grandmother had sensed a goodness to him when he first walked up Pencarreg's drive, so I always knew he was special. Love? That came in Aberporth. I remember the moment. We were sitting on a bench overlooking the sea, and I glanced up at him through my hair. In that sunshine I just knew it was true. The streetlights in the city used to fuzz on pinkly and grow stronger and stronger – love, I decided, felt like that. It was steady rain, the sort flowers open in. My age doesn't matter: that was one of the clearest moments of my life. It felt planned, perfect. I finished my ice cream knowing it. I have never been anything but sure.

Daniel kissed me first, not the other way round – in the middle of Carmarthen market a week or so before Christmas, the year before last. It had been a wet, cold, miserable day until then. Numb hands and cold ears, and when we resurfaced Daniel said, 'There'll be some people who'll object to this.' But I just wrapped my arms round the back of his head and kissed him back.

So who objected? Gerry. Not overtly, but when I told him he sat in silence for a while. When he spoke it was to say, *Then have you always loved him? Always?*

Mrs Watts was incensed. She appeared on our doorstep the day after my pregnancy was announced and said, 'Eve, he's as good as *family*.' That made me angry – it had never, not once, felt that way. She shook her head at me and said, 'Sixteen years! *Sixteen*!'

'Fifteen years, nine months, twelve days,' I replied, and casually shut the door in her face.

As for Reverend Bickley, he nodded gently at the news. He asked me if I was happy, and I think my answer must have contented him because he sent us a joint Christmas card that year. We went down to the carol service and found him there, watching his successor lead the choir. I saw him as tired and old. Daniel went up to him and pressed a cup of mulled wine into his hand. They talked for a good while. After the last carol the Reverend touched him on the shoulder and said, *Take good care of that one, won't you now?*

Billy is no longer around to speak to, but he, too, knew all about love. I didn't realise it when I was eight. I had no idea. But if I'd only opened my eyes a little wider I'd have seen all the signs of a saddened heart – solitude, quietness, a lethargy that sat alongside a desire to protect all that reminded him of her.

What was love to him?

It was flowers. Learning their Latin names from a library book to impress a brown-eyed girl.

And it was peppermints. It was spending his allowance on them and stuffing his jacket pockets. Why? Not because he loved feeding them to horses – that's not the truth. The truth is that my mother rode there, every Saturday morning between nine and twelve thirty, from the age of eleven right up to eighteen. Plaited hair and bobbled riding gloves. Those mints were just his excuse for being there.

The Fire

So how did this end? If indeed it ever really ended?

The last week of July. The gorse was now out and the sheep picked up thorns. The last of the hay rotted. One evening I heard a nightjar burring down near the Brych, and it made me feel sad. Owls, too, were out. Our cattle were checked for bots' eggs, the flock for flystrike. Ragwort was tugged up. Our wild rhubarb was wilting, and the leaves had turned soft. But I could still crawl underneath them and hide.

School was over. I returned from our cows to find my grandmother standing in the yard, her arms at her side. 'Grandma?' I whispered. She seemed far away. There was sweat on her forehead, her eyes on the sky.

'We need thunder,' she said. 'I have a headache' – she touched her temples – 'just there.'

I found Gerry on the ridge on the Tuesday. He was hunched against the hut, resting his chin on his knees. He took his time in telling me what was wrong.

'It's not been like this before,' he said.

'What hasn't?'

He meant his parents, and their fighting. He pressed his eyes into his kneecaps and I just sat there, unsure what to do. Wales ran out before us, looking brown and thirsty. Even up there, there wasn't much wind to be found.

The next day, when I crept down to the pub to buy a glass of lemonade, I saw Mrs Hughes for the first time in months. I stood and stared. I thought of the lambs with broken legs who sweated in the grass, knowing their fate. She was like that. She stumbled as though a gun had clicked into place. She made it past the oak tree, and was nearing the White Hart when she collapsed. Her head dropped forwards, as if too heavy; her knees gave way. I heard a crack as they met the ground. The noise she made was incredible. A final groan, a bellow. I stood there. I thought she had died.

Men from the pub came to help her. She was lifted under the arms and carried into the shade. It looked as if she was made of wax, and I could see her pores, the veins in her neck. Then a wail. That mouth opened itself to form a huge black hole. Not dead then, but not really living. They were saying, *It's OK, Mrs Hughes, we've got you now.*

And one afternoon as I slipped past the shop I felt a tap on my shoulder.

Broken veins, a broken nose. He said, 'I want a word with you.'

Others would probably give you a better account of what happened then than me. My memory is almost too full now, I think, as if it's smoke-damaged, or as if the heat of the summer curdled it. To imagine it, Mr Phipps and I face to face, my shoulders in his grip, is hard. I see us, but we're blurry. As though we're under water.

And it felt like that, too. I remember that much. Outside the church, yet the spire seemed so far away. Noises were slow. I struggled for breath. He shook me and I swayed like a strip of weed. *What did you tell them?* He spat. I saw his mouths form the words, *little Irish bitch*.

My brain told me to kick. That wasn't hitting, it wasn't breaking a promise, and although he held my arms tightly my legs were free so I used them. I opened my mouth and screamed at him. I kicked till he let go.

And then I had no choice but to run.

Through the churchyard, over the back gate, ducking through the bramble tangle, vaulting tree stumps. Then I followed the Brych, splashing through its shallows so that my shoes were sodden, and clambering up onto the far bank, pounding over the cracked earth of our cow field so that they skittered away from me. I just wanted to get away, to be in a safe place where there'd be no hands, no words, nothing, so I went spinning through the crisped dung, darting down towards the beech trees, and I threw myself under the wire.

But I was clumsy. The wire caught me. I tore my arm on a barb and fell into the nettle bed.

For a moment I was still. I lay there, panting.

Then my hands felt the nettles. My thighs, my knees, my face. The stinging began.

I whimpered. I was shocked, confused, and when I lifted myself up I saw welts were already appearing. White lumps on pink skin. My arm was bleeding. A thread of red snaked down to my wrist.

I blinked through my sweat and shouted his name.

He was there. He was in the sunshine, sitting on his tree stump, turning something over in his hand. When he heard my voice he looked up. His eyes clouded when he saw me – my blotched legs and glossy arm. I stumbled towards him with my arms out. My palms were skyward, showing their wounds.

'Evie,' he said, 'what happened?'

I said I was a liar. An awful, bad liar, and that I was in trouble, all sorts of trouble.

'What?'

'Mr Phipps. It wasn't him, I made it up, it wasn't him. I know it wasn't, but I said it was. I . . .'

Billy studied my arms, my legs, the underneath of my chin that was puffing up with nettle rash. 'This is bad,' he said. He pressed my hand against my cut. 'Keep that there.'

'I've told lies, Billy, I'm' -

'Dock leaves,' he said, 'are the thing for nettle stings.'

And with that he left me on the tree stump, clutching my own arm, as he moved through the grass towards the beech trees, saying *Rumex crispus* to himself.

Billy. Decent, kind Billy with a handsome face beneath his scarlet mark.

Forgive me for what happened next.

What must Mr Phipps have seen as he followed me across the field?

This.

Me, aged eight, wearing a white vest top smeared with old strawberry juice, damp with sweat, and blue towelling shorts meant for boys. Me, with freckled limbs and bramble scratches and hair tied into bunches with pieces of string. Me, flushed from my run, breathless, nearly weeping, with one hand out for balance, the other shyly holding up the inside of my shorts.

And Billy Macklin. A tall man in a waxed jacket too heavy and hot for midsummer. An odd man, a loner, hunched over my leg – over my pale inside thigh, to be precise – one hand pressed against it, his cool white fingers spread over my skin like a web.

From that distance, no one would have seen the dock leaf.

Can I blame Mr Phipps for thinking what he did? For all his hatred of me, his fear, can he really be blamed? If I were faced with the same scene tomorrow, *exactly the same scene*, would I not think it, too?

So easy.

The perfect scapegoat. A simple man. A man no one could vouch for, and who no one would miss. And who would believe the shouts of an eight-year-old who told lies and fought other girls and spent half her life in detentions? Whose father was a thief through and through?

I didn't know I'd been followed. I had no idea.

I just remember the evening sun, the long shadows, how a blackbird sang from the roof of the barn. How Billy shifted from one foot to the other as he dabbed my skin with the dock leaf. *Is that better?* he'd ask.

Twenty-one years on and the guilt still rushes me. It makes me double over, like a blow to the stomach. I could go mad with it. I deserve to.

I didn't get the chance to say sorry, and I owed him that. He was trying to make me better, and what did that cost him? Too much.

My fault.

If only I hadn't fallen in the nettles.

If only I had not told lies.
If only.

Say his name, say William Macklin in Cae Tresaint, and the stories are of a crazed loner who lured away Rosie, who took her, killed her, dumped her somewhere she would never be found. A savage man. Evil. Children will tell you he was an ogre. Adults will tell you he was corrupt, sly, malevolent – the devil himself, perhaps. They'll tell you that Eve Green, that red-headed woman from Pencarreg Farm, was often seen with him.

Quite a friendship, they had. If you follow.
No wonder she keeps herself to herself.

But he wasn't evil – you know this as well as I. He was a man whose found breezes helped his headaches, who knew where the pigeons nested, who kept to the unused paths of Cae Tresaint so that no one would see him but the occasional lost sheep. He left the flowers on our doorstep in the dead of night – those flowers were always from him. And he left them for me – not for my grandparents, not for Daniel, but *for me* – because I was Bronwen's, as simple as that, and so he took care of me. She was gone, but I wasn't. He watched out for me, and liked me, and the hoof of a grey mare smacked everything out of his brain but his basic, stark sense of love. In that way, wasn't he the best of us? Wasn't he the least likely culprit of all?

On the last day of July someone set fire to the derelict barn. I couldn't tell you exactly who lit the first match and held it in his cupped hands before leaning down into the old hay. But I can guess. I can see his face illuminated as the hay kindled – his sour face. His bulbous nose. Gerry's father was there, and the pub landlord, Lewis, and Mr Wilkinson, and the man with the pea-green eyes. Other fathers, men who spilled out of the pub half drunk, half mad with the heat, and with a hunger for some sort of violence.

I was in the yard at the time. It was a clear, airless night. The stars were out. My grandfather and I sat side by side on the bench by the porch, studying the sky, sharing an apple. He carved out the seeds with a penknife.

We chewed quietly.

I stopped.

He looked across at me. 'Are you all right, *cariad*?'

There was a distant, low rumble. Almost thunder, but not quite. Almost a freight train, but too steady for that. Could I hear voices?

'What is it?' I asked.

Did I know my mother would die? Did I feel the ripples of her death in the moments before I found her, tilted on her side in the bath? Did I? And what about Rosie? And the drought? Did my heart and stomach feel them coming closer? Can the future be detected, the way the diviners sense water, or the way the dogs know when an earthquake is coming?

To this day, I don't know.

But I know that I dropped the apple on the ground and ran out of the yard. I charged down the lane, into the dark, my feet slapping on the tarmac, thinking, *No! No!* My head screamed the words. My heartbeat pounded in my ears, and over my forehead, and I ran poorly, not breathing properly, my arms flailing. My grandfather called for me. I heard him, knew he was standing by the cattle grid, under our limes, frowning, but I didn't stop. I couldn't. I knew I had to run. Something carried me, something made my legs panic. I ran towards the Brych, threw myself over the gate of the cow field, and then my knees buckled. I cried out. I dropped into the grass like a doll.

The blaze was already under way. It was huge. The flames were orange – a hard, incredible orange – and they leapt higher than the alders or the single oak. They twisted up each other, throwing red sparks high up into the sky, and the whole field was lit up, as if it were daytime. The stars were lost. Our cows kept close to the lane, moving uneasily, lifting their noses for air and groaning to themselves. Their black eyes reflected the flames.

The noise of a fire is immense. I somehow never knew it. Or maybe I forgot. Maybe I'd never seen a fire this tall, this angry; maybe I'd never seen one uncontained like this, untended. But I could hear branches snapping, logs bursting, how the hay snickered into life. I could hear the beams crash down into the barn, throwing up new sparks.

And I could see the outlines of men to my left, down by the beech copse. Ten or twelve men. Shirt sleeves rolled up. Waving their hands against the sparks and the smoke, as if swatting flies. Watching. Nodding, perhaps. Content with their handiwork.

I saw Mr Phipps. Arms folded. Proud.

I thought, *Billy.*

I thought, too, as I stumbled down the field towards the burning barn, that ash flutters back down softly, beautifully, without a sound, the way confetti might, like red-edged butterflies.

The men didn't see me at first. After all, they didn't expect me. They didn't think that I'd erupt out of the brambles the way I did, screaming. Waving my fists. Hair loose.

I wanted to be in that barn. I wanted to find Billy and pull him out. I knew he was in there, I knew it, and so I ran at the fire, but the heat was too fierce. It felt like a wall, so hard that it knocked me backwards. Yet I tried again. I ran at it, and burst through. My eyes pricked and streamed. The noise roared around me. I saw nothing but fire, hauled smoke into my lungs, and I screamed out his name, screamed through the flames, wanted to pull him out, pull him out of the dark, drag her out of the bath, wanted to save her and have her back, and I threw back my head and shouted out his name, shouted, *Billy!*

Then I fell. And as I fell I saw something shine. Something glittered through the smoke, and I reached out for it with my left hand, straight into a hazy wall of heat. My skin burned. I saw flames wrap round my wrist like fingers. The pain was so much it was almost nothing. I remember just watching it burn.

And I remember somebody's arms.

They wrapped round my chest. Strong arms, arms I fell into, hands I knew, and Daniel shouted my name into my ear. I heard him through the noise, and fought him for a moment or two. I kicked him, went to bite his arms. I pleaded, tugged at his strength. *Billy*, I was telling him. *Not Billy*. But I was eight. I was exhausted. I never could have fought him.

I did my best. He tells me this, too, even now. *You did what you could, Eve. Let it go.*

Daniel hauled me away from the barn that night. He kept his arms around me as we watched the barn collapse. It threw out a shower of sparks, a huge push of heat.

He carried me down to the Brych and thrust my left arm into the water. I was crying. And I kept crying long after the flames grew smaller, and the men had gone. I sobbed till my head hurt and my lungs ached. Daniel let me. After a time he took me back into the field, away from the smoke where the grass was cool, and let me. I nestled into him. My skin was red, my hair was crisp, and I sobbed until my heart hurt, until I wore myself out.

My fists slowly uncurled themselves. He said nothing. He didn't tell me it was all right, or that it was over now. There was no need, and no point. He just waited.

My grandparents found us, scooped me up and took me home. An ambulance was called.

The fire engines came too late, of course. I heard their sirens through my shallow sleep, and learnt a few days later that all they found amongst the embers was the frail remains of a green waxed jacket, and a silver charm bracelet, somehow unblackened by the flames.

Nobody looked for him. As far as everyone was concerned, the barn was empty. It had been empty for years. As for arson, it was shrugged off. Fires can happen without warning when there is old hay and hot sun, when a summer without rain has left everything as dry as tinder.

To this day I don't know where Billy's gone.

But he must have made it out of there – because wouldn't there have been bones? Wouldn't someone have found a charred, dented skull? I like to think that we all missed him creeping out into the dark, minus his coat, that he made it up to the main road, turned back to see the fire that he'd escaped from, and then held out a thumb for a lift. That he got away from here. Maybe he reached the coast, after all.

Anyway, he has never been found.

Nor has Rosie.

But one good thing came of this. Just one. Mother Nature is a strange, silent woman. She finds a sliver of goodness in the worst of things. Fire destroys, but it also creates. These days, when I walk down to the place where the barn once stood, there are flowers. They took seed where the grass had burnt, and now the whole field is beautiful. Columbine, red campion, pinks and bindweed all grow there. Ox-eye daisy, too, has taken root. And most prolific of all, running over the charred beams and the blackened slates, lies the *Myosotis arvensis* – or, in layman's terms, forget-me-not.

On a square of pink paper my mother wrote:
It's yes. Due at the end of December.
And unusually for my mother she drew something. I can't be sure what it is – either a one-eyed smile or – my natural preference – a simple bundle tucked snugly into the crook of an arm.

BOOK THREE

Red Hair

The sycamore seeds are finding their way indoors now. They spin through open windows, or catch on our clothing and are carried in. I found one under my shirt yesterday. I watched it twirl forlornly onto the bathroom floor.

And there are conkers. What child never liked conkers? I loved unsealing the spiky shell and finding its treasure, as shiny as an eye. My grandfather and I used to pickle them in vinegar. Like scientists, we would peer into a bowl, test them in the morning, and those conkers were often the hardest at school. I'd come home with red knuckles and a victor's smile. 'How did that one fare?' he would ask.

This too is blackberry season – or the end of it. They grow as big as my thumb by our turning circle. But those berries are rarely picked now – the hard climb sees to that, or maybe it's just that no one eats blackberries any more. Maybe they've lost their allure. They're left for the birds, mostly. As it should be, perhaps. They speckle our windscreen with their purple droppings.

I like that October is not far away. It's my favourite month, with its crispness and first frosts, its rowan jelly and apple festival, and the fact that suddenly everyone is wearing scarves and gloves again and the shops start to play Christmas music. My grandmother hated that. She'd grumble to the checkout girl, *It's three months away, you know*! But it makes me smile to hear it. In Birmingham, I could almost believe that Christmas was ten weeks long.

And I like hoarding up on coal and sheep feed and dog biscuits, as if the coming winter might never end. I like retrieving the winter duvet from the attic and selecting which ewes we should make mothers in the spring. And I even like the rain at this time. It's just a quiet patter. It shows up the cobwebs in between the wires on the dog cage.

I think a good month for a birthday, all in all. This coming Christmas will be quite an event. I think it deserves a proper tree.

In the aftermath of the fire someone put a brick through Mr Phipps's window. I couldn't be blamed; I had an alibi. Nor could he really grumble, because there were worse things to think about. Rosie was still missing, after all.

I stayed in hospital for three days. I remember the cracks in the ceiling. I was drugged, wheezy, blistered, and my grandmother never left my side. She was amazing. She was my favourite nurse, my comforter. I'd wake to find her securing my dressing, whispering *It's all right, go back to sleep*.

As for my grandfather, he was awkward in hospitals. He shifted from one foot to the other, sat on chairs as if they weren't to be trusted. When he asked me if my burn was sore I lied to him. I said no, but it was. Despite the thick cream and gauze, it still felt hot. I caught a glimpse of my wrist when the dressing was changed, and I couldn't believe it belonged to me. At night I'd picture it – bubbled, luminous, soggy. It itched and throbbed. I knew it would leave a big scar.

And Daniel visited every evening. He'd bring a bag of sherbet lemons or a comic book. He said little. Sometimes he slept in the green plastic chair by my bed. I'd watch him, remember the walls of flame, and I'd sink under the blankets with Dog. I'd cry there a little, in my own private dark.

But I got better. Time heals – or does a good job of trying. I came home the afternoon of the thunderstorm, and I sat by my open window watching it. The lime trees rustled and I was sure I could hear the earth drinking. I wondered what it would feel like to unpeel my dressing, hold out my arm, and let the rain fall on my damaged skin.

My scar was an awful thing at first – scarlet and angry. But it's almost pretty now. It looks like a bracelet, at its thickest under my thumb. The rest of my hand is unmarked, as if the fire tried to throw on shackles. I neither hate nor love it. It just exists. As Daniel says, it's a story to tell. And isn't it? That's what a scar is – proof we've been through an event worth writing down.

The man with the green eyes whose name I never knew lived in Cae Tresaint for another year. But when I was nearly ten his white terraced house was sold and he slipped away. His departure wasn't really noted by anyone but me. I watched the removal van creep up the hill, out of sight, and I sat down by the war memorial with a sudden relief. I could finally stand in front of his house and stare at it – the peeling paint, the solitary cracked windowpane. He was not missed by anyone. He was neither popular nor reviled – the most boring sort, in a way. Who will remember him in the years to come, save for me? And even I have learnt to let him slide. If a wood pigeon burrs into life without warning I might, briefly, think of him. But my bad dreams are rarer now. Mrs Maddox was right: there's no point in fighting what has gone. Hold the past up into the wind, unclose your hand and let it go.

Gerry denied throwing the brick. To this day he rolls his eyes when I question him, and says, *Not this again . . . No! OK? It wasn't me.* So who? Not hard to guess. I see him limp over the shattered glass. I see him on a bus heading to a new place, his chin on his chest, not happy, but not quite sad.

So my father? A man called Kieran Green. No middle name. Born and raised on the west coast of Ireland, not far from Limerick and the youngest of seven, so I've now learnt. Red-headed, of course. Blue-eyed and freckled. A charmer; the owner of knowing hands.

He was only twenty-three. Not old. People have their whole lives ahead of them when they're twenty-three. Life's a stone not yet carved on, an unwritten page. As my grandfather told me towards the end of his life, that's a magical, flowering age. Anything is possible in your twenties, he said.

These are sentiments Kieran must have shared. He must have felt alive, ready, adventurous, for he took the Dublin ferry through the spray to Holyhead at the end of the summer of '68, caught the train inland, climbed Snowdon, camped in its park, and began hitching his way south past Bala and its lakes, the copper mines and slate caves, over the River Dyfi into Cardiganshire and to the far end of the Cambrian Mountains when, in August, on a road leading to Lampeter, he glimpsed a weathered sign through the cow parsley stalks that led him to wander past the red telephone box and into Cae Tresaint with his backpack, hands in pockets and a wide, easy smile.

My mother called him beautiful. *Not just a woman's term.*

Over a pint in the White Hart Kieran was offered a job at Bryn Mawr. He slept there, amongst pitchforks and mice droppings, and Bronwen Jones saw him for the very first time as she turned up for her weekly riding lesson. Straw in his hair, perhaps. How do I know all this? Billy, naturally. He was there, too. He saw the glances between them and understood. Never subtle, my mother. Cae Tresaint knew she loved Kieran long before she knew herself.

The rest I know. She has written enough – the bonfire kiss, the day at the coast, the secret night in a dark hotel where she wrote down poetry. The meetings in the empty barn. My conception, up at the Tor.

But there is so much I'll never be sure of. In that shoebox are mysteries: an inch of blue twine – what does that mean? There is a pink strip of paper covered in numbers that makes no sense to me. And the crisp bones of an oak leaf – why? Just because it was lovely? Did he hand it to her? Did it fall on her as she waited for him?

Sometimes I feel a lot older than twenty-nine. I feel I've lived for a hundred years, that I'm as old as the house and just as weatherworn. I've come a long way, I suppose. I look at that first school picture of mine – the boyish hair, the foolish grin, and I feel sorry for the girl. *You have so much yet to come,* I tell her. *Enjoy your mother. Hold on tight.*

Yes, I've been angry. My teenage years were peppered with my resentment, like ink blobs over a blazer's lining, and if I were ever to meet Kieran I know that sharp words would jangle in my mouth for a while. I'd spit; I'd snap. I'd curse him the way my grandmother – unwittingly – taught me to.

But that wouldn't last. It couldn't. How do you resent what is half of you? What you see in the mirror, gazing back? How do you resent a man you've never met, have never looked in the eye and spoken to? Having never heard his version of things?

She could have had anyone, my grandmother had whispered. Isn't that the way? Billy loved her, our vet did. Daniel thought her wonderful, always. And Mr Phipps was so transfixed by her that when she refused him, as any sane woman would, he changed his love to bitterness. *Those bloody Joneses*, he'd call us. *That filthy Irish bastard. That red-headed bitch from Pencarreg Farm.*

Men would have given up everything, if she'd asked them to. They would have put their hands on the Bible and lied, if need be. But Kieran? He showed her seven months of what life should always feel like. He showed her what her body was for. And in May, as the dragonflies came, he left without warning – the night after learning I had been made.

Only twenty-three.

Still, I suppose it comes down to this: just as we love, and can't help it, so we can't help it if love's not there.

He'd be in his fifties now. Over half a century on this earth. Greying at the temples, perhaps, a slight middle-aged paunch. I believe he's alive and well. I did think, for a time, he might have a life in the sun somewhere, involving yachts and palm trees, but that was naïve, because our skin is too sensitive for that. He'd burn in such places. So maybe he's back in Ireland. Or maybe he was in Birmingham the whole time.

*   *   *

274

Does he ever think of me? I have decided yes – but in a hazy, casual way. I could be a boy or a girl to him; he never stayed to find out. So it is a faceless ghost of a child he thinks of – a shadow that flickers through his head at Christmas time, when he passes a playground or sees a Welsh flag. Perhaps he looks at his other children and wonders if I look at all like them; perhaps he worked it out, added on nine months and drinks more than he should at New Year. Perhaps the mirror scares him. Maybe he always looks twice when a redhead enters the room. Each knock on the door stops his heart for one split second or two.

Who's to say? No one. It is all speculation; it is the dregs of wine in a bottle I've stored in my cellar for years. But I am sure of one thing: somewhere inside him, when he can't sleep for heat or noise or drink or worry, Kieran Green too stares at the ceiling and thinks *What if . . . ?* Because everyone asks that once in a while.

And that's enough for me.

Full Stop

A *thing with teeth and claws*, my grandmother said. I believe it. I will be the mother who watches the clock when my child's due home. I will study the water until my child resurfaces. I will kill wasps on sight, will teach road safety, will read up on meningitis and measles and head lice and glandular fever. I'll watch for signs of bullying. I'll hand out deep, embarrassing kisses without warning. I'll enforce seat belts and discourage lies, and yet all the time I will perfect a casual, breezy air so that they don't see my belief that the world is not always a place to be trusted. Back by five, I'll call brightly over my shoulder, whilst thinking, *by five, by five, or before, if you can.* As she, my grandmother, must have done.

She died of a huge heart attack at the horse market on a drizzly Tuesday afternoon when I had just turned nineteen. I was in the yard when the phone rang. I looked up at the house, at the bare lime trees, and I knew. So did my grandfather. As I replaced the receiver he appeared in the doorway, his fist to his chest. He said, *Is it Lou?*

I drove us to hospital in my dusty orange Metro. The

277

windscreen wipers switched on, switched off, and he sat on his hands as a child might. I wondered when I last really talked to her. And I didn't know.

It's hard to believe doctors when they say a death is instantaneous, as good as painless, but I stood on the blue and beige tiles of the hospital waiting room and chose to believe it. I would believe it, without question, and it would become the truth.

And my grandfather changed, of course. I'd expected it, but his loss showed itself in little ways. He took to sleeping on the sofa for a while. He'd fail to notice when I entered a room, or left it, and he became forgetful – coffee grew cold in its mug, the dogs were not fed, and I found him barefoot in the kitchen once, blinking down at his cold toes. I worried for a while, and chose to cry alone. But grief changes its face gradually, as a year does, and in time he was sleeping back upstairs in the marriage bed again – although he always kept to his side.

People told him, in their way of comfort, it had just been her time. *Lived a full life,* they told him – as if seventy was a respectable age, and it should somehow lessen his grief. But they were so wrong. It isn't like that. To him, she had never been seventy – she was still the brown-eyed girl by the coconut shy.

His turn came nearly nine years later, and in a softer way. Arthritis and a bad cold took him to bed when he was almost seventy-seven. I went downstairs to make him some tea, and came back up to find his head on one side, and the blankets still. His last words to me had been about the crack in the teapot. A good way to go, all in all.

And Rosemary Hughes? What happened to her? Nobody was ever arrested. Billy was the nearest thing they had to a suspect, but he was never tracked down. I'd have read

278

about it in the papers if he had been. Such an event would have been frontpage news. So it all remains unsolved – the worst, saddest of things.

If they found her, that might change. A stray hair, a drop of blood – DNA amazes me. But the search for her continues. I've done my part. I suppose all we can do is keep our fingers crossed, hope that one day a badger will unearth her, or a man – with green eyes or otherwise – will walk into a police station as I did, and announce, *I have something to say.*

Cae Tresaint has never been the same since that summer when I was eight years old. To a new eye it might seem normal enough – there are still weddings at St Tysul's, quiz nights at the pub, and whilst the shop has gone there is a garage up on the main road within walking distance, so ice creams are still licked by the war memorial and most people still know who is who. But scratch the surface and Rosie's face is undimmed. When I tread over a carpet of pine needles I still think of what might be lying underneath.

Nor did anyone find out who owned that field that our cows once grazed in, where the old barn was. It's seen as Billy's though. Daniel and I refer to it as such, and we glance over its gate whenever we walk past.

But let's not talk of death. Let's talk of birth. Let's talk of the birth that's coming closer, of the home-made cot and the sanded doors, of the black-and-white scan we keep tucked in the spare toast rack. Grainy, blurred, fish-like, and yet I know where its heart is, where its hands are. Good-looking, says Daniel, before kissing my skin.

Let's talk of Billy as I remember him, sitting on a tree stump with his hands relaxed; of how Mrs Maddox and I would clamber through ditches and trespass just to pick the best sloes; of Joe's parched kiss; of how I woke one morning to find my grandmother deadheading the rose bush in her dressing gown whilst waiting for the kettle to boil.

Let me think of how Daniel towelled his hair dry after his swim in the lake; how the Tor changes colour; how our sheep shimmy their tails and spill out their dung; how good those pears are; how my first kiss with Daniel was a lovely rainy opening thing; how I get lost in his hugs; how his hair smells of earth; how my mother and I used to wave at the trains from my bedroom window and share cones of chips on a Friday night; how her last entry in the shoebox had been just three neatly inked words – *we leave tomorrow*; how the cows shake their ear tags; how Wales changed utterly, incredibly, when I walked out of the bathroom eight months ago with a white stick in my left hand that bore two blue lines.

I know this: we will have a son with an innocent name. And his hair? Neither brown nor red, but a colour all of his own.

I am indebted to so many people who have helped and encouraged me throughout the writing of this book. There are too many to name individually. To all my family, and to my friends from York, Norwich and home – thank you.

Extra special thanks must go to my agent Vivienne Schuster and my editor Clare Reihill, for their belief, patience, expertise and for taking such good care of me; Sarah Thomson, for her invaluable advice; Mary Allen and Sarah Bower; Vicky Bragg, Katy Brumwell and Catherine Ballard; Helen Carpenter; Guy Essex; Tom and Patrick Hawkes; Susie Fletcher; my wonderful grandmother Claudia Dick; and the three people to whom the book is dedicated, for all their support and love.

P.S.

Ideas,
interviews
& features . . .

Finding a Rhythm

Eithne Farry meets Susan Fletcher

'I love poetic language, I love trying to get a sense of rhythm to the sentences.'

'It is the strangest, most baffling time for me at the moment,' confides Susan Fletcher. 'I have no idea what I did so right. I am thrilled to bits, of course, although it makes concentrating on the second book (or on anything, for that matter) pretty hard to do.' The 25-year-old author is understandably excited: her debut novel *Eve Green* has just won the Whitbread First Novel Award, a pretty big deal in the book world. 'I never expected to win anything, and will never expect it in the future. But it was wonderful to win this.'

Over morning tea in the quirky café in Liberty's in London Susan explains that the book took two years to finish and was started when she was attending the Creative Writing MA at UEA. 'I was trying to write a completely different novel, and it was going nowhere. My tutor suggested I try a short story to clear my head, so I began writing one, and it ended up being this.' She adds, 'I don't really write short stories. I think I get so involved in plots and characters that I like to keep going with them. After 5,000 words I don't want to stop. You can almost see the steam coming off the page.' That makes it all sound so, well, easy – an effortless flow of just the right words, conjuring up just the right atmosphere. Susan's rueful laugh tells a different story. 'Some days I try and nothing happens, nothing. I can just be staring at the same line for hours. And that's so demoralizing.' The only thing to do in these circumstances is to put on music, and catch up on some reading. 'I try and read a lot of poetry. I love a good poetic novel, and I love description. That's my real passion.' She explains how she could 'spend five pages describing the smallest things. So I have to be really careful not to go overboard in my own work, a paragraph perhaps, not twelve.' And if she's feeling fidgety about it all she'll head to the gym, go for a long walk, or meet up with some friends. 'If it's not going well, I seek company, I crave it. It helps to be among people who'll tell me this is just a hiatus, that everything will be fine. That I've done it once and I can do it again.' And if it's going well? 'If I'm really involved in what I'm writing, I could go for days without seeing anyone. I could go for days without even leaving the flat.'

Susan's flat is in Warwickshire, where she's 'writing full-time and living thriftily'. She gets up early and tries to work from 8 until 3. By mid-afternoon she's ready for 'big spaces'. 'I love getting out of doors and doing a lot of walking. I know I need that – fresh air and good views.' She laughs and says, 'That sounds so romantic.' And adds, 'I think I *am* quite romantic, but I'm also a very rational person. I tend to push my romanticism into some dark corner, and think with my head. And I do think time outdoors gives you a better sense of what matters.' And what matters to Susan, in her working life, is 'transportation'. 'I want to pick the reader up and put them in some other place, in ▶

> ❝ I love a good poetic novel, and I love description. That's my real passion. ❞

LIFE AT A GLANCE

Author photo: Jerry Bauer

Susan Fletcher was born in 1979. She grew up in Solihull, in the West Midlands, and went to St Martin's School, from 7 to 16. After that she joined the sixth form at Solihull School. She studied at York University for a BA in English and then took a year out to go backpacking in Australia and New Zealand. Back in England, she headed to UEA and their prestigious Creative Writing course and gained an MA. *Eve Green* is her first novel.

Finding a Rhythm (continued)

◄ someone else's shoes. And although I love writing description, it's also about emotions, how to deal with emotions. You want the reader's empathy.'

Susan grew up in Solihull, and her first hobby wasn't writing. She says, 'I loved horse-riding. I used to be absolutely fearless. I used to just charge over hedges, and if they put me on a difficult horse, I wouldn't have minded at all. I would've relished the challenge.' She read horse-care books and magazines, and she remarks that it was 'all-consuming, a real passion'. A little like her attitude to writing? 'It's different with the writing because some days I loathe it, I get so fed up with it. I think, "What am I trying to do?" But then there are the good days, the days when you've written something you like, even if it's only a single paragraph or a line . . . the sense of achievement, the excitement. I get so excited when I've written something I'm proud of, the elation can keep me going for weeks.'

At the moment, after winning the Whitbread prize, it's difficult to settle. Susan's working on her second novel, and 'got the bones for a third'. 'But I'd have to go off and do some more travelling before I did it. I'm getting itchy feet again.' Susan took a year off after studying at York University and before heading to UEA to backpack around Australia and New Zealand on her own. 'The night before I left I felt so daunted. I remember being at Birmingham Airport with my mother and feeling awful. Just thinking I wouldn't be seeing family or friends for six months. But it was incredible.' She travelled around the Northern Territory,

4

saw Ayers Rock, and front-crawled in a crocodile-infested river. 'They weren't the man-eating type, so I was safe – but it was so strange swimming there, knowing that there were crocodiles underneath you. That was a very primitive fear.' Her bedside notebook will accompany her – 'I read somewhere that the really creative part of the brain is only active in a state of extreme relaxation, so I always have a pencil and a book by the bed, just in case.' But rather than sit up and turn on the light, Susan scribbles her thoughts down in the dark. 'And in the morning when I try to read them, it's a scrawl . . .'

Tea drunk, Susan's heading off to the shops in search of the perfect pair of black trousers. 'I love coming to London for the day, wandering around, and visiting friends . . . but at the same time I'm glad to go. If I lived here I'd miss open spaces too much.' ∎

TOP TEN BOOKS

The English Patient – Michael Ondaatje

The Poisonwood Bible – Barbara Kingsolver

Beloved – Toni Morrison

To Kill a Mockingbird – Harper Lee

The Blind Assassin – Margaret Atwood

Jane Eyre – Charlotte Brontë

The Hunchback of Notre Dame – Victor Hugo

Lolita – Vladimir Nabokov

Death of a Naturalist – Seamus Heaney

Selected Poems – Robert Frost

A Richard & Judy
Summer Read

From Amanda Ross, MD of Cactus TV and Head of the Richard & Judy Reading Initiatives, on behalf of the Richard & Judy Summer Read selection team, notably Natalie Fox and Lauren Ebel.

Part of the ethos of Summer Read is to support new British authors and this book is a fabulous first novel, set in the British countryside. We think the imagery in *Eve Green* is exceptional. Susan Fletcher writes with both affection and sincerity about the Welsh community that Eve finds herself living in after the sudden death of her mother. The characters are lovingly drawn and we felt an instant connection with both the adult Eve, who is about to give birth, and the young Eve, who suddenly finds herself in a strange town with grandparents she barely knows. The bleakness of the small Welsh community is almost tangible. We delighted in the warmth of the Welsh summer floating through the pages, and could imagine reading it during our hopefully hazy summer days, being at once frightened and enthralled. There was tremendous competition for the six places in Richard & Judy's Summer Read selection, but *Eve Green* was an obvious choice for us as it really stood out. We think it will encourage readers to be less instantly judgemental, and to examine their own memories and how they affect the present. It's an effortless yet immensely satisfying novel and one that we are delighted to recommend to our viewers. ■

Becoming a Writer
Q & A with Susan Fletcher

When did you first realize that you wanted to be a writer?
At university. Until then, I had only written privately – and I had never considered it as a possible career. But at university, I read far more than I ever had done before. I began writing for a student arts magazine, sharing ideas, and finally putting my own work up for criticism. I realized I wanted to take it further. I wanted to try my very best at writing – and so applied for a Creative Writing MA.

You studied at the famous writing course at UEA. What was it like? Were you ever daunted by all of your famous predecessors?
Not as such – although we all knew of UEA's reputation. The atmosphere could have been extremely competitive, but it wasn't. I learnt a lot through the workshops, certainly, but the greatest thing of all was being around other dedicated writers for the first time. We spent a lot of time in the Grad Bar, talking books. To suddenly have that enthusiasm, and mutual support, was invaluable. And fun.

How did you find the time and money to write before you sold your book?
A third of the book was written at UEA. After that, I returned home to a very understanding family, who didn't mind me staying there for a further year. I wrote part-time, worked part-time – at a local video shop. At times, it was all deeply demoralizing. Friends were in good careers, earning, ▶

> ❝ The greatest thing of all was being around other dedicated writers for the first time. We spent a lot of time in the Grad Bar, talking books. ❞

Becoming a Writer (*continued*)

◀ buying houses, and I often felt I was wasting my time. But I had moments of real conviction. It was a difficult year – but it definitely paid off.

How did you get an agent?

I did my research. I discovered which agents represented my favourite authors, and which might enjoy the book. Then, when *Eve Green* was nearing completion, I sent my first three chapters to a handful of them. I was very fortunate. The agent I had always hoped for replied straight away. She was very enthusiastic, and asked to see the full novel. Within a few weeks of that, I was signed.

What was it like to get your first publishing deal?

Incredible – not least because it happened so quickly. I began September with no agent, and not much hope: I ended the month with an agent, a publishing house and a book deal. I'd always felt that at some point in my life I might make it into print. But I never believed it might happen so soon, or in such a way. I was both shocked and overjoyed. I know I've been very lucky.

When did you first hear about the Whitbread nomination, and how did it feel?

I heard about the nomination from my editor, who rang me when I was in the Lake District on a long weekend with a friend. We were above Ambleside at the time. I remember shrieking, and frightening a field of cows. Not long afterwards, I fell into a bog and we lost our way – but it didn't matter. It

❦ I began September with no agent, and not much hope: I ended the month with an agent, a publishing house and a book deal. ❞

was the perfect place to hear such news. There was plenty of wine consumed in Ambleside that night.

What was it like to win the First Novel award?
Astonishing. It still doesn't feel real. Just to be nominated was wonderful. I never imagined I would even get that far – I certainly never thought I'd win. I think it has changed me. I have more confidence as a writer now. It's confirmed that, at the moment, I am doing what I should be doing. However, I do feel, too, that the Whitbread prize has put more pressure on me – even though most of that pressure is self-imposed. It's always been rumoured that the second book is the hardest to write. I am definitely finding that now. But it's a challenge, which I'll enjoy – and I will do my best to meet it.

How did you feel on the night that the overall prize was announced?
I was delighted, in that the winning book is superb. But I admit I felt a little relieved, too – it would have been incredibly hard to follow on from such a win, as a first-time author. I'd feel I'd never match it. Now, at least I have something to aim for!

Do you write with a pen or a computer?
I carry a pen and pad with me, wherever I go. Also, I keep paper by my bed, for I often have ideas at night that vanish in the morning. But primarily I use a computer. I have no idea how writers managed before they could cut and paste. ▶

❝ The Whitbread prize has put more pressure on me – even though most of that pressure is self-imposed. ❞

Becoming a Writer (continued)

◄ With silence or music?
Almost always in silence – else I feel the
rhythm of the words gets lost. Occasionally,
when editing, I may listen to music. But even
then, it has to be lyric-less.

**Is there any book that you wish that you had
written?**
Many. And almost every book I read will have
at least one line in it that I love, and am in
awe of. But in terms of sheer beauty, I wish I
had written Michael Ondaatje's *The English
Patient*. It is poetry. It grows richer every time
I read it.

What do you read when you're writing?
Anything – unless it deals with similar
themes to my own book, in which case I'll
avoid it, for fear of losing my voice. With *Eve
Green* I read a lot of poetry – particularly
rural poems. If I was blocked, or had lost my
faith in the book, they'd reinvigorate me.
They'd remind me of what I was trying to
capture.

What is your guilty reading pleasure?
Magazines. And I love trivia books – my copy
of *Schott's Original Miscellany* is very well
thumbed. ■

If You Loved This,
You Might Like . . .

The Member of the Wedding
Carson McCullers
A classic coming-of-age story set in that
'green and crazy summer when Frankie was
twelve years old'. Frankie spends her days
mooching around, tomboyish and
impulsively purposeless. Her passionate
imagination seizes on her brother's wedding
as the event that will allow her to escape her
humdrum, lonely life. But her plan goes
alarmingly awry, with melancholy
consequences.

A Complicated Kindness
Miriam Toews
For Naomi Nickel, all the usual fun teen
things are forbidden – sex, drink and drugs –
but so are dancing, make-up and staying out
past nine. Obviously life just sucks if you're a
Mennonite in Manitoba. Especially if your
only prospect of a job is on the killing floor of
Happy Family Farms' chicken abattoir.
Slouchy, cool and funny, this debut novel
rocks.

The Poisonwood Bible
Barbara Kingsolver
Told by the wife and four daughters of
Nathan Price, a fierce evangelical Baptist who
takes his family and his mission to the
Belgian Congo in 1959, *The Poisonwood Bible*
is the story of their tragic undoing and
miraculous reconstruction over the course of
three decades in postcolonial Africa. Like a
nineteenth-century novel this grand sweep ▶

11

If You Loved This, You Might Like ...
(continued)

◄ of a book deals with sin and redemption, and all the muddled territory between.

....

Something Might Happen
Julie Myerson

On the first page there's a murder and from there on in it's heartbreak all the way. The setting is the Suffolk seaside, the weather's moody and changeable, and the mood is, frankly, devastating. Lovely, small-town values are fatally disrupted. Even domestic squabbles, the kind that would usually have as much impact as lightly thrown marshmallows, become as supernaturally charged as haunted houses. The tension builds up slowly and stealthily until every sentence rings with hurt. Devastatingly good.

....

Drinking Coffee Elsewhere
Z. Z. Packer

In just eight stories Ms Packer reveals herself to be a writer to be reckoned with. Ditching mannered politeness and pat happy-ever-after endings for more unpredictable outcomes, her tales crackle with electric energy. Brownies, runaways, teachers and college students find themselves in tricky predicaments. Not only are they hampered by their own vexed emotional dilemmas, they also have to deal with racism, prostitution, miscreant students, a drunken dad; and in the title story, a year's worth of psychiatric counselling after an off-the-cuff comment is taken a little too seriously. Slangy, elegant and graceful, this collection is remarkably good. ■

Find Out More

CREATIVE WRITING COURSES

The MA in Creative Writing at the University of East Anglia (UEA) is the most famous writing course in Britain. Graduates include Ian McEwan, Kazuo Ishiguro and Tracey Chevalier. The course description and requirements can be found at www.uea.ac.uk/eas/admissions/course profiles/w800t.shtml.

Similar courses exist at universities around Britain including Birkbeck College, Cardiff University, and Manchester Metropolitan University.

WHITBREAD PRIZE

Full details of all the winners in 2005, as well as previous years, and the history of the prize is available at www.whitbread-bookawards. co.uk

VISIT WALES

If Susan Fletcher's lyrical descriptions of Eve's home have inspired you, why not visit the source of her own inspiration. The Wales Tourist Board's website is divided into areas rather than counties (e.g. North Wales Borderlands; Snowdonia and the Coast) and offers detailed and comprehensive information on history, sights and practicalities (www.visitwales.co.uk or www.visitwales.com).